The Immortal Philosophers

CHRONICLES OF DYLAN EAGLEGOD
BOOK TWO
LOST BETWEEN THE LANDS
OF HERE AND THERE

THE IMMORTAL PHILOSOPHERS
Chronicles of Dylan Eaglegod Book Two
LOST BETWEEN THE LANDS OF HERE AND THERE
by
ALEXANDER ANTHONY CASILLAS

Lost Between the Lands of Here and There Chronicles of Dylan Eaglegod Book Two and *The Immortal Philosophers* is a work of fiction. Names, characters, places, and incidents are the product of the author's imagination or are used fictitiously. Any resemblance to actual persons, living or dead, events, or locales is coincidental.

Published in the United States
by Four Elements Press LLC, New Jersey.

To request permission, contact
contact@fourelementspress.com

Edited by Angelica Martinez

ISBN 978-1-965996-10-2 (Hardcover)
ISBN 978-1-965996-11-9 (Paperback)
ISBN 978-1-965996-12-6 (e-book)
Edition One

Published by Four Elements Press
fourelementspress.com
theimmortalphilosophers.com

THE IMMORTAL PHILOSOPHERS

CHRONICLES OF DYLAN EAGLEGOD
BOOK TWO

LOST BETWEEN THE LANDS OF HERE AND THERE

by

ALEXANDER ANTHONY CASILLAS

FOUR ELEMENTS PRESS

CONTENTS

For all who string-pull to
survive,
the world belongs to you.
Pull on.

PROLOG

The black curtains of chest-length hair fell heavy in front of the concealed face of Solomon Ibn Gabirol as he emerged from the shadow of the hall and into the brig of the dry docked cargo ship. His steps were swishing whispers against the grated floor despite the heavy soled shoes and gold jewelry adorned around his tight-cuffed and fitted gray checked suit.

"You called?" Solomon said into the steel walled room, his voice deep with impatience coded into each syllable. The resentment for his association with the selfish American was an aura all its own, emanating from Solomon like a presence difficult for anyone to ignore. But he needed the former FBI Director as much as the American needed his expertise.

"So, you did get my message?" came the slick and eely voice of John Edgar Hoover. "I had to wonder." He leaned across a wooden table engraved with a map of the Mediterranean coast. A number of shining gunmetal gray auric cruise ships floated across the table like ghost ships bobbing in the sea. The darkness of the brig cast Hoover's pale face with a sickly shade of silver in the glow of his auric energy. Behind him was the warm window-framed Málaga bay at sunset, glistening with turquoise waters and catamaran boats where the mountains tumbled into the sea. But nothing could make Hoover appear any less greasy in his navy blue suit with his gunmetal circular lapel pin that Solomon swore he would never wear.

"Must I go through this again with you?" Solomon said.

"I'll work with you, not for you. That includes finishing what I'm doing before rushing over to see what you need of me."

"This job is bigger than the both of us!" Hoover said. "Why does everyone else around here understand that but you? This is no small job. This is the one that will change our lives forever. We'll have the power to do whatever we want. We'd have the power to get to the Moon, Mars, colonize Atlantis or wherever else we might want to go. Do you get that?"

"Atlantis?" Solomon said. "Are we back in the 16th century?"

"We'd have the power to build Atlantis from the very essence of history itself," Hoover proposed. "Our power of limits will be limitless."

"And what good would that do us?" Solomon said, his body still and unresponsive to the Hoover histrionics that Solomon loathed behind the shades of his hair. "I've been everywhere I've wanted to be. I'm where I want to be now, doing what I want to do, aside from right this second and every moment that I spend with you, of course. I am living for what I want, and I'm living for more than what you busy your mind with everyday. With surviving. It's an American curse, of course, survival as a lifestyle. I'm happy with my Mediterranean pace of life and with how I maintain my immortality. I know what I am, and I do what I need to do when I need to do it. Existence isn't my whole identity. My only gripe is with the world infesting my city, and for that, I thought we already had a plan. So, what do you want with me today?"

"Have you always taken for granted the gifts you were given?" Hoover asked, moving his body in a shimmer of gunmetal auric energy as he peered closer at one of the auric ships floating across his miniature Mediterranean.

"My gift came with a heaping of humility," Solomon said,

tracing every scar on his boil riddled body with his mind. "But I'm not sure if any amount of humility could counterbalance your American penchant for feeling like you're constantly at a lack of something. I've survived hundreds of years just the way I am, with no need of going to the lengths you feel you must go."

"But you'll do it for Portendorfer?" Hoover asked, staring Solomon dead in the eyes.

"Portendorfer wants a place in this world, not the one you envision," Solomon said.

"Gabirol," Hoover said, laughing. "You're naive even in your old age. This world is an illusion of millions of different forces pulling at the wheel, all trying to direct the way we go. To want to live in this world, is to give up your hand in bending the world to your vision and to accept that of somebody else's. Portendorfer gets that, and if he doesn't, he soon will. I'm ready to start loading the crew. And then the guests."

Solomon couldn't fight the smirk forming in the shadows hiding his face.

"Everything and everyone will be on route," he said. "I'll send Portendorfer over with a list of names and auric levels. We'll soon both get what we want, it seems."

"One way or another," Hoover returned, turning around to take in the view of the orange glowed, crystal blue bay and ship spotted sea.

CHAPTER ONE

MEANDERERS OF MÁLAGA NIGHTS

Spanish melodies lingered out from the well of the guitar and brass horn of the saxophone, smooth and warm in the sweet Mediterranean Sea breeze that blew into Plaza de la Merced, slowing time as the spell of the music ebbed against the restaurant table where Antonio and I sat watching the musicians perform for us and Picasso. Who sat in cast bronze on a marble bench behind the performers, and to whom we drank. It had been a little over an hour since Antonio and I landed in Málaga, and, despite Aurelius's wishes, Antonio wanted to have a special birthday dinner together to celebrate me and my first night in Spain.

We chose the drag queen bingo paella restaurant with the Spanish music and drag queen servers. While the vibes felt right, I actually chose the place after catching sight of the steaming mixed mushroom paella as we browsed the bookshelf of the old Spanish facades lining the perimeter of the square plaza. The outdoor seating was spectacular under the dimming haze of the pink and purple sky. I felt like I could see the sun move as it set behind the ornate decorations of the roofs and the shrub spotted hills beyond the valley of the city.

Actually seeing the hills of southern Spain for myself made me understand Hemingway when he compared them to white elephants. The whole terrain of southern Spain looked to be made up of the tight hunched curves of elephant backs, herded close enough to one another that bridges were needed to connect roads against the slopes. All I wanted to do was enjoy another night of free life without the pressures of the world building around me, despite being brought to the city for work.

We spent the summer together at the bungalow in Ocean City after surviving Joshua's hunt for me. The old salty bungalow on the beach became a real home for us by the time September came to a close, and it was hard to leave the peace of the routine we had built for our days there. I felt, perhaps, the most put together I had ever felt before.

My mornings and evenings were full of training sessions with Antonio, Kana, Ikkyu, and Zenda. Aurelius had left for Spain shortly after our victory. Leaving Ikkyu and Kana to even give me weekend lessons on hand to hand combat and sparring with different metal, wood, and auric weapons. But the best part about living on the beach was the access to unlimited ocean water to pull from and blast at Antonio in battle, while Zenda kept our training concealed from mortals behind a bubble of mirage.

But just being with Antonio was enough to make me want to keep that life forever. I'd waited so long to feel what it was like to have someone like him around. Someone who was unafraid to love me and to show me a way to start loving myself after growing up around so much hate. I could depend on Antonio if I needed to in ways I could never do with anyone else before. The rhythmic breathing of his sleeping body beside me every morning and night as I straddled the boundaries between the days was the constant and assuring presence I never knew I needed until it was mine. I didn't want to go without him for a day, and he was teaching me how to better accept and be a part of the little family of the five of us Ocean City immortals.

"How's this for a birthday surprise?" Antonio said, before taking a sip of the red sangria he held by the bowl of the glass, wrapping his finger around the straw at an angle that kept the dried fruit inside the glass enough for him to gulp down a large swig of the sweet red sloshing juice at the rim. While the saxophone dipped in tone and climbed back up to the high ringing bells of heaven above.

"It's verifiably the best I've ever had," I said, sipping my sangria in turn. It was my first glass in Málaga, and the wine of Spain was already the best I'd tasted. It puckered the mouth, but was as sweet as a grape skin fresh from harvest. The dried citrus fruits floating around between the ice cubes looked to be mostly for decoration, but added a slight hint of matured zest that held on the palette, making the wine dance along my tongue with a delightful zing that still gripped me after I swallowed.

"Every year at school I hoped the guys wouldn't notice my birthday coming up," I said. "Joshua would always humiliate me extra on the lead up to the day. One year my parents sent an edible arrangement, and he took the time to carve every piece of fruit into the shape of a penis before bringing it to me, singing 'Happy Birthday to the ***.' It was disgusting."

"I bet you devoured that fruit though," Antonio said, lifting his eyebrows at me with an amused smirk.

"Of course I did," I said, rolling my eyes as I laid to rest the pain of Joshua's 'jokes.' "Back then, I never imagined I'd be here, though. In Spain on my birthday, with the most handsome man on Earth by my side."

"You're right about that," Antonio said, smiling at me with the soft confidence that love seems to bring.

"You've made my birthday more special than anyone, honestly," I said, thinking about his sweet jokes about the airport vegan food and the way he held my hand as the plane took off.

"Well, that's my job now," Antonio said. "Birthdays, holidays. I'll make them the best you've ever had."

"My life's so different from how it used to be, now," I said, thinking back to the prefilled birthday postcards my parents would send me from wherever they were traveling in the world.

"After everything you've been through," Antonio said. "I'm sure you'll be able to handle me and my antics, but it's the other immortals you'll have to watch out for."

"I'm ready for that, no question," I said, palming his shoulder. "I've been excited for this trip since you brought it up. I just didn't want to end our summer together faster than we had to."

"I didn't want it to end either," Antonio said. "I had a lot of fun with you. It was the best summer in my life, even if it did have a rough start. But these European immortals are *real* philosophers. Like, drive you to the brink of madness type conversations and situations that they put you in. And all for their own purposes of philosophical exploration."

"Are they really that bad?" I asked.

"I mean, I can handle them," Antonio said. "They'll mess with you though. It's in their nature. Right away, everyone's going to want to hear your first hand account of the power you used in Joshua's cave," Antonio said, flashing a grave look of reflection. "But only because they're impressed with your abilities, of course. And because they're just nosey oldies."

"I figured they'd want to know," I said, half of myself wanting to forget my first week down the shore, while the other half still felt proud of myself for getting us out of Joshua's mess alive. "I didn't want Aurelius to tell them until I was here."

"It was for the best, but it's driving them mad I'm sure," Antonio said, jittering with laughter. "I know I'd go crazy not knowing the end after reading that report."

"I'm sure Aurelius's kept their curiosities under control," I said, having faith in the man I couldn't help but see as a titan among the rest of us.

"He's good at keeping everyone in check," Antonio said. "But dissent among the ranks festers in obscurity. That's true among both mortals and immortals."

"We forget who we are when we're left in the dark," I said, watching the fountain in the square plaza spit water that blazed with the burning like of sunset.

"Saying things like that makes you sound like a philosopher already," Antonio said, impressed enough to take another sip oof his sangria in cheersed recognition. A drop of the purpled wine dribbled from his bottom lip down his chin, and he wasted no time wiping it with his fist as if it was blood from a fight.

"How safe is this city, actually?" I said.

"For gays," he said. "It's ranked more safe than most, but for immortals, it's a battleground."

"You didn't want to mention that before?" I said, my heart sinking in my chest as the metallic taste of auric energy soured my mouth. I was always a master at maneuvering myself around the dangers of my life, but my new power felt like the carbonation of a shaken soda bottle primed and ready to pop at the first slight slip of control.

"Whoa," Antonio said, taking a slow sip of wine and

grabbing my hand across the wood and tile table, before withdrawing it in the next moment. "Conceal your energy, or we really will be in danger. All of Eurasia and Africa are battlegrounds for immortals. That's why Aurelius set us up in South Jersey. Ocean City is our sanctuary, but out here we always have to be on alert. Europe is not like the Americas. There are threats here in every city that have survived centuries because they're experts at surviving. They have survived wars, genocide, famine, and all sorts of issues in between. We have to be just as smart as they are and try not to be noticed."

"It feels like I'll never get to a point where I don't have to think about hiding my energy at all times," I said, cursing my slowness to master control of my energy despite everyone's talk of how powerful I was supposed to be.

"You'll get it," Antonio said. "I have us cloaked head to toe from any abilities that could detect our energies. I can conceal you to an extent, but when we live our lives in the open, there's no room for error or mistake after tonight. Every moment of this is part of your training. Soon you will need to master the control necessary to keep yourself safe at all times. If I ever fall unconscious again, I'll need to know you'll be able to keep yourself safe and make it through."

"I did alright last time," I said, smiling at him, and holding out my glass in cheers, but I couldn't talk about that night without reliving the tragedy of the loss of life of Joshua's innocent cousins and the baby Joshua lost years before.

"It's a tough spot for you to be in," Antonio said, watching me as he spoke. "I don't know if I would be strong enough to be here if I were you. You've seen some of my memories of different missions, so you know the risks even beyond the ones you've learned first hand. I admire your strength and confidence."

"Thank you," I said, surprised by his confession and turned on by his admiration and honesty. "There's no point in backing down anymore. Not when backing down is to go against my will."

"That's right," Antonio said, looking pleased with me, even if our reality was as much a nightmare as it was a dream.

"I need to be able to protect you too," I said. "I couldn't live with myself if I couldn't protect you and something happened. Until then, I'm a liability. I came to train and push myself. I'm ready for it to be difficult."

"If you're that determined," Antonio said. "Then you might just learn faster than all of us."

"I will," I said, ready to be on the other side of Immortal Philosopher Boot Camp already. I thought after graduating from NYU I would have had all of the tools I needed to live my life, but the corruption of the world always seems to show us how underprepared we are for what comes next for us.

"I love you," I said, acknowledging the feeling that had been blossoming in me for months. The love confession was something I had said first, because I wanted him to know in case he didn't feel the same. His nature of letting me ask and say things first frustrated me, but only a little. I couldn't blame him for not telling me everything he thought or knew while there were so many things he knew that I've been trying to catch up on. There are only ever so many hours in the day to share the most crucial information we get to share with each other. Movies do a good job of fictionalizing the American spy in Europe as a high stakes lifestyle, but to really feel the stress of being in the field is an experience like dodging bullets in a war zone after dark. Predators could be everywhere.

"I love you too," he said with a kiss in the air in my direction that left an impression on my cheek through his auric power that felt as magical as it was.

The thing about traveling while gay is that, no matter how romantic a place you find yourself in, you never hold your partner's hand or hug them in public, god forbid kiss. You never know if being gay is accepted or if there are hate-supremacists ready to act against our 'evil' influence. You never want to end up dead for crossing the invisible line between straight and not. We end up coming off more guarded and paranoid than ready to enjoy a carefree vacation, but it's all we got to work with.

And as the guitar at the restaurant next door took us into the beautiful and rhythmic strumming of flamenco, I wondered how deprived of love we are as a species who shun the most basic forms of affection from the public experience? Homophobia seemed an American export compared to Europe, but the signs of hate were spreading fast with the viral nature of US based toxic Bro-Podcasters.

"Is Picasso one of us?" I asked, taking another sip of red while I analyzed the cast contours of the statue of the artist staring back at us from his bench.

"We're not entirely sure on that one," Antonio said. "There have been some reports, but we've never been able to verify. If he is, he probably painted himself into one of his paintings without a reason to come back."

"That would be something," I said. "How would we even know which painting?"

"I think we'd be able to figure it out as immortals if we tried," Antonio said. "If you'd like, we can take a trip over to the Picasso Museum one of these days. It's inside his old Málaga home."

"I didn't know Picasso lived here," I said. "Maybe we'll find some clues about him. I'm ready to try out some of my powers in the world and see what mysteries I can uncover. My story can't be the only one like it. I have a theory that tortured artists are a lot like philosophers and might have had more tendencies to actually be immortals or to be afflicted by predators because of our auric energy in our work. Could an artistic muse be another form of predator?"

"You're probably more right than wrong," Antonio said. "You'll have to talk to everyone else about it. A few of them might know some things to help your theory. Aurelius met Picasso during Picasso's life. He met Dali, too. He tried teaching me everything he knows, but you can't condense centuries of life into the amount of conversations we've been able to have. You'll have to talk to Stein, too."

"And here is your paella," came the voice of the waiter over our shoulders as he placed down the yellow rice dish in its searing serving pan, and I was relieved by the delicious smell to replace the pervasive cigarette tainted air.

"I'll have a second cup of sangria, please," I said to the waiter after he asked us what more we needed. I liked the service in Málaga. It was more casual than in the United States. Everything felt more casual. I felt like sitting in my seat for hours observing the city at night, and it seemed like everyone around us was determined to do the same. It helped too how Spanish came to me as quickly as Antonio could teach it to me. Somehow my auric power made communication easy without thinking much about interpretation and translation. What I heard from people, I understood. When I spoke to people, they understood.

"This paella really looks amazing," Antonio said. "I've had some good paella in the past, but these mushrooms look better than Mario Kart trophies. You have to squeeze the lemon before you take any."

I stopped myself with the serving spoon in hand and dumped the yellow rice back onto the dish where I scooped it from. "Lemon sounds like a nice touch," I said, grabbing the lemon between my fingers and squeezing its juice over the baked rice and meaty oyster and lion's mane mushroom strands that had been tinged with the burning red of the Spanish saffron the dish was mixed with.

"You're going to love this," Antonio said, and I was happy that the dish was the size of half the table. We finished the lime green olives and hummus that we ordered for an appetizer shortly after the waiter had set them in the center of the table. Training as an Immortal Philosopher made my stomach feel like a never satisfied pit of starvation. Every other thought that popped into my head was of how hungry I was ever since the shock of our battle with Joshua wore off.

"Mmm. You're right," I said, impressed by the flavors and texture of the rice's bright citrus and herbal profile. I breathed in the perfume that filled the air with the earthy musk of saffron, rosemary, and garlic. "This is so good." I said, as my body melted from the head down as the flavors tingled my taste buds and travel-slugged mind.

"It feels like home," Antonio said. "That's why I get it."

"It does," I said. "Like how I think home should feel, at least."

"Like how you felt at the bungalow?" Antonio said, taking another bite.

"Yeah, just like when you'd sneak up behind me with a hug every time you caught me staring out the kitchen window at the sand dunes," I said. Antonio laughed and smiled.

"You did love that," Antonio said.

"Not as much as you loved scaring me," I said, skewering a thick slice of mushroom with my fork and scooping some rice up with it to try the meal as a whole. "But yes, I love most of the things that you do." The mushrooms were a burst of umami juices as I chewed. They blended with the fragrant rice and took the dish to the next level.

"It's hard for me to find something you do that I don't love," he said. "But I'll let you know when I find something."

"If you do, I might have to do it more often," I said, laughing. "But honestly, I could eat here every night. They have paella with seitan-chorizo I saw on the menu that I want to try, too. I haven't had vegan chorizo since I left Manhattan."

"We'll definitely come back, but not every night," Antonio said, with a laugh. "This is the one city I've actually spent enough time in to know where to take you for dinner and fun."

"Oh really?" I said.

"Really," Antonio said between bites. "Why do you love to ask me that? Do you doubt me?"

"No," I said. "'Oh really,' is my favorite way to invite you to share more."

"I never know if you're interested in a good or bad way when you say it," Antonio said, staring at me with a narrow look.

"That's because I never know how I feel about things until I get enough information to know how to feel," I said, shrugging. "Call it a defense mechanism from dealing with life in a homophobic frat house hell hole where one of my closest friends secretly wanted to kill me everyday of my life and used his secret knowledge of my closeted gayness against me."

"Considering everything you've been through, it's not the worst defense to have," Antonio said, nodding his head in agreement. "Considering the circumstances, I don't know if

I would have been able to deal with it for as long as you did."

"It's something you have to get used to," I said. "Aurelius raised you with love and shared all the parts of his life with you that he could. And he still teaches you. My parents had me babysat until I was old enough to go to boarding school. Joshua and I were bound together from childhood on. Elementary, middle school and high school were all the same story. I thought college might have been better, but my parents offered everyone to stay with me in the brownstone. It was all that I knew, but I felt paralyzed against making changes until I had my degree."

"And look at you now," Antonio said, leaning back in his seat as if to get a full view of me to admire.

"I'm not sure I'm much to look on with such admiration," I said. "Not yet, at least."

"If we only ever appreciated the final successes of an individual, we'd never learn about the struggles that it took to get them to their peak," Antonio said. "I admire the work more as it's being crafted. That is the true miracle. The finished product is nothing without the work that it takes to become."

"And what if you work your whole life and never reach a finished product?" I said, raising my fork with my eyebrows to checkmate him, curious about what he'd say.

"We're never a finished product," Antonio said, smiling at me with the warmth of every summer morning we woke up together between the sheets. "Those who settle themselves into stagnation are not a finished person, but someone who has given up on the possibilities of their potential."

"Like a statue cast of bronze?" I said, settling my eyes again on Picasso.

"Exactly," Antonio said, and for the first time of the night, the musicians set down their instruments for a quick break. They laid them in the hardshell cases they had set out between themselves and the roped off section of seating, but music was everywhere in the plaza to fill the air.

As we chewed into our thoughts and the paella we shared, a troupe of six guitarists and three drummers came marching into the plaza wearing matching white pants, shirts, and jackets, all playing their instruments loud and in coordination with one another, while singing along in Spanish. The beat was quick and felt made for dancing. The crowds around the plaza all stopped to face the musicians as they stomped further into the square, heading for the fountain while performing their music. They were a welcome energy to the evening as the sky darkened and the plaza lights lit up along the walkways and around the center fountain. As if on command, the crowd started clapping and dancing along as the performers spread out around the fountain, all moving their feet to the beat.

Antonio and I watched along, sipping our sangrias and finishing our paella. The nine performers in white played, sang, and danced around the fountain, while some of the crowd got involved, making their own ring around them, spinning in the opposite direction of the performers but with just as much energy and enthusiasm for the music. They all kicked their legs with their hands in the air. It was a performance that felt great to be a part of, even as a seated observer. Everyone enjoyed it, locals and tourists alike. Everyone was smiling and moved to show affection to the loved ones they were with.

I wasn't sure why there wasn't street music like it in the US and wondered if we were lacking some part of culture that clearly made everyone feel so good. I had only perhaps seen something like it in Disney World, but all of that was scripted in Disney culture and not something unexpected. In the US, live entertainment at bars and clubs were common, but there was something about the public display of entertainment for the sake of it being a part of life that felt different.

As the troupe finished their song and dance around the fountain and started up another song, they took their performance once more through the plaza on their way down another pedestrian avenue of restaurants and shops, turning the heads of everyone they passed.

"That was great," Antonio said, as the loudness of the music died down and we could hear each other again.

"I loved it," I said, already impressed with the city and its people. "This place is something special. It's hard to imagine it as a 'battlefield,' like you said."

"Thankfully the battling is only done by immortals," Antonio said. "If mortals were involved, the fighting would be far worse. We've seen that in history already."

Now, Kana has arrived, but where are you two? came the thoughts of Aurelius in my head.

And now the fun is over, Antonio thought back. *What's up, Dad?*

Only the mission I called you two over for, Aurelius thought. *And the fact that you're now late for the main event. Ready or not, I'm sending Kana to pick you both back up. And happy birthday, Dylan. This will certainly be one to remember.*

CHAPTER TWO

CLÚB PUERTO

The music thumped from the bouncing minivan sized speakers framing both sides of the stage, shaking the corrugated metal walls on their clattering screws. The cargo ship hangar that doubled as the Málaga Port Dance Club was the biggest party I had ever shown up to and stayed at. Antonio led me through the sweat, smoke, and perfume rising from bodies like an atmosphere off the dense collection of dancing clubbers as they fought to ride the vibes. Their funk was an aura impenetrable by even the airplane wing fans cycling the air above, where the private guests lounged on couches with bottle servers and dancers in fancy ruffled flamenco gowns of all colors, who stomped their heels into the grated floor as the music drifted from techno, to hip-hop, to 80s throwbacks, then to today's pop favorites. Antonio was leading us through the crowd to the steps that led up the wall to the lounges. But over the music, I couldn't hear a word he or anyone else was saying.

I can't hear you, you know, I thought to him, his face flashing in and out of darkness and blinding light in the beamed light effects behind him.

I was telling you my embarrassing first clubbing story, Antonio thought.

Can't that wait for later? I thought. *I want to hear it, but I can't focus. Aurelius is counting on us. This mission seems more important than he's letting on.*

The missions are always more important than he lets on, Antonio thought back. He moved forward, pushing his way between people where he could without getting an elbow to the face, which I appreciated in the flailing crowd. Everywhere was the dance floor except for the stage that connected to an outside building where the musicians took and left the stage that stretched out from the wall at the midpoint of the building. Bars ringed the perimeter, while the stairs up the walls to the private booths stood guarded by secret service type security guards in suits and earpieces, looking to make our mission a lot more complicated than it needed to be if things got bad.

Is Aurelius here yet? I thought, slipping past a man in only a long linen poncho, dancing sweat soaked and dripping from whatever made his eyes roll back in his head while he shook the universe with his hands stretched up toward whatever heaven he saw above him. *This is not what I expected.*

I can't be there, thought the voice of Aurelius in my head again. My powers of detection were improving, but I still wasn't sure when he was listening in or not.

You sent us here alone? I thought. *On my first mission?*

Antonio slid me a look that let me know he was offended.

You have each other, Aurelius thought. *Last I checked, that's all you two really need. Kana's still in the car outside waiting for your escape.*

You're right, Antonio thought. *We're fine. Aren't we fine?* Antonio turned back to me, waiting for an answer before continuing to bring us closer to the stage.

I don't see why we wouldn't be, I thought. *I should be ready for anything after summer training. I guess we'll have my birthday celebration later.*

I have to ask a lot of the two of you before we'll have time to celebrate, Aurelius thought. *I needed you for this mission because myself and the others have already been identified by the group I have the two of you pursuing.*

So, you've all been compromised, and you need us to save you? Antonio thought.

It's more than that, Aurelius thought back, sounding doubtful of Antonio's simplification. *We need you to smuggle a celebrity out the back rooms without the predators noticing.*

Who's the celebrity? I thought, wondering who would be the most likely to be mixed up with a bunch of predators.

Elliot Cutcas, Aurelius thought.

No way, I thought back, disbelieving the name.

Really, Aurelius? Antonio thought. *You want us to kidnap the one celebrity the entire world is talking about right now? Why?*

It's too complicated to explain mid-mission, Aurelius thought. *But yes, we need what he knows.*

Why can't we just extract it right from his mind like we normally do? Antonio thought. *What's his story?*

That's what I'm still trying to understand, Aurelius thought. *There's energy around him keeping us out. Darker energy than I think he's capable of generating himself, and there're signs something bad is about to happen. We sprung a trap when we tried penetrating his mind ourselves. We were only just able to get out before our energies were lost and locked inside of whatever charm they placed on him. He needs to be lured away from them, like how Dylan removed himself from*

Joshua's influence enough to take control of his own power.

Who's controlling him? Antonio thought.

We're not sure anyone's controlling him, Aurelius thought back. *He could be acting of his own will, but someone's helping him. Dozens of tourists have gone missing, and they all followed the dark energy trailing off of him. It's more than a hunch we're working with, but not quite a fully concluded theory.*

So just, don't die. Abduct the world's most famous person. And bring them to the Palacio? Antonio thought.

Yes, Aurelius confirmed.

I'm not so sure about this, Antonio thought, looking back at me.

Why not? I thought, feeling now that nothing was more certain to me than needing to meet Elliot Cutcas and offended at the proposition we might leave without seeing him. I was never a celebrophile, but something about meeting Elliot Cutcas felt right. As if I should have been expecting my whole life to meet him then, smack on my twenty-third birthday.

You think you're ready for this? Antonio thought to me, looking at me with annoyed concern. I knew his annoyance wasn't with me, but the presence of his attitude was enough to annoy me too.

Yeah, I thought. *I guess you don't?*

I never thought that, he thought back, as the techno turned to a pop track I knew well. *Where is he, Aurelius?*

Above you perhaps? There should be elevated VIP booths around the hangar, Aurelius thought.

I know where he is, I thought to them both, as the voice of Elliot Cutcas cut through the choppy rev of the crowd that grew charged with *raaaa*'s.

"Baby do you remember?" Elliot sang, and the dark

stage lit up where Elliot stood in the orb of the spotlight. He held up five fingers and counted them down while staring at the floor as the instruments met the chorus of the angelic harmony of his background vocals. "The stars shining in the sky. And how they mesmerized me. Reflecting in your eyes."

For the love of immortality don't look him in the eyes, Aurelius commanded, and I felt Antonio tug me in his direction. But my feet didn't want to move. They were glued to the ground, as I stared through the crowd at Elliot Cutcas for the first time. He was performing shirtless, as always. Showcasing his Elvisesque looks and what he called last month 'the carved vessel of Greek godliness' in an interview with independent bro podcaster and influencer, Jordy Portendorfi, aka Portendorfer. I was starstruck and surprised. I was as helpless to Elliot as he described himself being to the person in his song. It felt like reverse psychology, or even a cast spell, the way my body turned to cement under the pressure of the chiming music and enchanting background harmony.

It felt like I'd lost myself, when Antonio finally grabbed my face and kissed my squeezed lips hard. He snapped me out of my daze, but as my eyes closed on Elliot, I didn't want his song or our suspended moment to end. Still, I bent to Antonio's lips and pushed myself into him more, forgetting the crowd, the city, and the Immortal Philosopher still whispering things into my head from his Málaga palace.

We're too late, the thoughts of Aurelius came through after the buzz of the mental cocoon I was stuck inside of subsided.

Too late? I thought, kissing Antonio more as the memories of his body rose in me, once again making him all I could think about. But something in the feel of his final few kisses felt different as he pulled back and his lips and nose brushed my lips, as if he wanted to avert his eyes from me too.

Change of plans, Aurelius thought. *This could still work, but now it's a lot more complicated. How does the crowd look?*

They look fine. What's really going on Aurelius? Antonio thought.

I looked around at the crowd, keeping my eyes off of Elliot as I scanned faces. I wanted to stare at Elliot. I wanted to listen and take in every decibel he offered me, but something strange captivated me when I looked at him before. It made me afraid to look at him again, as if part of me knew he would wrap me into his charm once more. At the catching of my eye. The faces in the crowd staring up at Elliot, though, seemed unaffected by what he held over me.

Everyone looks fine, I thought, hoping Aurelius would give us the answers we needed. *What were we supposed to stop?*

Elliot's song, Aurelius groaned in thought. *The group he's been hanging around. The group we were hunting and are now being hunted by.*

Everywhere he's performed in Andalusia he's enchanted the crowds so that they've left their cars, their families, and their lives to board and work for the cruise ships Elliot's been touring around in. There's no sense or reason to the decisions. There's no contact from whoever joins him, and now they'll have enough people to work their third cruise ship for Elliot's eight port Mediterranean tour he's embarking on TOMORROW.

No need to yell inside our heads, Antonio thought. *We can hear you just fine.*

I yell for effect, you know that, Aurelius thought. *To emphasize the critical nature of this predicament.*

I kept my mind focused on the thoughts of Aurelius and

Antonio in my head instead of thinking for myself. I didn't trust myself not to let Elliot capture me as his first song reached its climactic rise in emotion and the storytelling was turned on itself in the only conclusion possible for the song, yet you never see it coming.

We'll go with plan C, came the thoughts of Kana.

More like plan D, Aurelius thought back. *This mission's been resurrected more than I've been.*

Resurrected? I thought, not wanting to let the topic go.

After Elliot's set, we'll take him out the back door, Antonio said. *Kana, just have the car ready for us to get out of here fast. There are predators all over the VIP booths. We're not going to stay hidden for long if they were able to discover the rest of you guys, Aurelius.*

It's true, Aurelius thought. *You don't have long. We'll see you all at the Palacio. Keep me informed. I trust in you.*

We got this, I thought. *World famous celebrities ain't got nothing on us.*

I hope you're right, Kana thought. *I'll have the car ready where you exit. I'm tracking your every move. It'd be a shame on all of us if you didn't make it through your first night in Málaga alive. Especially on the day you came into this world.*

Really, Kana? Antonio thought. *We don't need those thoughts right now. Let's go, Dylan.*

And Antonio pulled me along through the crowd as on one of the screens, Elliot pulled out a black baseball cap from his back pocket and slipped it over his dark haired head, backwards, for his song, "The Drama I Write."

The close up of his face in the video feed was the same as the perfect photos I saw of him on social media and in magazines. The close up was unfiltered, unchanged perfection, and it was like no feeling I had ever felt for a person before. It wasn't a feeling of love, or even of lust. It was a magnetism that he in his song best described as mesmerizing.

We moved through the crowd, my hand in Antonio's as he moved with more speed now that some of the people who were dancing were pale faced and frozen, staring up at Elliot the way I did. I moved between them, feeling from them the excitement charging through them moments before, now extinguished. They all felt empty, except for their attention on Elliot.

This is something different, I thought. *It's gotta be him. He's gotta be charming them with his songs.*

It looks like it, Antonio thought. *But I'm not sure he could be powerful enough to hypnotize the entire crowd. What do you think?*

The people who are the most hypnotized have the strongest auras, I thought, observing it throughout the crowd as we made our way toward the door near the stage with the fire red 'backstage sign' lit up above it. Elliot's aura was the one misting the room with silver light. *It'd be hard for him to do, but that voice is a gift.*

I guess we'll see how strong he is when we try to grab him, Antonio thought.

I was just thinking the same thing, Kana chimed in. *This would be a new one for me. Celebrity cargo ship warehouse rave party abduction. Humanity always finds ways to surprise me.*

I never thought someone like Elliot Cutcas could be as dangerous as he is, I thought. *His songs are so deep. You'd think predators would want to stay out of the spotlight.*

Some need it, Antonio thought. *The best and oldest predators are probably by large percent billionaires and dictators just by their nature of existence in this world, where the biggest criminals hold the most power.*

You know, when he became best friends with Jordy Portendorfi I was afraid he'd fall down the rabbit hole of the hopelessness of the internet bro-sphere, I thought. I didn't think it'd happen this fast though, considering he's gay.

Nothing means anything when the world is a confusing place for people who've been hurt, Antonio thought, bringing us to the wall at the edge of the crowd where the red door to backstage guarded by a squad of heavy breathing, buff men who all looked like carbon copies of the stereotypical FBI agent. They had black suits, snot stringy ear piece cords reaching down their backs, and the double edged way about them that made you nervous to trust them with your back turned.

I followed Antonio along the wall in the direction of the door, letting my attention finally fall away from infatuation with Elliot to focus more on the threats ahead. Antonio looked unworried by the guards, so I did my best to feel unbothered by them as they eyed us up behind their sunglasses glasses as we approached. Their auras moved in faint veils of hazy energy. Clearly mortal. Clearly not the threats we were used to, but still they managed to be intimidating.

The guards straightened up as Antonio and I reached them, and I noticed they all wore silver gunmetal pins on their jacket chest pockets. Antonio grabbed the arm of the nearest one who reached with his ear to try and hear what Antonio was saying. Then I saw Antonio's aura get to work. His sky blue energy tainted the aura of the big guy and speckled into the guard's weak auric core.

The other guards shifted on their feet with agitation at Antonio as they waited to know what the two of us were up to. The place was so loud that sound vibrated off the walls and echoed back into our heads in a distorted mess. It was no wonder the guards were so on edge.

Let's go, Antonio thought, and the bodyguard he charmed turned to lead us through the overpainted, drip dried, crimson shine of the backstage door.

In the hall, with the door shut behind us, the sound of the crowd and music outside was muffled by the fabric covered red walls and thick shag carpet. My ears felt clogged and busy as my hearing adjusted to the new sound level as we followed the guard down the empty hall. When we reached the door at the end, the guard held it open for us after he hulked himself through the smaller frame.

Backstage was a shadowy maze of tall hanging curtains and wires. White doors lined the back wall, each hanging with golden stars, while a group of stage hands near the stage observed Elliot performing. The group felt absent of auric energy, making my stomach sour with the oddity of the sensation. Over the summer, Antonio had trained me to project a false aura to trick predators without sticking out. But where their auras should have been in the auric current, there was nothing. I wanted to identify them, but I couldn't catch their faces before following Antonio to the back by the dressing room doors beside the building's exit in the corner.

Good, we'll have a way out for extraction, Antonio thought, but not to me directly.

I see the extraction point, Kana thought. *Now, make it useful.*

Antonio directed the guard toward the dressing room door nearest the exit. I sensed Elliot's energy around the door too, so it made sense as the most likely room for Elliot to return to.

How do you feel about the group by the stage? I thought to Antonio.

Not good, he thought back, but he kept his face forward, watching the guard as he led us to the dressing room.

When we reached the door, the guard hesitated after grabbing hold of the handle. He turned to Antonio, scrunched his brow into an unflattering mess of rivulets and hair in a silent plea to keep the door shut.

"Go," Antonio said, and the guard turned the handle and pushed open the door, stepping into the room and obscuring the two people talking inside.

"What's this?" I heard from the voice of well known country singer, Calamity J. I never thought she could be the real Calamity Jane, but now I was certain she was one of the predators involved in the entire conspiracy, which meant we were up against someone with more than one lifetime of experience.

"Sorry to bother you," the guard said, holding up his hands as Antonio and I were still not visible behind his large frame.

"Without even a knock," came the other distinct voice of Jordy Portendorfi, another person I was hoping wouldn't be involved.

"I lost my focus," Calamity said, and I heard her get to her feet from her seat on the floor.

"We can take his energy," Jordy said. "Since he came to us of his own free will. I feel a strong pulse deep inside his reserves."

"It won't be enough, but we might as well," Calamity said, clicking in her boots as she approached the guard.

Fight or flee? I thought.

"He's finishing up his performance anyway," Calamity said.

"Hoover's not going to be happy with you," Portendorfi said to the guard.

"With me?" the guard asked, caught between the rivers of the energies of Antonio and the two predators. The room was thick with the auric mist of radiation green, gunmetal, and the bright red of bargain store branding and discount stickers.

"We can take a little bit," Calamity said. "If we take too much, I'm sure Hoover would notice. Shut the door, and we'll get started."

"Shut the door, oaf," Portendorfi said, and Antonio let loose his control over the guard, letting Portenforfi take over without detection before the door shut.

What now? I thought, happy to calm my pulse as the anticipation for battle started to wear off. But I was still on high alert.

Behind us the music continued, but Elliot's voice was absent from it. From near the stage, though, Elliot's voice cut through. It was him talking. He was arguing with someone behind a curtain off stage, stomping his feet.

"I don't understand what's going on," he shouted. "I tell you I need things to be the way. I tell you they need to be my way because I'm art! And this is a show! This is art! I'm an artist, and you're all my instruments! Without you, I'm nothing, but with you I'm everything we believe I can be. I can be anything we convince them I can be. When you fail me, we all fail them, and we fail ourselves. We fail to be what we truly are, and I can't have that! I won't! Jordy said you'd be great, but I don't know what's so great beyond your suits and hair. You won't even look at me, you're so distraught. I'm sorry, but I gotta go. I'll let you know when I'm ready to make more art, if I don't find better tools out there to exercise."

What in the world? I thought to Antonio. *I didn't think he'd be this bad. I don't know if it's worth abducting him. Our ears might fall off.*

We might not have to abduct him, afterall, Antonio thought. *And you're going to have to keep him talking once we get him out of here.*

'If' we get him out of here, I thought, as the floor stomping turned to a set of muffled steps heading in our direction.

Action, Antonio thought as Elliot Cutcas himself rounded the backstage curtain, running his fingers through the Elvis-like flop of hair that jiggled like a wave over his forehead. He was black haired and silver eyed, with a Mediterranean tan that darkened his olive skin to a toasted tone. Then the smile I saw everyone talking about everywhere lit up between his lips, completing the heart stopping effect that nobody else had ever had on me. Somehow, not even Antonio.

"I think we might be able to help you out," Antonio said, directing himself to Elliot while I struggled to gather myself.

"I was very much hoping you'd offer," Elliot said, seemingly refreshed by the sight of us. "Is this some sort of gift from Calamity? Or a joke from Jordy?"

"Neither," I said, feeling comfortable with Elliot's surprising turn to flirtation. "We're stage managers and pro-moters for the Mediterranean music scene. We heard you could use some help."

Good call, Antonio thought, while Elliot listened and considered our words, making his way across the hall.

He had the look of a man who knew what he wanted before he wanted to speak it into existence, taking his time to think while he approached, and closing the gap between us. He didn't feel like a threat, but how he talked behind the curtain was concerning.

His instruments, I thought to Antonio, reflecting on Elliot's words.

I know, Antonio thought to me. *But I'm still not sure he's behind all the aurics.*

"I could use a lot of help," Elliot said. "Especially from the likes of you two. What's the pitch? I want to hear it. I'm interested," he said, stopping so close to us that it felt like we were back in the rave crowd. The perspiration off his skin was a sticky perfume of the orange blossom scent of Málaga city, with the slight saltiness of sea air.

"No pitch," I said, leaning in and speaking past his neck. "Just come to our studio and check us out for yourself."

My body was hot and charged with the tension of my face being so close to his.

"Take me," Elliot said. "You two are going to be a lot of fun to work with. Jordy and Calamity are never going to believe this," he said, trying to move past us for the door handle. But Antonio and I held our ground.

"Better to return with stories of glories than to spoil the surprise," I said, charging a stream of auric energy into the suggestion.

"How enticing," Elliot said, not noticing my power, if he could sense it at all. "I could use a break from them all, actually. All they do is complain. I'm ready, then."

Kana, you got the car ready? Antonio thought.

Right outside, Kana thought back.

"We've got a car this way," Antonio said, leading us to the exit door.

We're walking him out now, I thought.

Without an explosion? Kana thought. *What kind of immortal abduction mission is this?*

One that's kept under control, Antonio thought. *You should take some notes.*

Oh, I could give you notes on a thousand missions I've completed without my body even leaving home, Kana thought. *You two babies ain't got nothing on me.*

Well actually, I thought, feeling Elliot's breath against my neck as I led us out the exit door. *I think we seduced the most world famous pop star ever. Is that something you could say?*

That, I'm happy to say, I've never even attempted, Kana thought, and we were outside in the darkness of the back car lot.

The streetlights of the cargo yard lit up the gates around the port, while Kana sat idling in the humming black Euro-Chinese electric sedan.

This is weird, Antonio thought.

"Here we are," I said, reaching the car door. "The name's Dylan, Dylan Eaglegod."

You didn't have to give your real name, Antonio thought.

"Dylan, nice to meet you. Elliot, Elliot Cutcas," Elliot said. "I'm sure you knew that."

"You're very right," Antonio said. "We know you. My name's Antonio. Now, let's go. We have a lot to show you."

"I'm ready for you, too," Elliot said, laughing to himself as he slid in to join me in the back seat.

And finally Antonio, looking reluctant to climb in, joined our tight squeeze and shut the door.

"Cozy," Elliot said, slapping his hands down on each of our knees, smiling with his eyes forward.

Let's get out of here, Kana, Antonio thought.

"To the studio," he said, against the silence.

"Yes, to the studio," I added, unsure of how much of the act we'd continue to keep up now that we had him.

"Right away," Kana said, and then I realized Elliot's eyes were on mine in the rearview mirror the whole time, tempting me into a love sick pit I never expected to find myself in as Kana pulled the near silent car away from the building.

As we pulled out of the parking lot, the door to backstage blew open, and the security guard stumbled out while Calamity J and Jordy clamored around him, their auras blazing their toxic green and discount red.

Here we go, I thought to Antonio and Kana, and I sparked my cobalt aura to life around me.

Jordy and Calamity both blasted beams of auric energy at our car, sucking at the weak aura of the bodyguard for extra fuel.

You boys got this, Kana thought, directing us more so than asking us.

We got it, Antonio thought, but out of instinct I already expanded my aura around the car, covering the metal with auric armor that I hoped would withstand their blast.

You bastards! came the thoughts of Calamity J through the sea of thoughts.

When the blast hit the car, I charged everything I could into keeping up our defenses as I struggled to absorb their attacks. While I shook like seagrass in the wind against the strain, Antonio was taking an offensive approach to defense, by channeling his sky blue aura across the ground in their direction. When the energy wave reached their legs, his aura shot like a missile up their bodies and down their arms, gloving their hands in cyan gauntlets that exploded in gender-reveal blue clouds of smoke.

"You don't have to be nervous," Elliot said, not noticing a second of the attack as Kana floored it down the bayside boulevard and out of sight of our attackers. "You'd be surprised how many people shake when they meet me. It's an energy vibe thing, I think."

"I'm fine," I said, relieved the assault was over. "It's definitely an energy vibe thing."

"You're not the first, and you're not the last," Elliot said. "I'll make sure you feel comfortable."

Can someone shut him up? Kana thought.

Took the thought right out of my head, Antonio added.

"Thank you," I said, keeping my attention out the side, front, and back windows of the car as the city of new-modern and old-intricate buildings passed us by. "I'm fine."

"As long as you say so," Elliot said, laughing to himself for some reason I felt better off not knowing about.

My skin was still burning like it had been blistered from absorbing the attack. Before we fled, I noticed the mass of concert attendees marching single file out of the concert hall, lined up, and heading toward the docked cruise ships in the cargo harbor. But that too Elliot didn't seem to notice.

Did you two see the crowds? I thought, my mind finally catching up.

I sure did, Kana thought. *I hope Aurelius has a back up plan for this. It doesn't look like missing Elliot will stop them now.*

They seemed frantic about missing him back there though, I thought back.

If this dope is the key to their success, they should have kept a better eye on him, Antonio thought. *I think you're right, Kana. I'm starting to doubt even more that he's the criminal mastermind Aurelius thinks he is. But let's hope this is mission-complete and we can get back to our Málaga celebrations.*

CHAPTER THREE

POPSTAR PROBLEM CHILD

"This is your place!?" Elliot said, rounding his words with a rapturous amazement that I felt, too.

Kana pulled the car through an iron gate off the corner of a cobblestone street and down a snaking marble driveway with old gnarled-barked and tropical palm trees that obscured the world above and around us. Broad leaf ferns and bright purple flowers carpeted the groundspace of the walled garden with the density of a spring meadow that I imagined I could expect the comfort of a well made bed if I laid upon. Twinkling garden lights popped in and out of the darkness like auric insects or micro-fairies, and somewhere between purple flower bushes, a fountain gurgled into the humid atmosphere around us. At the end of the driveway, the marble erected into a wedding cake-like palace. Adorned in the center of the columned portico above the door with the shining words, 'Palacio Asturias' inside a marble crest depicting a cliffside castle and standing lion. A marble crown topped the upper roof with grape leaves and bushels of grapes where the crown's points held up the sky.

"Welcome to the studio," I said, containing the stagger of

my own suspended shock and remembering the false plot we needed Elliot to still believe in.

"This place is awesome!" Elliot said, as Kana wound the car around the marble driveway. "I saw this place from the helicopter earlier. It's got a green roof. I *need* a tour. I *love* MTV Cribs. You have no idea. I watch reruns all the time. I bet there're hidden rooms and passages all throughout, for sure. If there's a city-underground, I'd be surprised if it wasn't connected to some other buildings in the city. We'll have to get lost in one of the rooms, though, and I might have to give you a little tour of me, too," he said, lifting his arm over my head and resting it behind my back. Pulling me closer to him by my shoulder as he talked.

"Yeah, it's usually hard for people like you to get in here," Antonio said to Elliot, peppering attitude into each word.

"It's usually harder for people like you to get me to leave places like this," Elliot retorted, and he moved his other arm from Antonio's knee to behind Antonio's shoulders, too. "The tour's available for you as well, don't worry."

Get me out of here, Antonio thought, and I struggled not to laugh. I was on the precipice of a childish dream come true in meeting Elliot, but still teetered by the discomfort of Antonio and my love for him. I knew that if we weren't on a mission, meeting Elliot would never have happened. But it was hard for me to even remember the mission with the ramblings of romantic possibilities engorging my mind and body.

Can't take the flirtation? Kana thought to us as she pulled under the portico, where the ornate wood carved doors of the palace entrance stood thicker than walls.

He's nothing but a problem child, Antonio thought. *A*

popstar problem child.

That's how we feel about all you first lifers, came the thoughts of another immortal that felt almost like the voice of the palace energy itself.

Strachan? Antonio thought back, as Kana hurried out of her seat and around the car to open Antonio's door, keeping up the facade of the experience for Elliot.

"And who, here, is at my door?" called the pompous voice that matched the thought voice. It was a mustached man exiting the palace door who called to us as Antonio jumped out of the car to escape Elliot's hold, only to stumble into the arms of Kana as he flailed.

"It figures you're the first one out here," Antonio said, regaining his footing as Elliot and I joined them under the portico.

"I felt you cross the gate, of course I'm here," Strachan said, twisting one end of his mustache with a narrow gaze as he looked us over.

The energy inside the walls of the palace grounds had a nature to it that felt like the tightly collected and fermented particles of vinegar and wine in an aging bottle. The concentration of power here was intense, making the air thick with a buzz of enchantment, but it was an enchantment I wasn't sure was from the natural land or if it was made from the housing of so many immortals for so long.

Some of the energy seemed shared with the aura of the neat, silver haired Strachan at the door, with his round and mischievous eyes that scanned like TSA agents at the airport. The shimmering milky marble gray-white energy of the garden moved through him as if one with him as it also moved through the ornamental facade of the building's face. He looked to be one with the property in a way I didn't know was possible before, but that I noticed a bit with Zenda's home in Ocean City.

Before it was my turn to exit the car, Elliot slid out and held his hand for me to hold as I took my turn exiting.

"I wouldn't want you to fall, too," Elliot said, charming me despite the strangeness of the night. "You're way too precious."

"Thank you," I said, taking his hand without refusal. Checking off another day-dreamed thought of mine made true.

"My pleasure," he said, adjusting his hand around mine to more of a hand holding fashion as we followed everyone to the palace door, not loosening his grip a smidge.

"Welcome, new faces. Welcome," Strachan said, now sounding more like a delighted host. "Hurry in, hurry in. Aurelius is awaiting." As he spoke, he waved his arms to beckon inside, where his aura really bloomed around him. He wasn't the strongest immortal I'd met, but his energy was more grounded to his surroundings than others, which made me wonder if he would feel weaker away from the garden and palace.

Who is he? I thought to Antonio as we gathered around him.

Why don't you ask your new boyfriend? Antonio thought back. I'd be lying if I said I'd forgotten Elliot's hand in mine. You never forget when a popstar is holding your hand, and it felt as normal as you wouldn't expect it to feel. But it still felt like magic.

Oh, please, I thought back. *Whatever fantasy is playing in his head, I have nothing to do with.*

I'm more worried about the fantasy playing out in your head, Antonio thought back.

I didn't know what to say, and I couldn't tell how serious he was. But my thoughts froze as I took in the paradise inside the Palacio around us.

Bouquets of a hundred different flowers lined the walls and center of the entrance hall, making the room feel and smell like the freshest spring meadow, baking in the sun after a short rain as everything opens up and exhales with moisture and the essences of wet dirt, bark, and sticky floral pollen.

The large blue stained glass windows in the ceiling bathed the entire room in an aquamarine blue that made me feel like we were on clouds high in the sky. The floors ran in reflective polished designs of white and gray rippled marble tiles. Strachan gathered us around a circular table in the center of the room holding a large potted stumpy palm tree with bark the color of shiny charcoal. It was full of sharp, dark green leaves that made it look more like a plant made of petrified bone or dried alligator leather than it did a living palm, but the leaves of the canopy of the giant palm were fresh with a new growth that I could almost see growing in a mirage of impossible movement as I watched it. Near to it, I breathed in the scent of charcoal and oxygen, which wafted into the air, like a filter adding energy to the space we breathed.

"This is the nicest studio I've ever been to," Elliot said, drawn in by the magic of the room as much as I was. But not enough to let go of my hand.

"This architectural and artistic masterpiece," Strachan said, holding up his arms as if in prayer. "Is El Palacio Asturias, my crowning jewel. And I..."

"We need a private room," Elliot interrupted, holding up our hands. "I'm here to see the studio. I don't need the whole shabang. If I see what I like, I'll bite. Are you like the groundskeeper or something?"

"That's exactly what he is," Antonio said. "The studio is on the top floor. You're going to like what you see, don't worry."

Strachan looked between the four of us, more confused than I'd ever seen an immortal, until a thought registered in his head from Antonio or Kana that made it clear he was not needed.

"Very well," Strachan said, ushering us further into the building with a flourishing arm. The next room looked even bigger than the first. "It's always my custom to introduce new faces to the operation. But I'll move you along right into the studio without delay."

"Appreciated," Elliot said, pulling me to follow the group into the grand hall.

Everything about the first room was there, but even more elegant. The ceiling was the same, but bigger and taller. The columns around the room formed a square where a quad of sitting areas were set up with velvet couches and coffee tables in their symmetrical corners.

As we followed the walkway down the center of the hall, I glimpsed at the artwork hanging around the room. The complexity of the medieval Islamic mosaic patterns in the archways, floor, and walls depicted histories I hadn't yet learned but felt pulling at my mind to dive into. Through the back of the building was a large bookshelf lined ballroom, with tall glass doors at the back-end that opened up to an outdoor patio where the Mediterranean Sea bobbed up and down the lights of ships in the far distance of the night.

Antonio led us to the back left corner of the grand hall and into an area with a set of golden elevators and marble stairs that led up and down in ornate fashion, with a banister carved to resemble a smooth spiraling tree trunk. We stood in the golden reflection of the elevator door as Strachan called it down with the button. The Palacio looked ready to house over a hundred immortals if the occasion required, but the main floor was as silent as a midnight church.

"Take it all the way to the top," Strachan said after the elevator doors clunked open. "Aurelius is waiting for you."

"Thank you," Antonio said, and we loaded in without Strachan. "Be sure to start on something to eat. Elliot just performed and Kana hasn't eaten since this morning."

Strachan looked around himself to see who Antonio was barking orders at, before realizing he was the one Antonio was directing.

"Since it's been so long," Strachan said, his expression softening. "I'll fix something up, homemade."

"Perfect," Antonio said, and the doors clunked shut on the four of us.

Kana and Antonio were up front, side by side, leaving me in the back with Elliot still holding my hand between us. I was starting to wonder if he was bullied a lot on the playground as a kid, or if he was the bully growing up. The type of bully that would demand others be their friends and hold their hands without letting them escape. The type of bully that I found Joshua to be, but the feeling from Elliot was more of interest and infatuation rather than the pure essence of hatred I'd grown accustomed to. I still wasn't sure how much of a threat Elliot was, but I was happy he wasn't throwing fists or any other appendage, auric or not, at us. Things were getting complicated enough for one night.

"And here you all are," came the voice of Aurelius as the elevator doors finally opened. The sweet orange blossom air outside cycled into the elevator, and we joined Aurelius and a short-in-stature friend with tight pulled hair wearing a frumpy dinner suit who stood beside him on the patio of the Palacio roof. At this point, I didn't know what to say. I didn't know if we were continuing the ruse for Elliot or not, but Aurelius noticed as soon as Kana stepped aside, the hand of Elliot around mine. His head cocked to the side, causing him to take a second to rub his neck in thought before saying more.

"Another butler," Elliot said, stepping out of the elevator with me. "You have one on each floor? And you," Elliot said pointing at the protruding stomach of the stern looking woman in the suit. "Are you familiar?"

"No," the woman gruffed. "You'd know my name if we met before. I'd be sure of it. Stein. My name is Gertrude Stein."

"Gertrude Stein?" I said, in slight amazement. Antonio hadn't given me specifics on the names of the European immortals, but I had read about Stein and her wife in an English course in highschool. Only because she worked with more famous straight authors, like F. Scott Fitzgerald. Her gayness was never mentioned. The knowledge of her wife came from self-directed after-class research. It was a fact apparently not important enough to make it to the class discussion.

"And I'm not quite a butler either," Aurelius said, with the calmness of an assistant principal. "This isn't what you think it is. And before I forget, happy birthday, Dylan."

"Dylan?" Elliot said, looking more confused than I'd yet seen him.

"Dylan's my name," I whispered to Elliot.

"Oh, yeah. I forgot," Elliot said, sounding annoyed. "Happy birthday, anyway. Birthdays deserve special kinds of nights, you know. This should be the best yet for you."

"Yeah, thank you, Aurelius," I said. "And thank you too, Elliot. It's certainly been interesting so far."

"Well, don't count your blessings before you hit the pillow for the night," Aurelius said. "It's good to have you with us as well, Elliot."

But Elliot wasn't listening. His eyes were focused on the Mediterranean in the distance. "Wait, that's my ship!" Elliot said, dashing across the patio as if he could catch the blue lighted cruise ship in the distance as it rounded the glowing white-stone walls of the wedding-cake like Málaga lighthouse.

Aurelius watched him, but I ran after him out of instinct, still attached to the mission until told otherwise. And Antonio was with me, back running at my side.

"What do you mean your ship?" Antonio asked, heavy on each word, as if the weight of them were meant to slow Elliot down.

"I mean," Elliot shrieked, reaching the marble rail, and nearly flinging himself over from the momentum at his back. "My concert is leaving without me! How could they do this? It doesn't make any sense, but… No… Solomon wouldn't." He looked more troubled with every thought. "Jordy wouldn't, at least. That's for sure, I think."

"That's a lot of uncertainty," Antonio said under his breath, and rolled his eyes.

"And there they are," Aurelius said, coming up behind us. "While, here you are. There is much we need to discuss, Mr. Cutcas, and I want to assure you, we will get you to your next show."

"Why would they sabotage you like that?" Stein asked, gliding up to us from behind Aurelius.

"Did they pawn me off to you guys?" Elliot said, not taking his eyes off the drifting cruise ship. "This is cuz of Gabirol. I knew I couldn't trust him!"

"Au contraire," Aurelius said. "Gabirol knew of your dis-appointment with him, and look." Aurelius pointed out past the crowns of the lit frond puffs of the palm trees across the street, past the crescent strip of beach, and to the water beyond.

"Your private ship has arrived. The White Seahorse. See the amber lights?" Aurelius said, and as he spoke, I found the gleaming white yacht with three sail masts, careening into the crescent bay. The amber lights dotting the deck gave the distant ship an antique amber glow that didn't match the futuristic billionaire white-yacht exterior, but did seem to match the elegance of Málaga Bay.

"I see it," Elliot said. "Let's get down there. I can't miss my shows. My fans need me."

What is going on? I thought to Antonio, looking between him, Elliot, and Aurelius for some kind of sense making. Kana stayed by the elevator, watching us with the bored expression of the bodyguards from the concert.

Not sure, Antonio thought back. *Just keep playing along. Seems like you're enjoying it enough, anyway.*

I am actually, I thought, lying to spite his attitude. The months of agreeable communication left me unprepared for the ugliness of his surfacing jealousy, and I found my mind erecting the same defenses I used to hide myself from Joshua and my school friends.

"It's a sin to take an artist away from his art," Stein said. "I feel for you, my son."

"As do I," Aurelius said. "But we'll head right down. It seems everyone is right on time."

Good, he's your responsibility then, Antonio thought back to me.

I can handle that, I thought, returning fire and seeming more up to the challenge than I honestly believed I was. But the way Antonio was acting put me on antagonistic autopilot, and I was helpless to the death spiral of my triggered emotions.

"We'll walk down together," I said to Elliot, collecting his soft hand in mine. "Where are your shows at?"

He was panicked, and if Aurelius wanted to keep up the charade, I needed him to settle down. After a few seconds, his expression softened, and he looked down at me, taking his eyes off the horizon for the first time since we stepped onto the roof patio. His silver eyes caught mine like magnets, sending my heart tumbling over the rail of amorous confusion.

"Thank you," he said, his eyes glinting like moonlight around his pupils, while his silver aura dazzled like stars in the air between us.

"Of course," I said, feeling breathless as I spoke. I wanted to crash on one of the half moon sofas on the patio, staring up at the stars together until the sun came up. I wanted to drink a drink at the bar off to the side of the roof deck, and I wanted to ask Elliot a thousand questions about what it was like to be so famously himself. There were rumors, of course, about his taste for fine men, but there was nothing ever admitted to in public. Up and coming actresses and singers still found themselves trying without luck to catch the interest of the hard to get Cutcas, but it seemed like he didn't take notice unless you were gay and, in my case, already involved.

"Delightful," Aurelius said, breaking the awkwardness of the moment I didn't realize Elliot and I had created for everyone else. "Let's go, then. Our captain, Grace, is waiting."

Then Aurelius and Antonio turned to make their ways back to the elevator. Antonio, visibly more unhappy than ever. Every move he made was a jab or stab or darting of eyes. The veins of his neck and arms were thick with blood and pulsing fast.

"Don't leave me tonight," Elliot said to me, pulling my attention back to him. "I don't do good left alone."

Startled, I wasn't sure what to say. Stein was still staring at me with her beetle like eyes, and I felt seen by her in a way

I've only ever witnessed art be analyzed. I was toying with how I'd lie to Antonio later about feeling nothing at all for Elliot, but for now I wasn't sure what my evening would look like. And I wasn't sure how to handle a pop star sex icon who had obvious trauma around being alone with himself.

"I won't leave you," I said, tugging his hand in the direction of the elevator as I silently wished Aurelius and Antonio were still within earshot for help. "We'll figure all of this out once we board the ship. Don't worry."

"Such confidence, for such new recruits," Stein said, and I wanted nothing more than to get away from her. She stood with her hands clutched below her belly, and penetrated me with her eyes to the point that I solidified my mental defenses just to ward her off if she was trying something I couldn't see.

"Thank you," Elliot said, grinning with genuine and innocent pleasure at me. "I knew I could count on you."

I didn't respond beyond a nod as I broke away from his gaze and dragged him toward the elevator. He moved with me as I walked him across the patio under the burning stare of Antonio.

"Are you coming, Stein?" Aurelius called from the elevator with Antonio and Kana.

"No, Aurelius," Stein called back. "I'll say my goodbyes here. I'll watch you off and keep you covered. The Palacio is in good hands with Strachan and I."

I see things have gotten a little messy, Aurelius thought to me as Elliot and I stepped into the elevator.

I'm trying to figure out how to be useful, I thought back. *Elliot's not really what I expected.*

"You're a true friend," Aurelius called back to Stein with a wave and a smile as the elevator door cut her off.

I can see that too, Aurelius thought, as the elevator lowered us to the ground floor.

Even though we could implant thoughts into each other's minds, we all kept our private thoughts private and safeguarded from one another. It was one of the first things Antonio made sure I could do after Joshua. I learned how to close my mind to immortals at least as strong as Zenda and Kana, who were two of the strongest immortals I knew. Even Ikkyu couldn't penetrate my mind after he recovered from his head trauma.

You'll figure it out, Aurelius thought when I didn't respond.

I wasn't sure what to say, and I was happy he didn't know what to say either. I didn't want the matter settled. I liked the uncertainty of the feeling. Something deep down was drawing me to Elliot, and it was clear something was drawing him to me, too. I had to figure out what it was, and if Antonio couldn't understand that, I wasn't sure what he was doing. He was acting so different from who he was in Ocean City.

Is Elliot the key to the mission? I thought to Aurelius, ready to prove I could be more than just an inconvenience or annoyance for Antonio during our first worldly mission.

I don't think so at this point, Aurelius thought. *I don't see why they would leave him unless they got what they needed out of him. Which could be just as bad as if they still had him. Penetrate his mind and his past. Get close to him while he's with us. He's a first life immortal, too, you know.*

The man who has everything even has eternal life? I thought, with disbelief at the lottery of life.

He wasn't born with everything, Aurelius thought. *I identified him as an immortal in his infancy. Elliot's mother was murdered by his father, and the state took care of dealing with the father after a short round of trials. Elliot's grandparents weren't sure they could care for him, but I convinced them to try their best while our philosophical coffers covered his and most of their expenses. I was raising Antonio at the time, and I wasn't sure if I had made the right decision in raising him as an immortal from birth. I didn't know if I should try raising another boy the same way, as brothers, at that point. His grandparents accepted our offer to help financially, so I thought the matter settled itself. They raised him with love, and I had them guide him towards his other talents. Singing was his passion, and his auric power found its crowd-mesmerizing outlet. He didn't need us, until recently. It's hard to know when to upend someone's life with the knowledge of us until it's necessary.*

Are you ever oblivious to anything? Or do you really know everything? I thought back as the elevator stopped to let us out and my mind filed away the information into the context of everything I knew about Antonio, Aurelius, and the Immortal Philosophers. The fact that Antonio and Elliot almost could have been raised as brothers was a startling fact that Antonio hadn't mentioned before.

Does Antonio know all this? I thought as we stepped out into the hall of the ground floor. Antonio led Elliot, Aurelius, Kana, and I back into the great hall of the palace, before turning into the dark ballroom in the direction of the glass wall with the view of the pool patio and Mediterranean beyond.

"Farewell, Strachan," Aurelius said back to the curious man as he wheeled a cart of food trays behind us.

"Looks delicious," Elliot said, checking out the spread as we continued on our way.

"Save it for next time, Strachan," Antonio said, smiling through his uncontrolled, frustrated expression, causing him to look more in pain than Strachan looked hurt.

"As they always say," Strachan said, petrified by our fast leave.

"Look after that old man up there," he said, pointing at Aurelius.

Antonio knows nothing, Aurelius thought, groaning in his mind. *Not that I identified Elliot early, or that he almost had a brother, which in hindsight might have been good for him. But I could never have allowed Elliot to pursue his music the way he's found so much success in doing. The life of an Immortal Philosopher is not an easy path to follow. Especially so for a child. Antonio had as good of a childhood as we could have provided, but there's so much that he missed out on, too.*

The ballroom floor continued past the glass doors and onto the raised patio outside, where terraced sitting areas branched out on either side of a grand marble staircase that led down to the sapphire crystal blue pool and ground lit garden.

The palm trees danced in the light above us in the breeze off the water as we passed the blue lighted pool. Aurelius led us to the door along the street-side property wall and opened it with the flash of a tyrian auric blast at the lock, where the energy sank into the metal and clinked the door to a groaning open. On the other side, we crossed the palm lit Málaga street and were on the paved path beside the beach.

The amber lights of our ship were closer now, and it looked bigger than it looked from the roof deck. About a dozen sails were glowing from three masts, but it was still bobbing far out in the bay.

"We swimming out?" Elliot asked, and I wasn't sure how to answer as we crossed the beach in the direction of the water.

"We'll walk, of course," Aurelius said, lighting up all of our feet with his purple aura as he hopped over the low waves at the break and landed firm with glowing purple on the water surface.

"Cool," Elliot said, as the two of us leapt onto the water to join the other immortals. "I saw this in a Shortvid once."

We landed on top of the water, and followed behind Aurelius and Antonio, while Kana took up the rear. There didn't seem to be any threats. The beach was empty aside from a few couples walking, and there weren't any people to run into over the water, so I figured we were in the clear. If there was danger, Aurelius, Antonio, and Kana would know before I would've.

"This is the craziest thing I've ever done!" Elliot cheered, as we picked up to a jog across the water, our feet feeling as if they hit ground where we landed. "I knew I'd walk on water one day. You guys are the best. It feels like a song. You make me feel like / I could dance on my own vibes / Across the tide zones / On my way to your home."

As he sang, he slowed his speed and turned to me, stopping the two of us so he could hold my hand to his chest and pull me closer to him with his other hand on my back, until he kissed me on the water. Once, twice, three long unbroken times while the moon spot-lit us against the darkness.

You mesmerized me, I thought to him, and I felt his lips curl against mine into a smile. I kissed him back, without hearing the splashing footsteps of the others stop to watch us in our unprompted affection.

After the moment of feeling like one of my dreams had come true, I knew I messed up worse than Antonio would forgive me for, for the night at least. And when I opened my eyes, he had blasted forward in a trail of cyan light, already nearly at the ship.

"We have to go," Aurelius said, studying Elliot as he stood waiting for us. "Water walking can't last forever."

CHAPTER FOUR

THE WHITE SEAHORSE

As we reached halfway across the bay, the size of the yacht really started taking shape. The three masts and sails were nothing I'd seen on the billionaire white walled yachts before, making the whole ship more impressive than others without them. There were four floors of sleek black windows below, the main and upper decks, with a platform off the back where Antonio climbed aboard.

"It's nowhere near the size of the cruise ships I'm used to," Elliot said, as we water walked our way across the crescent bay to reach the group of immortals greeting Antonio. The smile across all of their faces brought a light to his face that only a true family could bring. A light that I brought to him every night except this night. I watched him turn again into the charming coffee shop owner, delighting each other immortals with a phrase or two that warmed their hearts and brought them together in hugs.

"It's not what I'm used to either," I said, unsure of how the rest of my birthday night would go with Antonio justifiably angry with me.

But once we reached the deck, I was treated with the same

warmth Antonio received. It was almost like Elliot never existed. Antonio helped me onto the ship with an outstretched hand and charming smile that wiped away any doubt I had in him, and he pulled me into the crowd of new faces to introduce me to everyone.

"Dylan, this is your Captain," Antonio said. "Pirate Queen Grace O'Malley. Captain, this is Dylan Eaglegod, my boyfriend."

"What a stunner," Captain O'Malley said. "I'm perked to 'av you aboard, and I heard you've brought us a birthday to celebrate, I hear?"

"Oh, yeah. I turn twenty-two today," I said, blushing from her sincerity and the embarrassment of Antonio's arm around my shoulders. I wasn't much for PDA, but I couldn't risk shaking him off after everything that had already made him annoyed with me. It actually felt good to be back under his arm after everything with Elliot, making me almost forget the feeling of his lips on mine and the way I kissed him back. "It's nice to meet you, captain."

Captain O'Malley's three cornered captain's hat reminded me of Johnny Depp's Jack Sparrow character from my childhood, but this Captain seemed like a much more put together sailor. And not only because she was a queen. She wore an amber blouse, brown long coat, and trousers that looked medieval and brand new at the same time. Her hair was a bouquet of red curls that looked as though they never came undone from their thick coils, and behind her, Kana was greeted by a Greek looking woman with a smooth teal aura and short black curly hair, adorned with a smaller black pirate's hat atop her head. Kana and the woman hugged each other for longer than I thought Kana would hug anybody, finishing with smiles that reached deep into each others' eyes.

"I'm happy to be aboard the ship, thank you," I said, watching the captain's gaze fall on Elliot coming up the deck behind me.

"And who is this familiar looking face?" O'Malley said, lifting the brim of her hat to get a better look.

"You should all know him as world famous pop star, Elliot Cutcas," Aurelius called to us, making his way over to us with the other immortals who still needed an introduction. Aurelius walked with his arms raised and gathering the attention of the dozen or so of us all congregated on the deck. "I want all of you to know, we're here to help Elliot get to his next destination."

"Welcome aboard," O'Malley said, reaching out her hand to Elliot for a shake.

"Wish I didn't need ya," Elliot said, looking around at the immortals. "But I'm glad I have a ship and crew to get me where I need to be. Just promise you won't leave me behind like my old crew did."

"No sailor gets left behind on the White Seahorse," O'Malley said, with a deep dig of emphasis that told me she was serious. "What's all this going on, Aurelius?" O'Malley asked, moving Elliot out of her way with an arm.

"He's mixed us up in some real shit this time," Antonio said, referring to Aurelius and rolling his eyes for O'Malley to get the message.

"Hyp, come here," O'Malley said, turning around to see Kana and the other woman finally parting their reunion. The taller woman, 'Hyp,' heard and flashed a smile at O'Malley that when Kana saw, her glowing face fell into a hard mask.

Hyp dropped Kana's hands and made her way over to us without another word to Kana, who stayed behind the congregation near the sliding glass door to the inside lounge of the main deck cabin. She looked small in the massive frame of the retractable wall, and more defeated than I'd ever seen her. The lounge behind was plush with curved sofas and a bar in the back, all bathed in amber light, with everything made of golden walnut and amber suede. The lights even cast us in the glow of Captain O'Malley's light.

"We have Elliot here, and we need to save his show," Aurelius said, as if explaining a plan everyone should already understand.

"Not stop it? What kind of silly mission is this, Aurelius?" said a hunched over Europeaner with lush, unbrushed and frizzy brown hair. His crazed eyes were glassy and wide, as if they saw the totality of his visual field and processed it all without the need to focus on anything specifically. The aura around him was egg yolk yellow and a density that made him look surrounded in powder.

"Mission?" Elliot said. "What's with you people and missions? That's all Gabirol would talk about, too. That's why I never wished to be one of you. This is a tour. Not a mission. You immortals are all the same."

"What did you say?" Antonio asked, staring hard at Elliot as everyone else watched in stunned silence.

"What do you know about immortals?" Aurelius followed up, grabbing Elliot by the shoulder and turning him towards him.

"Jordy said everyone Gabirol employs is immortal," Elliot said, with a look of shock and disgust from being handled. "That's the most I know. Jordy's one. I'm the only one around them who isn't, so I figured you all were too. Your lights are stronger than regulars'. That's how I knew Gabirol hired you." Elliot looked down at me from his few-inch taller height, smiling at me and again scooping up my hand, which everyone's eyes darted to before looking over to Antonio.

"Grace," Aurelius said. "Get us en route to Ibiza. But stay

behind that cruise ship enough for us to go undetected. They might not expect us. Leibniz, cloak up."

"Right away, Aurelius," Captain O'Malley said, grabbing Hyp by the shoulder and steering them both into the warm amber glow of the luxurious cabin.

"Shouldn't they expect us though? Even if they left me on purpose, they can't expect me not to show up at my own show," Elliot asked, finally looking confused for all the wrong reasons.

"I'm not sure, exactly," Aurelius said. "I'm a bit confused with all this, too. What else did they tell you about immortals?" Aurelius asked, releasing Elliot as the other immortals gathered closer for answers.

"I learned that I'll never be one," Elliot said. "They're born with magical light powers. I know Jordy and Calamity are ones. A few people I never learned the names of who Gabirol knows are immortal too. I'm a pop star, though, and I felt like they all wanted to be me, anyway. I didn't see a need to pay much mind to their talks of magic. My voice is my gift."

"And a gift it is," Aurelius said.

"An immortal gift," said the tall North African man with the olive skinned, kohl eyed woman standing with unspoken elegance under his arm.

"I think you're right my love," the woman said in a soft and silky voice, placing her one hand over the man's chest and looking between Elliot and I with a sharp and unmoving stare. Behind them, the lights of the coastal Spanish cities were ablaze, with their reflections shining off the rippled sea between the boat and land.

"Dylan, Elliot. This is King Juba and Queen Cleopatra Selene of Mauretania, the seconds of their names," Aurelius said, waving for the couple to step forth.

"Call me Cleoseléné," the Roman, Greek, and Egyptian Ptolomey said, smiling with the glow of the moon between her lips as she parted them to reveal a bright, stunning smile. "We're here to help however we can."

"And call me Juba," the king said. "I was expecting to only meet one new immortal today. Why didn't you tell us you were bringing two new members, Aurelius?"

"Two new immortals?" Elliot asked, looking at everyone with a slick smirk as if it were a joke to only disbelieve.

"Um, yes," Aurelius said. "Your voice is not your only gift. It's very clear to us that, with some training, you will be a full fledged immortal. The born that way type, and not the predatorial stealing life from other people type of immortality that's enjoyed by Gabirol and your friends Jordy and Calamity."

"And you're sure about this?" Elliot asked, looking down at whatever thoughts were going through his head, while I held my breath for the emotional explosions I came to expect from him.

"Haven't you come to some conclusions yourself about the gift of your voice?" Aurelius asked. "Your song *Mesmerized* is a powerful spell of a song, and when you do sing it live, it's been reported to have entranced people into catatonia."

As Aurelius questioned him, Elliot's lips spread wider and wider into a smile the corners of which he was unable to pull down. His face might as well have been frozen.

"I knew it!" he shouted, startling half the immortals around the deck, myself included, but Aurelius watched on, smiling all the same.

"You were right!" Aurelius said, laughing. I couldn't get the secret Aurelius had told me about Elliot out of my head. I didn't understand why I had to live with a secret I couldn't tell the one person I needed to be one hundred and twenty percent honest with. Now there was no denying that I'd have to live with the curse of that secret being on my mind all the time, just waiting for the right time for it to be too crucial to keep from Antnio. If that time ever came.

"So, what now?" Elliot asked. "What's a predatory immortal?"

"Now, we keep you safe," Aurelius said. "Just like we keep every single one of us safe. We mostly have to keep ourselves safe from predators, as we call them. Gabirol, Jordy, and Calamity are all predators. They weren't born with immortality, but gained it through some kind of way. We've stopped thousands of predators who have gained immortality by feeding off the energy of born immortals and of strong-aura mortals. We've stopped predators who have survived off of the self-sacrifice of others, off of murder, off of old corrupted shrines, and through other ways. And, if we're right, it seems like your old friends had gotten close to you to prey on your auric energy, too. Auric energy is the light power you mentioned. That is the tool we can access as immortals and as predators."

"What about mortals?" Elliot asked, as if trying a theory.

"Some mortals have strong connections to their auras, too," Aurelius said. "But you're definitely an immortal. There's no question about it."

"Alright, alright. I knew it had to be true," Elliot said, looking at me for a reaction, and, despite myself, I nodded at him with a smile. It wouldn't have killed me to be nice to him, but I was afraid Antonio might have killed me if I was *too* nice.

"Well, considering everything we've uncovered, I'm thinking I should join Grace in the brig. From there I can keep these currents in our favor," Juba said, and Aurelius nodded confirmation.

"Not just yet though," Aurelius said. "Elliot, let's get you to your cabin while we make sure we have a plan to keep you safe. I'm afraid the dishonesty of your old friends has been as complete as it has been vague, and it's a shame you have to go through this confusion."

"Yeah, tell me about it," Elliot said, yawning with annoyance. "I'm ready for some beauty sleep, anyway."

"Good, you need it," Antonio said, just louder than under his breath, but everyone heard.

"I do," Elliot said. "It's part of the responsibility of looking this good. Someone with your aggressive good looks should understand. You don't have to be a pop star to take care of yourself."

"I do take care of myself, thank you," Antonio said, receiving Elliot's backhanded compliment with an attitude that the entire room felt. Antonio mentioned the power of his emotions being hard for him to keep inside and keep from seeping out into the people around him. And it seemed like it was getting the better of him the more his frustration with Elliot grew.

"Juba," Aurelius said. "Maybe you could escort our newest member to his quarters before you make your way to the brig?"

"It'd be a pleasure," Juba said, making his way toward the interior cabin. "I'll show you some parts of the ship along the way. Dylan, it's fabulous to meet you. I look forward to getting to know you a lot better on this journey."

"It's a pleasure to meet you too, Juba," I said, melted by the warmth of his voice and kind eyes as his deep navy aura shimmered in inky waves around him.

"You coming with?" Elliot asked, looking back at me after taking a step.

"I can't now," I said. "But I'll visit you later," I added, seeing the disappointment overcast his gaze.

"Be there by the time I get out of the shower," Elliot said.

"I want to see you before I fall asleep."

"I'll try," I said, knowing I'd need more time to discuss everything with the other immortals. And then Elliot went without another word, following Juba into the decadence of the interior of the ship.

"I'm cutting out of here too," Antonio said, surprising me once again for the evening. I'd wanted to be without Elliot to hopefully smooth things over with Antonio, but Antonio blocked my shot once again. I watched him say good night with a hug for everyone except me, and then he too disappeared into the ship without even looking back at me as he went.

"Well, now we can have a more cozy discussion than I thought we'd be able to manage," Aurelius said. "Let's get down to business. Why don't we have a seat on the sofa inside?"

"Sure," I said, feeling lost aside from having Kana still around. It surprised me how quickly a few months can turn a person hungry for independence, into someone comfortable in being supported as a dependent. Even around others who wanted only to help me, without Antonio, I was starting to feel lonely.

The group of us followed Aurelius into the interior cabin as the ship turned and coasted into the small waves. Before getting inside, I caught sight of the lights of the cruise ship we were supposed to be following. It was about two crescent bay stretches of beach away, drifting into the darkness of the night.

"I have a spot for you here, Dylan," Aurelius said, nodding to a space on the amber suede of the sofa beside him, so I sat next to him. The other immortals sat around the ring of couches, all vibrating with energy that was so intense that it took focus to keep my head from spinning.

"Thanks," I said to Aurelius, looking around at all of the new faces. But even without Antonio, I was feeling more firmly in the throngs of my new life and the immortal identity I was building. I wasn't a mystery to myself anymore, even if I didn't know everything about my new world. Whether Antonio was with me or not, I was Dylan Eaglegod, Immortal Philosopher, and these were my people.

"So, where should we begin?" Aurelius asked the group. The wine and liquor glasses in their hands made each of them heavy where they sat, relaxed, and amused. "I know you all have questions for Dylan, but I want to see where Dylan wants to begin."

"Thank you Aurelius," I said, interested in knowing who each of my new family were. "Everyone's names would be helpful."

"Great point," Aurelius said. "Let's see. So, I introduced you to Cleoseléné and Juba. The moon queen and king of tides. You spoke with Grace and Hypatia, yes?"

"I spoke with Captain O'Malley, and Hypatia?" I asked. "That's Hyp?"

"Exactly," Aurelius said. "Hypatia was a Greek Alexandrian philosopher with a more difficult immortal story than some of us, but not all of us. Now, watch out, because Hyp likes to flip. One minute they'll present as a female, and in the next, they'll present as male. However, to find one of the most difficult stories, I'll introduce you to Queen Moremi."

"Oh, Aurelius, drop the Queen already," the stunningly beautiful West African woman said with an accent I couldn't place but adored. Her high smile and timeless elegance of movement pulled me into her presence as she lit up our immortal circle with her speech. She wore a thin gold silk dress with her hair braided into a pyramidal crown atop her head, adorned with dazzling gold clips and figures of what looked like swaddled babies. I'd never thought the mother of humanity was a person to meet, but Queen Moremi appeared to me closer to that earthly mother than anyone I'd met before. Her aura had the same moonlight glow of Cleoseléné, who she sat beside like a sister.

"You'll never find a more loyal leader than she," Aurelius said. "Having sacrificed everything for her people, she is an inspiration to us all. Feared by all who cross her, she will be a teacher to learn from."

"Thank you Aurelius," Queen Moremi said. "It is a pleasure to meet you, Dylan. I'm excited to fight by your side and teach you my immortal ways. Aurelius likes to bring out all of the pomp and circumstance of royalty, but, please, call me Moremi."

"Thank you, Moremi," I said. "It's my honor to meet you."

"Now for the bachelors among us," Aurelius said, turning to the four unnamed men I was also curious to know.

"The world has to watch out for these four," Kana said, joking from her place on the other side of Moremi.

"I'll go first," said the second youngest looking man. His voice was full of the direct certainty that reminded me of TED talks and debates that made me want to hear everything he had to say.

"He hasn't heard of you," the youngest of the men said. His youthful Persian features made him as young looking as myself, but he had the gravity around him of a poet or religious leader.

"He will," the black man with the violet aura returned, and I searched for his face in my memory banks of history. "Dylan, my name is James Baldwin."

"Ah, I do know you," I said, happy to find him among the immortals. "I've read a few pieces of your work. It's a dream to meet you."

"Ah, please. I only crawled, so you could run, my friend," Baldwin said. "I go by Baldwin now. I dropped the James after moving to Spain. Names are such a fascinating thing for immortals living in a mortal world. I just transitioned into my afterlife before you were born, so I'm relatively fresh on the scene compared to the dinosaurs around us. But you remind me much of someone I wrote about long ago. I hope you don't mind me saying so."

"Are you making moves on the new recruit already?" the Persian interjected with a playful accusation that I would have enjoyed if I wasn't already in the throes of relationship turmoil with Antonio and Elliot.

"Oh, Rumi, it looks like he's got more meat on his plate than I'd dare try my hand at touching," Baldwin said back to Rumi whose parchment colored aura crinkled around him, and though I hadn't taken Baldwin's previous comment as anything more than a joke, this comment had me blushing like a timid child.

"Dylan, I feel for you," Baldwin continued. "I see the strife between you and Antonio, but it's not your fault. Antonio can be a hard ass sometimes. He'd have more fun if he'd loosen up, but I suppose that's always true. Being so loose ain't always better, though, and that's the fact Antonio can't get past. He has the discipline of his father and of Zenda combined. He didn't get enough of us fun immortals growing up, if you can still call us that. You always believe you see a shift towards a more kind world, but it's becoming more apparent that, though kindness might shine through, darkness never dies. As soon as there's an excuse for darkness to take over, it does. The guardrails of progress are always so timid and fragile when fought for the hardest. Aurelius knew this more than anybody. You can't be kind to those who prove themselves an enemy to you. There's no room for second chances or forgiveness of defection. It takes a shameless person to infringe on the rights and allegiances of others... Who are you, Dylan Eaglegod? You look like you just woke up out of a daze... Much like how I remember my first year of freedom with myself. Let's hope you make it to the end of yours in one piece with all these broken hearts you're leaving all over this ship."

"I agree," Rumi said. "On almost everything. Except, what is love if not for forgiveness? A lover overperforms, underperforms, gets distracted, and gets you upset. That fire that burns is there all the time. No matter what. Embrace what makes it burn hotter, lest the flame does die. Baldwin is correct in saying life need not always be so serious, but there's a balance one can have with looseness that's not all that damaging, but enriching. As with all things in life."

"And now we're in the thick of philosophical reasoning," Aurelius said. "But let's not have it at my expense."

Rumi and Baldwin both smiled at Aurelius with the love of gleeful brothers seeking mischief.

"Well, you should've taken our advice a long time ago, Aurelius," Baldwin said.

"I've been advising him for centuries longer than you," Rumi said. "And I'm convinced there's nothing that will break his conviction to the dullness of his stoicism."

"These two could get you into trouble," Aurelius said, looking at me with warning. "But they'll teach you how to be a more rounded person than I ever had the luxury of becoming. I'll give you two that victory for the night."

"Oh, and he speaks with such definitiveness," Rumi said. "I'm allergic to such style of language. You need to open your mind with how to think and speak about life. If you were a poet, you would have been known as the most depressed Roman emperor of all time."

"I think that's still claimed to be true," Aurelius said, again owning up to the pitfalls of his philosophy.

"Mortals hate the truth tellers among us," Baldwin said to me. "It's always been. The uninspired talk us down because we turn around their problems to show them ways out, just by ways of changing their minds. And then we're the bad guys. However, they figure."

"See, Dylan," Rumi said. "Us philosophers can talk ourselves in circles all night. This is why a little distraction is needed in our lives. Otherwise, we'd forget to stop our thoughts enough to live. It's nice to meet you. My name is Rumi, if you haven't picked it up. I'm still the greatest poet the world has ever seen."

"Well, now," Baldwin said, rolling his eyes.

"The two of you are such self-absorbed emotions and physical desire," said the hunched immortal with the Einstein-like frizzled mane of dark hair and white rosy cheeked face. "I'm Leibniz, Dylan."

"It's nice to meet all of you," I said, not sure of what else to say while still taking everything in.

"They'll never know what it's like to put all of that aside," the final unnamed man said. Another American, but way older than Baldwin and myself. He too presented himself as older, like Leibniz, but closer to the forty-five years of age range, with an untamed head of black and grey hair that stuck straight up off the top of his head. His eyes swam with more mystery than I ever imagined a person could hold.

"I knew the best of the best stoics who ever lived," the man said. "Their entire minds were geared to disassociate from the needs of the self, even from hunger, sleep, and pain. It took the mindset of a Buddha to survive the horrors of American slavery the way that myself and my brothers and sisters experienced it. Dylan, welcome to the Immortal Philosophers. My name is Frederick Douglass, and it's nice to be here to meet you. The one philosophy you need to keep in you, above all, is love for humanity and an intolerance for hate. I see that propensity for undying love in you now. Hold onto that, whatever you do. Please, call me Frederick," He finished, his golden aura swirling like honey around him.

"We often forget that the horrors of history are people's life stories," Aurelius said. "Thank you for that, Frederick."

"Your story is legend to me," I said to Frederick. "I read your autobiography early in my university years, and your life inspired me to know there was always a life worthwhile after difficulty. You helped me get to where I am today."

The corners of Frederick's eyes grew wet as I recollected the tortures he wrote of experiencing, as I looked into his face. I wondered which lines had been there since those years of his unimaginable enslavement, and I couldn't imagine how it felt to carry that history into everyday life as an immortal.

"Nobody again will ever let you believe that you are powerless," Frederick said. "Never forget that."

"Now that's a statement in line with Leibnizian logic," Leibniz said, sticking a finger in the air. "Impressively, we're all as powerful as everything else in the universe, naturally!"

"So right you are," Aurelius said, laughing back against the sofa. "Dylan, Leibniz here is going to be teaching you some things we hope can help us get a handle on your abilities and help you use your predisposition to moving through and viewing time, with the goal of helping you see more of the future. I think having you explain the rest of this past summer's story will help the others better understand the complexity of your powers."

"I understand," I said, tamping down the shock of meeting so many historical figures at once. It felt unreal to believe they'd be interested in my story at all after all they'd been through, but their strength finally made me feel ready to recount the part where Antonio and I were trapped in the prison of Joshua's cave.

CHAPTER FIVE

The Tomb of Terrible Memories

"When I came around to what happened, I realized the cave had buried itself deep underground, with us inside. But the power it was running on wasn't Joshua's. The space felt empty of Joshua's control, but full of an empty energy that felt different. It felt like the negative of what I understood energy to be. Then, I recognized it as the feeling of the greasy slime running down the cave walls."

"I couldn't sense anything outside or up above. I didn't know if Aurelius could feel us or get to us, but the pull of the empty energy felt strong as it pulled at our auras. I could feel it ripping energy away from Antonio, as he lay unconscious after hitting his head, and when I wasn't focusing on maintaining my armor, I could feel layers of my energy peeling off and watched it merge into the slime."

"So, I encased us both into an orb of my cobalt aura and expanded it to the limits of the cave walls. I wanted to see if I could absorb the cave's absent energy and secure it under my control. It felt like the only way to deal with the panicked and weak energy that was threatening us. It felt more desperate for power than even Joshua ever was. Even when he was at his weakest point on the beach after I took my energy back from him."

"I didn't know what to do other than try to pull from the void that it was pulling my energy into. So, I pumped all of the energy I could into focusing on flipping the direction of the energy current, working at it for I wasn't sure how long. At some point, Antonio woke up, and he let me working in silence as the focus I required was entrancing. Then he started fueling me with his energy, and my work doubled in effectiveness. Finally, the pull direction of the energy started shifting a bit. Then a little more."

"After a while, I shifted the entire pull until a current of pure auric energy that blasted out from the cave walls in a dazzling light so powerful and pure that it charged my tired aura as soon as it hit me. But when the energy didn't have anywhere to go, it collected in the center of the cave in a volatile, spitting plasma. I harnessed the energy as it came, directing it all upward. Hoping to blast a hole clean out to the surface."

"Where I aimed, the energy disintegrated the cave wall, clearing a way right through the ground and into the sky above our heads. Riding the current, I lifted us out of the cave, and we were back with Aurelius, who we found sitting in meditation on the forest floor."

"Behind us was the hole into the cave, but instead of sucking the life energy out of this world, it was pumping out streams of power into the auric current around us, like a tapped and unstoppable well spring. And it continued like that for as long as we sat studying the phenomena. We did what we could to cloak the well behind enchantments, but Aurelius said he'd never seen an immortal turn such a desecrated space into an auric well like that. Zenda confirmed the transformation we'd assumed happened and compared it to the tea trees her ancient tribe used for their auric spring power enhancements."

"And that is what brings us to today," Aurelius said, nodding to the group of stunned immortals.

"What a story," Juba said, having returned from the brig to stand behind Cleoseléné. "I've never heard anything like it. Aurelius, the others are alright up top. We've got the cruise ship on our radar, and the Costa Del Sol is on our port. The tides are in our favor."

"Perfect," Aurelius said. "Good work. Now, what are everyone's thoughts on this new power Dylan's discovered? Moremi? Cleoseléné? Rumi? Might any of you have insight?"

"I might," Cleoseléné said, raising a timid hand in the air as if afraid to acknowledge it. "But please, I want to hear from others first."

"There're holes like that all over the East Coast and Southern United States," Frederick said. "I heard about them when I was there. We all did. Portals to hell, we'd call them. The ones that pull at you, I'm talking about. Those ones I recognize. What you did to it, I never heard of. I always thought they were the curse of the land for the crimes done upon it. We sang songs about them, but even we weren't sure if they existed, or if they were just metaphors for the ones who disappeared at the hands of the white slavers and slave hunters."

"If this is true, then my brother might have disappeared down one," said Cleoseléné, demanding every eye in the room with her statement. "Long ago."

"What do you mean, my love?" Juba said, leaning over her with a hand on her shoulder. "You never told me this. Of Helios?"

"Yes, of Helios and Ptolemy both. I never thought that it was a memory," Cleoseléné said. "I always thought it was my imagination playing tricks on me. Making me believe in something so that I didn't have to believe that they were gone. But before they disappeared, he told me he found a place. A place in the bowels of the palace, deep down in the underground layers of what Rome had once been before it was rebuilt upon itself hundreds of times. I didn't know what he was talking about. I didn't want to know what he was talking about. I just wanted to find a better way to live. For the three of us. I told him to stay in the sun, that the darkness was nowhere to be for a boy who was a sun god, for a boy with a name as bright as his. And he asked me, in his comical, brotherly, way, if that was why I looked best in the dark?" She said, smiling at the memory.

"And that was the last time I saw either of them, before he disappeared. People said they were taken by Octavian. Sold, or worse. I was told shortly after his disappearance that he was dead, and that his death had been confirmed. With how dangerous Rome was for us, I didn't think he could have even made it to the place he wanted to escape to without being murdered for exploring, until now.

"When you're told a hundred different stories over and over again, you start to believe some of them. And sometimes you start to believe more than one at the same time. Until one day you decide that you can't bear to think about it at all anymore. Then you don't. And then you don't think of the person for millenia. Now, I fear I'll never have a thought without him."

"Oh, Cleoseléné, I'm so sorry," Moremi said, giving her friend a hug as tears fell down both of their faces.

"That dream sounds more like a nightmare," Juba said. "You really think he could have been swallowed up by something like that?"

"It's quite possible," Leibniz said.

"Tell us you have it all figured out, sir thinks a lot," Rumi said. "No mystery gets by you."

"I think I know exactly what's going on here," Leibniz said. "Obviously, Dylan has the ability to pull from the atrament, an ability I never heard of before. And, apparently can turn an atrament hole into an auric well."

"What's an atrament?" I asked, feeling more concerned after hearing the name.

"It's a term I made up," Leibniz said. "But, if you humor me, I'll explain. The atrament is the plane for unbodied immortals. The plane where energy is negative, as you experienced and explained. It's a vacuum that sucks at the energy of the auric current of our realm. A place where consciousness can exist in as many complexities as it exists for us here. Like here, though, it is a place that is fueled by competition. It's a dangerous place that not every immortal makes it out from once there."

"And here I thought you just sat in a chair for days because you were thinking," Aurelius said. "Have you been traveling around this atrament?"

The accusation looked exciting for Aurelius, as if he had struck gold for the first time in his many lives. I wasn't sure how right Leibniz was, but his answers felt possible.

"I wish, Aurelius," Leibniz said with disappointment pulling at his face. "It's not a place one can enter and leave from at will. It's a place outside of that. Dylan is the first one who I've known to hold control over anything related to it. It's possible your brothers could have been absorbed into it, Cleoseléné, the way Frederick has heard it experienced as a state of disappearance. Though, I never found or thought to look for a hole into it. It's always just existed in theory for me."

"I'm going to need you to work with Dylan on controlling and expanding this ability," Aurelius said. "If we can help him master this along with his dispositions to moving through time, we might just be able to help him become the most powerful immortal we've ever known. We might just be able to help him change the world."

"The ability to create an auric well," Juba said. "Now, that is world changing."

"But how do we guarantee that the predators won't be able to exploit the wells unless we monitor them?" Cleoseléné asked. "It seems like a big risk."

"No more of a risk than the naturally occurring wells," Aurelius said. "It's my assumption that these atrament holes are the real danger. They're the ones with the power to grant immortality through the contract of dependence. The wells would be temporary charging stations for us, capable of being corrupted by the energy of a predator, yes, but at least not creating predators by themselves like the atraments seem to do. That seems to be the case with Joshua Bailey, at least."

"And once corrupted," Leibniz said. "A predator has no ability to convert it back to a well. They don't have the emotional purity or the power or intention good enough to even try. Their exploitative nature simply corrupts everything."

"You'd think the wells would have their own powers of protection," Cleoseléné said. "Like the protective powers of the moon."

"Ah, like the blessing of receiving your lunar light?" Juba said.

"Yes," Cleoseléné said. "Simply channeling my energy protects me with the natural protective properties of the moon because it becomes a piece of me. Isn't it strange that an auric well wouldn't want to protect itself in the same way?"

"I think it does have some protections," Kana said. "I went to see the site after they told me about it, and behind their enchantments, there were disguises in place and barriers to get behind."

"Wasn't the cave where Johnathan hid on Long Beach

Island a hole into the atrament, too?" I asked, remembering the memory as if I'd lived it myself.

"Yes!" Leibniz said. "I remember that from your account. What a timely observation."

"But that's no different than how the shrines and temples have operated throughout history," Aurelius said. "Are you certain?"

"Ah," Leibniz said. "That's a good point. To think about it, you might be right. That was the difference between the reservoir-like cave near the lighthouse and the cave behind his home. There must be something more to the atrament-predator relationship."

"Like a curse?" Moremi said, swallowing hard. "A deal, or the contract Aurelius alluded to?"

"I'm afraid that's how we referenced them in our songs," Frederick said, sighing a long breath.

"One of the many avenues into unnatural immortality and salvation," Rumi said. "I've seen more of my share of paths to immortality than I'd like to admit."

"Rumi's specialty is attraction," Baldwin said to me. "And he's especially attractive to predators. Even if they can't tell he's immortal, they're drawn to his presence."

"Yes, but my real curse is my inability to refuse the moments of their passion," Rumi said, wiping his face with his hand.

"Ibiza has ruins and shrines," Juba said. "Why don't we search for an atrament there? Test his ability?"

"I'm not so sure we should be so quick to push him," Leibniz said. "I want to have a lesson or two with him first. The searching could be helpful, but I'm not sure we should mess with any of that until we stop the traveling predatory circus band."

"I agree," Aurelius said. "I don't want them getting their hands on that power. We don't need to help them. We need to stop them."

"It'd be fun to search," I said. "But I'm with Aurelius, too. I'm concerned about Jordy Portendorfer and Gabirol, whoever that is. Calamity J also felt pretty powerful. And all the people who just walked out of the rave yard and onto the ship. Something happened after Elliot left the stage."

"We'll have to find out more tomorrow," Aurelius said. "I knew of Gabirol before Portenforer arrived with Elliot, but I was surprised they were all working together. I wasn't sure how to break them up before Calamity J discovered me. She, like Rumi, has some pretty attractive qualities."

"You didn't, Aurelius," Rumi said, gasping and lunging forward until he was over his knees.

"I didn't, Rumi," Aurelius said. "I'm honestly not sure how she discovered me, but I was caught by her in the street, walking down the boulevard under the palms when she ran into me. She touched my hand and felt me for my power. It was almost like she knew she would find me to be immortal, but there was no way she could have known me for who I am. I knew then we couldn't leave the palace the way we normally would, hence keeping you all out at sea and bringing Dylan and Antonio over."

"You think they could have something planned for every show?" Baldwin asked.

"Well, it seems like whatever they needed from Elliot, they got," Aurelius said. "And that should frighten us all."

"Well," Juba said. "This has been an enlightening discussion. I think given this escalating change in circumstances, I should return to the brig."

"I think you're right," Aurelius said. "We should all head to our quarters from some sleep, as well. We're going to need it for tomorrow."

Elliot was awake in his quarters when Baldwin dropped me off at his door after Aurelius's instruction. I could feel Antonio asleep already somewhere on the ship, so any hope I had to talk with him before the end of the night was useless. Elliot had showered and changed into a thin white sweatsuit that made him look more like a loungewear model than a pop star, but I couldn't complain about the sight of things when I entered and he was splayed out across the bed.

"There're clothes in the dresser," Elliot said, pointing to the walnut dresser along the inside wall of the surprisingly spacious yacht suite.

"Thanks, I'm not sure what I want to do now, though," I said, staring at him laying back against a mountain of pillows in the amber glow of the bedside lamps.

"Well, you're not getting in this bed without a shower and change of clothes," Elliot said. "If we can share the room, we can share the bed. Plus, I really hate sleeping alone. I told you I don't do well on my own. It's good you're here for me."

"It's kind of weird, ya know," I said without thinking. "If you don't mind me saying."

"Well, I'm not the one who put you in charge of me," Elliot said, in defense. "I'm trying to make the best of this the same way you are."

"I'm not 'in charge' of you," I said, thinking of how to get myself out of this conversation and into the bathroom where I'd at least have space to organize my thoughts before saying something I couldn't take back. Bad stuff always came out when I was tired like this. "I've admired you for a long time. It's weird, the connection we have. That's all I meant. I've only felt like this with one other person before. "

"With Antonio?" Elliot asked, but without waiting for an answer he continued. "I've been drawn to you both, but he seems to not like me as much."

"I don't know if that's true," I said. "But anyway, I should shower. We'll need the recharge for tomorrow."

"The recharge?" Elliot asked.

"It's an immortal power thing," I said, moving towards the tiled bathroom. I kept having to remind myself I was on a ship, because nothing moved, and everything looked too nice to be actually put on a boat.

"You're going to have to teach me how to use my powers," Elliot said.

"I'll see about that," I said, making my way to the bathroom. "I'm not sure if I'd be any help without Antonio."

"Well, you better talk to him then, before I find different teachers," Elliot said, as I closed the bathroom door.

"I'll try," I said to the bathroom, knowing my next conversation with Antonio would be a dreadful walk through a minefield.

After my shower, I felt more refreshed physically. My brain and body still hurt from the auric battle with Calamity and Jordy, but the burning in my muscles and mind from before was now just a stinging soreness.

"Here," Elliot said, shifting himself out of the middle of the bed to make space for me to lay as I made to join him.

"Thanks," I groaned, as my heart pumped hard in my chest finally having to acknowledge the space next to him that I had to fill. I wondered if Antonio could feel my body awaken against my tired mind as I laid down and leaned back against the body of Elliot Cutcas, who only offered me just enough room to fit. A million guys and millions of girls would have killed to be there beside him, and I just couldn't wait for the night to be over. But still, something deep inside me wanted to feel every second of the mystery of what might happen.

"Thanks again for staying with me," Elliot said again into my ear as he leaned over me, big spooning me with the length of his body.

"You don't have to keep saying that," I said, wanting him to quit with the thanks and just say what was really on his mind, if he felt compelled to keep talking at all.

"Is that a way to tell me to shut up?" Elliot said, pushing himself back away from me. And as soon as he was gone, I wanted him back with his hand holding my arm and his breath hot on my neck.

"No," I said, unsure of what I needed to say. "I want you to be comfortable enough to talk. But why do you feel like you have to thank me so much? It doesn't seem like a popstar would be in the habit of thanking anyone."

"Well, I thank everyone," Elliot said, returning to where he pushed up against me. "Especially the people who see me for me and who protect me."

"Is that what Jordy did for you?" I asked, more curious now about their relationship than anything else.

"Not truly," Elliot said, sounding sad as he looked me over. "I thought I liked him, actually. He never shared a bed with me, thank god. He was kind of gross, but he pretended to be my best friend. Thinking back, I don't know why. There weren't many times I felt heard by him, but we take what we can get, I guess. He even said he'd never understand me."

"Jordy and all of his immortal friends would just tell me to shut up. But that pain's been in every part of my life since before I knew him, even with my fans. The rumors about my gayness spark outrage, and it makes me not know who to trust.

I've grown impatient with how slow the world is changing. To the point I'm not sure my happiness will ever catch up to me, or if I'll ever truly be accepted by anyone, let alone the world. So, I thank you for helping me feel more myself."

"I know what that feels like," I said, turning to see Elliot's face. He looked down at me as we laid together, and in the amber glow of the room I said, as if seeing him clearly for the first time, "I accept you. You're safe with me."

Then he closed his eyes, leaned in, and pressed his lips against mine, while my world melted into the silver of his eyes.

CHAPTER SIX

THE MYSTERY OF MEDITERRANEAN MORNINGS

"Something happened with the tides last night," Juba said to the group of us. All of us immortals were brought to the brig by Aurelius for a debrief on our mission for the day, but everything seemed to be going wrong.

"What happened, my love?" Cleoseléné said, emerging from the crowd of us to stand at his side. Behind them, the glass windshield of the brig showed only water in every direction, telling me we were still in the middle of the sea with no sign of Ibiza or the cruise ship anywhere.

"Where are we, Juba?" Aurelius asked with a grave edge to his voice while the rest of us waited in silence for an answer, the uneasiness of the morning thick in the Mediterranean air.

"Fifty or sixty nautical miles away from the port," Juba said.

"About three hours," Captain O'Malley said behind him, leaning on the big wooden wheel that looked like it was transferred from an old time wooden ship.

"Are we back on course?" Aurelius said, looking between the two of them for answers.

"We're on course, now," Juba said, the intensity of his

navy aura thick in the air around him, with roots reaching down into the cedar boards of the brig floor. "But I don't know what happened. We should be there already. All of the ship's instruments said we were on course before we took a few hours to sleep."

"I didn't notice we were off course until I woke up and saw water all around us," Captain O'Malley said, pulling off her hat and smashing in the center of it in frustration.

"So, nobody was watching our course?" Aurelius asked, his disappointment dropping like a weight on all of us.

"Well, Horus was watching," O'Malley said, moving to look into the nave of the ship's wheel, where the gold plate of what looked like an eyelid fluttered open to reveal a sapphire blue eye, centered with a white, spinning pupil.

"You called?" A voice spoke, but I couldn't tell where it was coming from. The voice felt as close as a thought, but it seemed to originate in my ear canal, where it settled like the sound from an earbud.

"Don't act like you haven't been listening the whole time," O'Malley said. "He knows everything that goes on around the ship."

"Who?" I asked, wondering what everyone was nodding about.

"Horus," the voice said. *I'm like an immortal without a body,* the voice thought in my mind.

An immortal in a sapphire eye? I thought back.

"For forever and eternity," Horus said to the group. "You're a clever new mind, Dylan Eaglegod. I should follow you around and teach you a little bit about what it takes to be called a god."

"Eaglegod," Elliot said, intrigued and eying me. Of course Antonio noticed and rolled his eyes toward the sea.

If Horus knew everything that went on around the ship, then he knew Elliot had kissed me the night before and that I didn't stop him. But Antonio didn't seem mad enough, so it didn't seem like he knew, yet at least. And I wasn't sure if I wanted to keep it that way or not.

"Thank you?" I said, unsure of how to talk to an unbodied person, if it even was a person.

"Absolutely," Horus said to the group. "Now, I'm not as perplexed as the rest of you. We veered so far starboard that we're far south of Ibiza. Something shifted us off course. Something powerful. Even I didn't detect it at the time."

"It must have been powerful to have overpowered me," Juba said. "I should have never gone to sleep."

"And the moon didn't warn me," Cleoseléné said. "Something's very wrong."

"And what of the cruise ship?" O'Malley asked, bending over to look Horus in the eye as he looked around the brig, honing in on each of our faces.

"The cruise ship," Horus said. "The cruise ship was faster than it should have been, honestly. Faster than most. Whatever was powering it could be the same energy that pushed us off course, but there's no way for us to know right now. If my calculations could be trusted, I'd say the ship made it to the port an hour or two ago."

"How fast can we get there with Juba and I working together?" Cleoseléné asked, with a determination in her eye that showed her strength as a queen who takes charge.

"I'll work with the two of you," Moremi said, crossing her arms in determination.

"Hmmm," Horus thought. "My recommendation would be for Juba to open up the currents at the bow of the ship, for the stern to follow easier. Cleoseléné and Moremi, you take the back of the ship, and boost us forward. Your connections with the rising tides will come in handy back there."

"I like that plan," Aurelius said, looking around at everyone. "Grace at the wheel, and the rest of us will be at the sides of the ship rowing us along with whatever auric tools you want to use. We have to get there as soon as possible."

"I'll take Dylan with us to show him our power," Cleoseléné said.

"Should I go too?" Elliot asked, cutting in when I'd forgotten he was even there. But it was nice to be reminded that I wasn't the least experienced in aurics among us anymore.

Is he really an Immortal Philosopher now? I thought to Aurelius, knowing he was the only one to make that call.

"Go and watch," Aurelius said. "Both of you. Elliot, watch Cleoseléné and Dylan. Your energy is strong, but you're not ready for this job."

He'll have to become one of us, Aurelius thought with a curious wonder and subtle hint of fear. *But I'm not sure how much about us we should share just yet. The predators might still have some sway with him. You need to make him see us as his greatest allies.*

I understand, I thought, feeling the heaviness of the responsibility on my shoulders. *Antonio is not going to be happy, though.*

I'll keep Antonio occupied, Aurelius thought back. *We all have difficulties with the responsibilities that come with this role, and Antonio is not immune from those difficulties. I'm not immune, and you aren't either. Just make this easy on our new recruit. His world has been turned upside down in ways he hasn't been prepared for. We can't let him fall before he even gets the chance to rise.*

"Let's get to it, then," Aurelius said, and with that everyone started to move to their assigned sides of the boat.

"Follow me," Cleoseléné said to Elliot and I, as she brushed past us toward the rear of the ship, her gold and maroon jumpsuit glittering as it hit the sun.

"Right behind you," I said, eager to learn from another master.

"You're going to get yourself into trouble around here, Dylan," Cleoseléné said back to me, making me blush with confusion.

"Well, I hope not too much trouble," I said.

"He's already gotten me *out* of trouble, actually," Elliot said.

"That might be precisely the problem," Cleoseléné said, leading us through the lounge and onto the deck where we climbed aboard the night before.

"I guess it's one of those things people agree to disagree on," Elliot said, more aloof than philosophical, but I didn't know a philosophical mind that would ever use such a refrain. And I was starting to feel like Cleoseléné wasn't joking with me.

"It's a dangerous game bringing such new immortals to battle," Moremi said, coming up behind us and joining the conversation.

"I agree," Cleoseléné said back to her, looking past Elliot and I as if we weren't there.

Are you trying to send me a message from Antonio? I thought, fitting puzzle pieces wherever I could fit them in my thoughts.

Nope, Cleoseléné thought back. *I'm sending you a message from everyone on this ship who loves him.*

Woah, I thought. *This is a job. The same way we're about to start bending some water to get us closer to helping people. Aurelius charged me with earning Elliot's trust.*

You can fool yourself, Dylan, but one cannot fool the moon, Cleoseléné thought. *I don't think it's Elliot's power over you, but you're enchanted by him.*

"We're going to use the water as our thrusters," Cleoseléné said, taking a surfer stance at the back of the boat and centering her body over her core, while Moremi did the same behind her. "We have to work together. Are you with us, Dylan? Elliot, stand back and hold onto something. Try not to go overboard."

As Cleoseléné's accusations settled in my head, I took my stance as I did a hundred times over the summer and used my aura to feel the water around and below the boat. The entire area was charged with the colors of our energies, spreading out the more we channeled.

"Now lift the tide and thrust us forward," she said, and together the three of us started moving the water. I channeled my cobalt energy from my core, pumping it through the water beneath us and to the sides of the back of the boat. As we pushed, I felt the resistance from the bow disappear, while the other immortals joined in from the sides of the boat, and the ship started gaining speed until we were blasting across the Mediterranean with ocean spray erupting in mist and wake behind us.

My heart raced as my body surged with power and the connected energies of the other immortals. Their auras felt like old and fermented wines, as if each drop of their power was stronger than the same sized drop of mine. But my few months of training was paying off, as I felt my power grow into a distinct force among the mixture of our combined will.

I didn't want to think about what Cleoseléné had said about me and Antonio, but I needed to figure out my thoughts on everything. And since she seemed willing enough to offer unsolicited advice, I figured it wouldn't hurt to ask a few questions. Plus, I couldn't hear Elliot's words over the roar of the water, which was a relief I never thought I'd need.

How have you and Juba stayed married so long and happily, it seems? I thought, hoping Aurelius wasn't making a mistake in making me Elliot's babysitter.

So, you're turning this conversation around on me, now? Cleoseléné thought back with queen-like elegance. *Is this deflection?*

I'm more so looking for some way of making sense of what I'm feeling, I thought, fueling my aura more heavily as my frustration with my combatting thoughts started to build. I wanted to make Aurelius happy and help out the immortals. The last thing I wanted was to fail at my first mission.

I respect that, Cleoseléné thought, her energy literally lifting the tide behind us and pulling at the tide in front of us. *You're going to need to be open to hearing a lot of things from us, and I say things with an 's' specifically. We'll advise you on your powers, your ambitions, your fears, and your heart. But we can't promise a life without hurt. In every aspect.*

I understand that, I thought. *But were you and Juba always happily together throughout your lives? At least with each other?*

I can't quite say it like that, Cleoseléné thought. *But we're together because we love each other for who we are and who we've been. For what we've done together. For everything we've accomplished and everyone we've helped along the way. The sacrifices we've both made for each other, as the urges of long life sway us with the cycles of history, astrology, philosophy have been difficult to weather... The urges and cycles that are so beyond the individual that they're almost socially communicable and almost destined, pull at our bond, but in the end make us stronger. To believe that mortals are the only ones bound by nature and the pressures of life would be a fallacy. Us immortals have the biggest responsibility in protecting the earth and humanity. But, in the end, those two things are quite the same.*

We both were soaked down with the spray of our auric engine, but I couldn't focus on anything but her voice in my head and the energy coursing through me.

These urges are what I call the inexplicable and natural rhythms of life that are beyond our control, Cleoseléné thought. Because I don't know what else to call them, and mostly because they're almost auric. Even mortals feel the power of the moon and stars that reflect this. Sometimes they spur cultural movements or social disruptions. Sometimes they overcast an era of mass war. Sometimes they lead you into love, and sometimes they lead you out of love. Sometimes you reach a certain point in your astrological cycle that it's time to partner, grow a life, have a family, and sometimes your immortal beloved is not on that same cycle.

Sometimes the urge calls for something new over the centuries and a break of rediscovery. And sometimes, your partner needs that too. Other times, you both decide you're all in for each other and take on the world side by side. Other times, you decide to sit back and disappear together, but alone for one reason or another. Or no reason at all. Just to exist with a shared longing for silence and the passing of the months in a forest garden.

All this to say that, sometimes you have to take a stroll, and sometimes you figure out there's nothing sweeter than returning home. Just because we're immortal, doesn't make us inhuman. We don't sell our souls like predators. We don't need to feed or leech or kill to survive. We only run the risk of running afoul if we reject the nature and urges of our unique and beautiful experience of the world. We need to live to survive. I'll always stick up for Antonio, but he's still learning as you are, I just see some hurt between the two of you now.

There's definitely some confusion, I thought. *And maybe some hurt. I still don't know quite how I feel about my new life, honestly. But I know that I love Antonio. Elliot is a different kind of person, and I've given into him more than I should, but I think I have to talk to Antonio so he'll help me instead of ignoring me like this. He abandoned me for no reason of my causing, right at the moment Elliot started leaning into us both. This is the first time he's been like this with me.*

I'm sure talking to Antonio about it will help, Cleoseléné thought back with a comforting tone. *He's going through some emotions for the first time too. It's not easy being in your first life. Emotions are so powerful and raw. Harness that sensitivity and never let it go. Don't let him lose it either. You might be the only one able to keep him from retreating into himself the way I've worried about him doing for a long time now.*

Are we all just picking up the pieces of the messes Aurelius gets us into? I thought, feeling unable to detach myself from finding Aurelius at the root of all of my present issues.

That's what family is, Cleoseléné thought, flashing a smile of understanding back at me. *Picking up each other's pieces and doing it with love. This is what we do as Immortal Philosophers. This is what matters in this life, helping those who find themselves in the jaws of predators and evils beyond comprehension. That has been the role of philosophers always. To illuminate the way into tomorrow.*

Nobody's put it like that for me before, I thought, feeling silly for questioning the purpose of what Aurelius does and how he leads everyone into being better for themselves while living closer to the light of helping others. *I can see how this all keeps us pure. I just hope Antonio will understand after we talk. This mission is littered with issues, and this hasn't even been our biggest one.*

Don't let the silence between you last long, Cleoseléné thought. *New love is sensitive, and immortality doesn't make it easier. And yes, you could have not made the mistake of letting Elliot sing in the first place, birthday boy.*

Hey, that also wasn't my fault, I thought back, letting a smile creep across my face. *Maybe that's why Antonio is upset. Maybe he feels guilty for everything. In all seriousness, I'll be patient with him, though. I just wish he was over this silliness.*

Well, Aurelius taught him a little too well, Cleoseléné thought, with a mental laugh.

After we carved across hours of the Mediterranean in a little over an hour, Elliot jumped up from where he was sitting just inside the ship. I didn't know what he was doing, but I hoped he wasn't coming over to bother me. The struggle of concentration on matching my auric output with Cleoseléné and the others was wearing on me, and I was forced into silent focus for much of our trip.

"I see land," he said, holding himself upright with his hand at the top of the door frame.

"Thank you!" I said, relieved at my hopeful reprieve. I wasn't out of energy, but using so much for so long felt like running a marathon while holding my breath. And my muscles were so sore and tight it was hard to hold my body upright again without feeling like a stretch band about to snap back into my crouched stance.

Great work everyone, came the thoughts of Aurelius in my head. *Prepare for departure, and meet in the brig.*

And with a shudder, the boat slowed down, nearly skipping on the water as it adjusted to the normal speed of the boat's engines as we all dropped our auric thrust. My energy burned as it adjusted to disconnecting from the others' energies, so I took a second by the back rail of the boat to realign my auric channels throughout my body so I could feel normal again.

"You're a natural," Moremi said to me, smiling with a hand on my shoulder. "I support you all the way. Don't let anyone get you down."

"Thank you," I said. "It feels good to use my aura with everyone. It really takes being a team to a different level."

"You're good at it," Moremi said. "You're going to learn fast with us, if you can keep up."

"He knows what he's in for," Cleoseléné said, giving Moremi a mischievous look as they both made for the cabin. "It's a tough life, the path of the Immortal Philosopher. It's not for everyone."

"Oh, remember our first lives?" Moremi said to Cleoseléné, waiting for her, and collecting the pharaoh under her arm to walk together. "These boys would have been in for it back then. I love them all, but life's been brutal to us women in more brutal ways than these boys can imagine."

"You're not wrong," Cleoseléné said. "Thank the moon those times have passed."

You all did a bang up job carrying this ship across the sea, the unbodied voice of Horus thought. *I guess it only takes about a dozen immortals to get us to our destination late. Who would've thought?* Horus's presence felt as invasive as Strachan's felt back in the Palacio, with them both knowing everything happening on their ship or on their grounds but always secretive about how much they actually knew.

Thank you, I thought. *But we would've already been there. On time. If you hadn't allowed us to run off course. You're literally the steering wheel of the ship.*

That's not my fault, Horus thought. *I was asleep as much as you were. Even an unbodied consciousness needs time to shut down their awareness and dream. I'm not just the steering wheel of a ship.*

Do we all have to listen to this, Antonio thought, devastating me by not coming to my rescue as he usually would, but I could handle Horus on my own.

Take it private, you two, Aurelius added. *We've got business to attend to.*

So, what does an unbodied consciousness dream about? I thought, disbelieving that Horus even slept or dreamt a day in his life.

Of having a body of their own, of course, Horus thought. *It's a consistent dream, expected, delightful, and, overall, relieving when I finally wake up, of course. I've never had to think of things like using the bathroom or eating food. I just had to make sure I had someone to talk to, otherwise the boredom of my jumping thoughts would consume me. At least when I make friends, they're people I care deeply about. People I love, cherish, and want to help as much as I can.*

So you're not like a god who needs worship to survive? I thought.

No, Horus thought back. *Don't you have enough men after your attention already to want mine too? I've got work to do too, and it doesn't involve you much more than being included in these little pop-ins, as I like to call them.*

Well, that's a relief. I won't keep you then, I thought, happy to be alone in my own head. Especially with Elliot coming over to complicate things further after chatting with Moremi and Cleoseléné.

"Great job," he said, smiling and shielding the sun from his eyes. We were all soaked from the ocean spray, and he looked funny in his wet and baggy grey shirt and shorts. But I couldn't leave him sopping wet, so I stripped the water from his hair, clothes, and body with a wave of my hand and flicked it into the sea. Then I did the same for myself, feeling fresher than a clean sheet out the dryer.

"Thanks," he added.

"No problem," I said, "That was pretty fun. Getting us here. Like nothing I've ever done before."

"It looked freaking awesome," Elliot said, running his fingers through his dry hair. "How long have you been learning how to use your aura? That's what it's called, right?"

"Yeah, that's what it's called," I said. "What's making you curious about me now? You've only talked about yourself since I met you."

He didn't look happy about my comment, but he didn't look mad or upset either. I wouldn't have minded if he did get mad at me, but I knew Aurelius wouldn't be happy if it happened.

"That's probably true," Elliot said. "I have that problem. I get nervous and just can't see anything or anyone except myself. Of course I see you, but it's cuz of what I like about you. I've been told to talk to a professional about it, but I've just been too busy. Pop star problems, ya know?"

"Yeah, I've noticed," I said. "Do you remember what you

even asked me?"

"How long have you been training your aura?" Elliot asked, eyebrows raised, and expecting me to be impressed.

"You're ridiculous," I said, laughing at his act that I couldn't help but feel charmed by. "I've been training for a few months."

"A few months?" He said, big eyed and open jawed. It was hard not to be entertained by his animation, but I still had to try to seem annoyed. "You're so powerful with it after only a few months of training."

"I am," I said, with all the certainty in the world. "I had great teachers. Antonio, Zenda, Ikkyu, Kana. You've met Antonio and Kana, remember?"

"How could I forget?" Elliot said, blushing a slight shade of red. "I didn't mean to offend you or anyone. Last night was hard for me. Thank you for being there for me."

"You didn't offend me," I said, wanting to be off the subject of the night before. "I just have to give you a hard time. If I can't enjoy this experience, you shouldn't either. And you shouldn't be trying to make it more complicated for me, either. And yes, I'm powerful because I'm a strong immortal. A very strong immortal. And I'm going to be one of the strongest, no matter if you or Antonio is there with me when I make it there. So you won't want to make me your enemy, either."

"I admire that drive," Elliot said. "If I was Antonio, I wouldn't've let you out of my sight. Especially if someone like me was around. You deserve that support from a lover."

"What did I just say?" I said, not seeing the recognition in his eyes that I needed as he moved closer and brought his hand up to cradle my jaw. I didn't want to break away from the mesmerizing glint in his eyes, and, despite myself, the taste of his mouth was still lingering in mine, while the clean scent of his skin brought me immediately back to the night before. Then, to my horror, behind him Antonio appeared in the hall inside the cabin where I sat on the sofas the night before.

"Antonio!" I called to him, swiping Elliot's arm away from my chin, but Antonio turned back the way he came without a word, leaving me there with Elliot and the water churning through the jaws of the engines beneath us.

"Portendorfor acted the same way," Elliot said. "Happy when I behaved and met his expectations, and silent when I didn't. Especially when I would ask him about his powers."

"I told you to stop," I said, growing frustrated. "I don't need things more complicated than they are. Europe is a battleground for immortals. You never know what could happen, and now… We need all the allies we can keep. We have enough enemies already."

"I'm sorry," Elliot said, looking more confused than manipulative, so I tried to believe him. "I can't control it. In all seriousness. My mind is not right these days. You make me feel like a kid again."

"Well, I don't know how that's possible," I said, lying. Because I knew exactly how it felt. I didn't want to acknowledge it to him, but I couldn't stop thinking about him either. My mind did feel not wholly my own. "Hopefully we'll get you to your concert and everything will be better."

"Everything's better in front of the fans," Elliot said, looking at the blue sky off the side of the ship. "I feel that way, anyway. I don't want them worrying about what happened to me if I don't show up. It's not right to do."

"Well, hopefully we're not too late already," I said.

"What else do you know about aurics?" I asked, curious and desperate to keep the conversation with him off of the topic of my love life. Antonio was never going to give me the opportunity to explain anything to him, and I didn't know what to say to even try.

"I saw Jordy and Gabirol use their powers for some stuff," Elliot said. "Calamity too. She showed Portendorfor how to conjure a revolver and make it fire. They play pretended duels like in Old Westerns. Her revolver was scarlet and shot bullets the same color. His was nuclear green, like a color you'd never want to touch. That should have warned me to stay away."

"We never know what we're sacrificing until we live with what we were missing," I said. "That might not always be true, but it sounds right, here."

"Do you think you might know why they kept you in the dark about your powers?" I asked, more curious about that than anything else.

"They were more secretive than your group," Elliot said. "And half the time you people just stand around looking at each other in silence."

"Hah," I laughed. "We think to each other sometimes. I didn't realize you weren't in on the conversations."

"That makes sense," Elliot said, thinking something to himself. As if rewinding his memory to explore his past with that context. "Jordy never told me about that power."

"They probably wanted to keep you under control," I said. "If you know of your power, then you wouldn't have felt like you needed them. But in reality, they needed you."

"Well, that was always true," Elliot said. "But they did

coach me on connecting with the audience more through my voice and with my skills on captivating people. I didn't know if that was aurics, as much as I think it might be now, though. They pushed me hard in those rehearsals. I just thought that's how agents and stage managers were as people. I haven't really had any other experiences than people in those positions sucking everything they could out of me without a real care at all about me as a person. They could never beat me up as much as I beat myself up, though. It's the artist's curse."

"I know what it's like to live with people like that," I said, feeling in Elliot how I felt living with Joshua and the other guys I lived with in Greenwich Village, making me curious about his rehearsals and the coaching of Gabirol and Jordy. I wondered if they were trying to learn from Elliot as much as teach him. "We're not like that here, though. We have respect for each other. There's a lot that you don't know, but we're all here for a good purpose. We want to help the innocent from people like Gabirol, Jordy, and Calamity."

"I can sense that, just from how nice everyone's been to me so far," Elliot said, and for longer than a few seconds it felt like he was going to kiss me again.

"We need to eat before we get to shore," I said, moving him aside and walking past him before he got the chance to hypnotize me again. "Let's check out the kitchen in the lounge."

Thankfully there were snacks in the cabinets and prepared meals on the shelves of the full size fridge behind the bar, so we ate until we were full. I kept my personal space personal while we prepared our own meals, and moved away from him when he got too close. I enjoyed his conversation and the way he brought up things about his past that

I would never think to mention given the danger he was under, but still he talked about the singers and musicians he idolized as a kid watching tv, his only portal to the outside world growing up on a farm with his grandparents. And how he thought the whole world should sing instead of talk because it would make life a lot more enjoyable.

Despite the distance I kept and his denials, the popstar I had dreamed of meeting for years was infatuated with me, and he was becoming someone more difficult to not fall in love with than I had ever imagined a popstar could be. I wasn't sure I could find a tune to play that would make Elliot, Antonio, Aurelius, and myself happy all the same time, but I knew I'd have to figure it out sooner than later if I was to find my own way to sanity.

CHAPTER SEVEN

THE BATTLE FOR THE BEACHES OF IBIZA

When we entered the bay of Ibiza, there were two different worlds on two opposite sides of the beach. On the right side of the beach wasn't a beach at all. It was a sea of people crowded around stages, food stands, and carnival rides, while on the left side, cut in half by a wall of rocks that jetted out into the water, was an endless strip of sand with beachgoers that curved around the curvature of the island and into the rockier ground in the center of the island.

Unfortunately, the cruise ship we were after already looked like it had been docked for hours. There was nobody on board, and as we approached the docks, we noticed in the crowd the uniformed crew of the ship everywhere alongside the suited security we saw at the concert in Málaga. Neither of this was typical, but Aurelius suspected it was bigger than just the crew. And when we got closer and noticed a second ship right beside the first, we knew we'd have to start expecting the worst.

Are there enough of us for this? I thought to Aurelius, seriously concerned.

There's never enough of us, he thought back, making me

wonder again how we let him lead us, but so thankful that he was there.

Aurelius split us into two different teams, one to try and figure out Gabirol's plot, and one to keep Elliot safe and allow me to train, since we were too late to stop the concert from beginning, once again. After I told Aurelius of how they instructed Elliot on how to use his aurics without telling him he was using it, Aurelius was more certain about needing to keep Elliot away from them. So one group was tasked with scoping out the concert, while the other was going to scour the rocky outcrop of the beach for an atrament.

I was put on the atrament team with Elliot, of course, while Antonio, to my annoyance, was put on the other team. I didn't tell Aurelius that he, the leader of us, was causing me problems with his son that were bigger than either of us could solve, but his separating us was making it harder for me to even attempt to smooth things over with Antonio. Even if I wasn't exactly yet sure of what to say.

You need to keep our secret, Aurelius warned as the group of us atrament hunters departed down the beach.

I will, I said, knowing he was referring to Aurelius's knowledge of Elliot and how he and Antonio were almost brothers. Seeing how Antonio was reacting with me made me understand Aurelius's hesitation in talking to him about the history. But I still had to deal, alone, with Elliot's annoyance with not making it to his concert for his fans.

"This should be fun," Elliot said, walking at my side with his hands around the straps of the backpack he stuffed with water and snacks enough for both of us. "Headed to look at rocks, while my fans suffer at the hands of my stage crew. What more could go wrong? What's a pop star to do after his entire fanbase is abducted? Get a real job? Sing back-up for someone with fans? Give up and return to the farm?"

He might have been a whiner, but the way he carried the backpack was proving to be useful. I couldn't deny that he looked good doing it too. I was relieved I didn't have to go into the mess of the concert crowd again and be under the eyes of predators. I wanted to know what I was up against before actually signing up to be in the battle this time. I know that's not how battles work, but the best ones are planned and strategic. Going in blind is never a good idea.

"This is a solid squad," Cleoseléné said from up ahead.

She, Moremi, Kana, and Hypatia were leading the rest of us, while Leibniz and Frederick walked with Elliot and I. Captain O'Malley was on standby on the ship, while Aurelius, Antonio, Baldwin, Rumi, and Juba took reconnaissance around the concert. I didn't know how Aurelius broke up the teams, but six other immortals felt like overkill for us, when their team was the one who was going to need the eyes.

It was also the first time I'd seen Kana and Hypatia together since their embrace when we arrived on the boat, and I wanted to see more of how they were together without Captain Grace O'Malley around. I don't know if it was one of my auric intuitions, but I'd always had feelings about people that always turn out to be right. And I was feeling there was something more complicated going on. If not now, then maybe in the past.

"Now, this isn't a lesson," Leibniz said, waving a pale lanky finger up at me. "But feel the energy around you, as if everything were just a different reflection of the same totality of the universe. Just presenting itself from a unique perspective. And in that mess of existence, feel for the familiar and natural pull of the atrament!"

"That's quite a way to put it," I said, recalling a discussion from the Buddhist club where students read excerpts of something that sounded similar to Leibniz's expressions.

"It's the only way to put it," Leibniz said. "And I'd reason with you until you believed it to be correct. If you don't already, of course."

"I'll take what you're saying and apply it," I said, feeling no harm in adopting his philosophy if it meant mastering my aurics.

"Good," Leibniz said. "And as for you."

He looked at Elliot with narrowed eyes. "I want you to focus on the well of energy in your gut. We call it the auric core."

"I sing from my core," Elliot said, rubbing his stomach.

"You might *sing* from your core," Leibniz said. "But to activate your auric core you need to do more than just open your mouth and belt. You need to focus on it. Be aware of it. Believe in it. Feed it. And eventually, draw from it. Try. The both of you."

"He won't give up until you try," Frederick said, walking beside me. Leibniz had taken the other side of Elliot and was poking him as he talked to emphasize his points. But where Leibniz was erratic, Frederick was stoic.

"I'll try," Elliot said, closing his eyes as he walked. So, I did the same.

"Just make sure I don't step on anything gross," I said, walking with my eyes closed and focusing on the energy sloshing around in my auric core. My energy was a thousand times more dense and heavy since I started my training, and I was able to pull from it in an instant. I channeled it into the auric current and felt around us and in the distance for the pull of an atrament. But I couldn't feel anything.

The beach was flat where we were, with a mess of beachgoers having family style fun that we walked around, undetected under a mirage of auric protection. Down the crest, the beach was breached by a wall of cliffs that reached into the sea on our left and rose up into hillsides inland. I kept up my auric-charged atrament search, and as we got closer to the rocks, something did pique the interest of my energy. But something felt off about the pull of it.

"I think I feel something," I said, moving my energy in the direction of the signal. It felt like the slime of Joshua's cave.

"Good," Leibniz said. "Very good. You're a natural at this, it seems. Is it speaking to you?"

"No," I said, hearing nothing like what he referenced. "It feels almost weakened... or disrupted. Evil, yes, but more than that. Like an oozing wound."

"Hmmm," Leibniz thought. "Lead us to it, and we'll see what's going on."

"Okay," I said, pumping more energy further away from my body, and attempting to tether myself to the pull of the atrament. "Let me see if I can get a firm connection to it."

"Be careful," Leibniz said. "We're dealing with dangerous energies here. Keep your emotions pure. Focus on love."

"Yeah, focus on love," Elliot added, and all of the focus I had on the atrament faltered. The connection I had with the vacuum was cut, and the feeling of the sourness of my tainted relationship with Antonio seeped into every part of me. I didn't know what to do besides give up and try again, but I needed a break from the exercise.

"Well, that was worth a shot," I said, opening my eyes and turning to Leibniz.

"Love doesn't help?" Leibniz asked, the curiosity

mangling his face with crooked confusion.

"I'm not sure," I said, knowing that love was not the problem and unsure of how to feel the way only Antonio made me feel. Loved. Not wanted, in the way Elliot wanted me, but loved, in the way Antonio honored me everyday we were together. It was a mutual worship, from the moments we woke up together, to the moments we went to sleep. Even in my sleep, his love warmed me through the storylines of my dreams. All summer, I was never without him. Until, Elliot.

And as I flexed my control over my aura once more, I realized that love wasn't going to be so easy to use as a leveling emotion as much as it was before. But one thing was clear, it wasn't love's fault. It was mine, for not knowing how to handle the situation.

"You need another kiss?" Elliot whispered in my ear as I helped pull him up onto the rock pathway in the canyon of the wall breach, but no matter how quiet he could have said it, I knew everyone heard it. There were no spoken secrets around immortals, but he didn't know that yet.

"No," I said, gritting my teeth in frustration.

I don't envy you, Cleoseléné thought. *These are going to be difficult lessons to master for you given everything on your plate.*

I'll figure things out eventually, I thought. *I have to.*

The pathway through the rocky cliffs wasn't long, and after a few minutes, we were across to the other side with the continuation of the flat stretch of beach in front of us. But the waves off the Mediterranean were so measly, I wondered if storms could even churn the water enough to make it as rough as the stormy seas of the Atlantic. For an October day, the sun was still strong on my skin and the air

LOST BETWEEN THE LANDS OF HERE AND THERE
was hot and humid when the breeze stopped, but I didn't
feel the atrament in front of us anymore. This was where
lone sunbathers were laying on towels and blankets in
various forms of nudity and bathing suit straps, all minding
their own business away from the festivities only a mile or
two up the beach.

"We should turn around," I said. "We must have passed it."

"Are you sure you don't want to chill on the beach here?"
Elliot asked, and I wasn't surprised anymore by his motives.
Especially after catching him pulling at his waistband.

"I'm sure," I said, cutting with the sharp edge of annoyance. Cleoseléné, Frederick, Moremi, and Leibniz were
testing me. But it was more than that. My power was mine
to master, and I needed to strengthen it for my own survival. It was the curse of being an immortal out in the world
where predators were on the hunt.

Say the word, and I'll put him in his place, Kana thought,
looking at me with serious eyes. *Nobody messes with my
nephew and gets away with it.*

Thank you, Kana, I thought back, feeling warmed by her
use of nephew. It wasn't the first time she used it with me,
and she truly grew to be someone I looked up to as an aunt-
like figure over the summer. *I can handle him. He's the least
of my worries at this point.*

You just let me know, she thought again, holding firm
her serious eyes before throwing an arm around Hypatia's
shoulders pulling her closer to her.

You need to get it together, I thought to Elliot, looking to
refocus myself from his distraction.

What? How? Elliot thought inside his own head.

You know what, and you know how, I thought back. *This*

isn't easy, and if you had any sense about you, you'd be trying to learn from me and everyone else here who's trying to teach you. This is about survival, and everyone's risking their lives to be here to help your fans from mistakes you made by getting too close to evil predators.

I... I'm sorry, Elliot thought, as if recovering some kind of sense that he'd lost. *I haven't thought of it like that. You're right though. It's just hard for me to keep my head right. I don't know what's going on. All of this is a lot to keep straight in my head. I keep telling myself it's not that bad, just to not feel scared, I guess.*

Well you should feel scared, I thought back. *I'm scared everyday and every moment, because I know I need to be better if I want to survive on my own one day and if I want to be able to help keep everyone else safe if something happens to them. This is our responsibility as immortals, Immortal Philosophers, and human beings working to live up to our potential and our obligations. It's not about making ourselves feel better or feeling good all the time. It's about being better and being good all the time.*

I hear you, Elliot said, looking up at me from the sandy floor he was locked on as I thought to him. *I'll do better. Thank you for helping me understand. I get the responsibility of the show, but I guess, for you and for these guys... the show never really ends... I respect that. I'm used to that. But I've never really been around people who understood that too. I won't let you down.*

Good, I thought. *Now, let's get a move on with this mission. People are counting on us.*

"I'm going to find it on the way back," I said to the group, turning everyone around to head back through the canyon.

"Will for a way out," Frederick said, and I stopped at the thought.

"And feel the harmony of the universe in your heart," Leibniz said.

"Thank you," I said, and I focused my mind. I scanned the canyon with my aura in a wave of cobalt energy as far as it would stretch, and I willed my mind to identify where the atrament was hiding.

"They're illusive for those searching for them," Frederick said. "But when you're searching to be anywhere but where you are, that's when they draw you in."

"Thank you," I said, feeling more compassion for that desire in me. I'd lived with it my whole life before escaping Joshua and meeting Antonio. I remembered the strength of the feeling that pushed me through my school years, and I called it up to help me now. The fresh feelings of wanting to disappear whenever Antonio and Elliot were in the same room together came up too. I didn't want to be alone again, but sometimes being alone was easier than dealing with the consequences of other peoples' problems. It was a selfish thought, but it was a self respective thought. My sanity was important. My feelings were, too. But secrets always complicated the lives of people lost in subjectivity, while I had a problem with seeing anything other than objectively.

I wanted a way out. I needed a way out. I never signed up to be under the palm of anyone, and I felt that feeling like a wave of longing, standing on the beach, searching for a way out.

"I think I feel it," I said. It felt like a pin hole in the exterior of a spacecraft, sucking all the oxygen and gases around it into the vacuum of its void, but something felt off about it. It was weak and muted, as if a filter was placed between here and wherever it led.

"Take us to it," Leibniz said, coming up beside me. "We're with you."

"This way," I said, and I led us all back the way we came, one slow step at a time as I focused on the atrament pin hole. I held the focus more, willing more with every step for an escape, and I felt it grow closer to me every time my feet touched the sand of the canyon floor. When we were about half way down the canyon, I felt something off to our left. Directly into the canyon wall.

"I think it's behind here," I said, feeling the wall against the palm of my hand. The dust caked my sweaty palms, and I regretted the touch as the dry minerality failed to rub off onto my pants.

"Let's see what's on the other side," Leibniz said, making sure the elder immortals were ready. "Lock in, and bring it down."

The immortals fixed their stances and activated the light of their auras around their bodies. Their energy charged into the ground, and with a groaning shudder, the rock wall started shaking.

"Take control of the monads," Leibniz said. "And bring the whole thing down."

"Monads?" Elliot asked, but the cracking of the canyon muffled out everything else. The immortals all brought their fists over their heads and struggled against the weight of the wall as they pulled down, sinking the wall into the sand as they worked.

I took the chance to help out and focused my energy on the sand around the wall, vibrating and softening it the way I broke Antonio out from under the stone he was pinned under at Trop. Just the thought of the memory charged my aura as I filled with the love and fear I felt that night. And in the next moment, the wall slid down into the beach, revealing a path between the rocks that led through an inland canyon.

I thought the pinhole might feel stronger once we passed the threshold onto the hidden path, but the pull remained as faint as it was before. Just barely there.

"It's further down," I said, knowing it to be true. I felt it between the rocks down the end of the curve of the canyon.

"Take us to it," Leibniz said, looking down in the direction of the path's unknown end.

"I feel something else," Moremi said, touching the back of her angled neck.

"Everyone be on guard," Kana said, encasing her hands in cherry blossom pink auric gloves. "Keep Elliot and Dylan safe as a priority."

As we made it halfway down the path, I felt the presence of something other than the atrament, too. I felt the energy of the filter as if it were something with a power of its own. A charged power that felt like it redirected the energy pulled into the atrament and kept it within itself, growing stronger.

When we came around the bend, the group of us froze. Down the end of the canyon, three short haired, rigid looking strong-men stood with a long haired woman and thin man with the stance of a gothic anime character in black and red plate armor. The tallest and strongest was clad from head to toe in heavy blackened-bronze armor that covered his face, while the two other warriors wore armor that moved in cosmic fractals of Milky Way purples, blacks, pinks, and blues that matched the woman wrapped in sunflower yellow and river green ribbons around her gleaming and dewy black skin.

"I've seen them before," Elliot said. "Meeting with Gabirol. Jordy said they were another band..." He sounded confused, and I was wondering what other important information he might know of that we haven't gotten out of him yet. Like, information that could keep us all alive.

"They're definitely not a band," Moremi said, readying herself in a flare of moonlight glittering auric armor.

"No they're not," Cleoseléné said, breathless.

"Now I smell something familiar," the woman wearing the fluttering ribbons said, her voice booming down the canyon walls at us.

"Oshun!" Moremi shouted, with a fierce throat scratching grit to her voice. "At last, your final day has come."

"I could say the same for you," the woman called Oshun called back, but the power of her voice staggered compared to Moremi's.

"We both know you've been avoiding me for good reason," Moremi said, thrusting her hands in front of her and materializing a moonlight gleaming shield and spear.

"I've kept your people strong," Oshun said. "I've held my end of the deal."

"Hundreds of years of exploitation and cruelty is not the deal that you held hostage my son for," Moremi said, the fury echoing from her throat. "It's time for the end of the terror you started. Our people are not prisoners for your profit. My son and the sons of all my sisters, I will save."

"Nice speech," Oshun said, drawing her cosmic energy into a slick armored coating around herself. "But now you must put your words into your fight, and we all know how that ended for you last time. Show us how much better you immortals really are now, if you dare. Or turn around and leave us to the business of wielding the power you all are too weak to employ."

"How can they be better?" their one square-jawed cosmic armored gladiator looking warrior said. "When we made them who they were in their first lives? I'm talking about you, Cleopatra Selene."

"Don't worry about how," Cleoseléné said, readying her lunar luminescent light energy around herself in a hooded gown with long sleeves and daggers she whipped around her body until a bubble of moonlight surrounded her.

Julius Caesar, Cleoseléné thought to us. *Hannibal, and I don't know who the other two men are.*

Well, I can help with one, Leibniz thought. *Elagabalus is the thin one. Though, I didn't know he was still alive after I encountered him last.*

"Leibniz, my old friend," Elagabalus said, leaning against his long-bladed staff. "Surprised to see me back in one piece?"

"Actually yes," Leibniz said. "You should still be broken up into particles across the universe."

"I know!" Elagabalus said, hunching over himself in maniacal laughter. "And if you'd cracked me into one more fraction of myself, I wouldn't be here whole. The miracles of life never cease to amaze me. Though, Caesar, Hannibal, and Oshun had a lot to do with helping me reconnect myself."

"I'm getting sick of these types of miracles happening only for people like them," Hypatia said to our group, readying herself in teal auric armor that fused with her pirate garb. "I had to sew myself back together with the thread of my aura and spend a century repairing my body in hiding before I could live a life again."

Focus, everyone, Frederick thought, covering his body in gold like a statue with irises of golden rings. *I'll take Oshun with Moremi. The rest of you, focus on the others. This isn't going to be easy.*

I'll do my best to keep Elliot and Dylan safe back here,

Leibniz thought, expelling egg yolk yellow energy haze into the air around us.

"You might have found our little secret power source," Caesar said, sheathing his gladius onto his auric belt. "But you'll never have the power to use it before we show you what we can do with it. Hannibal?"

"Kings versus queens," Hannibal said, smiling where his pointed helmet revealed his mouth and chin. "Let's show them what we've got."

Then, as if choreographed, Hannibal stepped forward next to Caesar, and the two of them held their hands toward each other without touching. Between their hands, started forming a circle of their cosmic, atrament corrupted energy that spiraled with eggplant purples, pinks, and deep navy blues. The light bended as the circle spun with a wild, lashing energy. It lashed out and spat like a solar flare erupting off of the sun, landing in splashes on the ground and the rock walls around them, glowing with white hot heat where it landed. Elagabalus and the unnamed giant in blackened bronze both stood back, but Oshun stepped up from behind them and stopped in front of the energy circle. Her serious face was only broken for the laughter she unleashed as she prepared for what came next.

In the next seconds, the energy Oshun channeled from behind the cosmic auric circle blasted through in our direction, pulling at the corrupted energy from Caesar and Hannibal. The energy hummed as it tore through the air in our direction, loosing lava-like puddles onto the ground as it blasted towards us.

But the egg-yolk yellow haze of Leibniz's aura wrapped around us in a bubble of protection that stopped the beam.

Their energy slid down the barrier with waterfall force, where it collected in a white plasma sludge that quickly started to grow into a lake between us.

The energy expense of the burning auric power steamed into a thick fog that rose to fill the canyon as Leibniz broke into a saturating sweat as he managed our defenses.

Kana, Hypatia, now's the time to hit the two distracted of them, Leibniz said. *I don't know how long I can keep this up. If you take out their guards, Moremi, Cleo, and Frederick can get an opening to attack once this blast stops.*

Copy, Kana thought, expanding her armor into her full samurai layers and pulling out the two katanas at her sides. *Let's go Hyp.*

Right behind ya, Hypatia thought back, and the two of them crouched out from the cover of Leibniz's protective bubble.

I'll cloak us from their detection until we strike, Kana thought again as they reached the canyon wall and broke out in vertical sprints in the predators' direction.

As the blast of corrupted energy continued to explode against the barrier Cleoseléné, Moremi, and Frederick moved to feed their energies into Leibniz, lessening the strain on him. But I could see that the predators' energy wasn't just brute auric force. It was almost like an infection, leaving veins of pulsing light that worked their way into the structure of the barrier. I felt their hunger to feed and cor-rupt the very core of the conductor of the defense.

Their energy isn't normal auric power, I thought, feeling my words as truth. *If it hits you, there's no telling what it can do. It wants to feed on us in the same way the predators do.* And as a precaution, I activated my cobalt aura around myself, feeling safer in my self-constructed roman styled armor that Antonio and I designed together.

"I feel it too," Leibniz said, struggling to get the words out even with the golden and moonlight charges from the other immortals.

"Do you have armor for me?" Elliot asked me, yanking on my arm like a frantic child needing calming.

"I'll try," I said, not taking my eyes off the spot where the predators' energy met the shield. It didn't look like a crack would form yet, but the energy flow was growing more intense the longer they held the beam.

After a few seconds of focusing on armor for Elliot, he was looking himself over in a suit of cobalt blue roman auric armor identical to mine. I surprised myself more than I surprised him, but I was relieved to know I could do that for anyone if needed. I was one step closer to my goal of being able to trust myself to be able to protect Antonio.

"This is sick," Elliot said, clapping his gloved hands together and sparking the air with his silver auric energy that now worked its way through the armor I provided.

Outside the shield, Kana and Hypatia were half way to our attackers, and from what I could see beyond the blinding lights and haze was that nobody on the other side had yet noticed they were there at all.

I feel your energy, Antonio's thoughts came to my head. *What's going on?*

You feel me, but not the massive corrupted energy beam blasting at us? I thought back, more fearful than relieved. I trusted the immortals I was with and myself, but the predators together were much more powerful than Joshua was by himself.

A corrupted energy beam? Antonio though. *You found the atrament?*

Of course I did, I thought, watching the void energy eat more into our defenses. *We got ambushed by a few predators. Caesar, Hannibal, Oshun. Elagabalus? And someone else. You know them?*

Only from the stories the immortals would tell me, Antonio thought. *We're battling a few now, too. As discreetly as possible between the crowds.*

I didn't think there would be this many of them, I thought back, as Elliot again slid his hand into mine.

I didn't either, Antonio thought. *I don't think any of us knew it'd be like this. I'll get to you as soon as I can. I need to see this corrupted energy in action. We need to know what we're up against.*

Thank you, I thought back, feeling the distance between us closing, but of course it was still there. Ever present as long as Elliot was with us and as long as I needed to keep secrets from him. I couldn't help but feel the corruptive reality of those truths every time I spoke to him. Even if I still loved him more than anything or anyone. *I love you,* I thought, feeling more honest than I'd been the last couple of days, but also tinged with guilt.

I love you too, Antonio thought back, feeling jealous of the honesty he could say it with and torn for having hurt him in the first place.

Not knowing what else to do, I refocused on the corrupted energy. If we needed answers about the atraments and the energy these predators used, I needed to be the one to find them. The truth was, I hadn't found the atrament itself. I felt it nearby, but I wasn't sure exactly where it was beyond the fact that it was behind where the predators stood. I could feel that the energy the two warriors and Oshun were channeling was tainted by the corrupting nature of the atrament, and I could feel the filter that I noticed before we found the group, which made me think it could be the tool they were using to harvest the atrament energy.

As I settled into my near meditation, Kana and Hypatia had made it across to the predator side of the canyon, and I watched them leap from the wall to the ground behind some boulders that looked like the remnants of a rockslide. A few feet from them, the two by-standing predators were watching with smug contempt and casual coolness of a job they seemed happy was finishing itself.

Now looky here, the thoughts of Horus came to me, surprisingly without as much distraction as while on the boat. I was starting to get used to his presence, and his aura actually felt like a comfort to feel around me.

Looky here, I thought back. *You ready to be impressed again?*

I'd love that, Horus thought. *To impress a god is to craft a miracle from imagination, Eaglegod. But I can tell already you haven't spent as much time with Aurelius as he would like.*

I haven't spent as much time with him as I would like either, I thought back, feeling if I had spent a few hours a week training with Aurelius throughout the summer, I probably would be further along in my training.

Well, Horus thought. *As still a god governed by your own rules, how will you see your way out of this mess you certainly found your way into?*

A wise American philosopher once said, there's a hole in the wall, it's a dirty free for all, I thought back, channeling my middle school dance memories. *I'm going to find that hole in the wall. I'll find the atrament.*

And how will that help, pray tell, my god? I cannot see the correlation to our problems at hand, Horus thought, sounding as if playing a game with me.

I can cut off their energy supply, I thought, seeing the correlation clearly.

That could work, I'd imagine, Horus thought.

"Dylan!" Leibniz shouted over the boiling rumble of the hot energy around us. "You can pull this off. You feel the corruption of the atrament, I know you do. Find it, and end their use of it."

"Yes, sir," I said, feeling more ready as Kana and Hypatia ambushed Elagabalus and the giant predator in blackened bronze. Kana's katanas struck the deflected blow from Elagabalus's bladed staff, as Hypatia struck the back of the giant's armor with a trident she materialized as she thrust with precision. The giant turned with a broadsword to break Hyp's strike, and sent her staggering back as Kana and Elagabalus clashed in a flurry of blows that sparked red and pink around them.

"I'm going to have to get in the action," Moremi said, staring Oshun down. She hadn't taken her eyes off the woman behind the corrupt energy ring. It looked like she hadn't even blinked.

"You'll get your chance," Cleoseléné said. "I can't imagine your feelings, but I'm furious for you. We'll get your son back."

"I will get my son back," Moremi said. "She's going to find out what I should have taught her lifetimes ago."

"She won't be the only one finding out a lot today," Cleoseléné said. "I've got a ton to teach Julius once they put down their toys. He was always the puppeteer behind Octavian's depravity against my brothers and I."

I feel where they're pulling from, I thought, finally locating the crack between the rocks in the back of the canyon where the atrament was vacuuming in all of the loose energy in the auric current. But instead of pulling the energy into the void of the atrament, the window revolved and redirected the energy into a thread of power feeding like an artery the energy the predators channeled at us. It amplified their power, threatening us with its poison on an auric level. *They're corrupting themselves with the void energy.*

I too can feel it amplifying their power, Leibniz thought. *I don't know how, but one of them must know.*

I don't think I can control it, I thought, considering if I could do anything with it.

Don't try to control it, Frederick thought back. *Don't even think about taking power from the atrament. That's when it takes you.*

But you have the power to uncorrupt it and convert it to a well of pure, positive energy, Leibniz added. *We know that's true.*

I might be able to cut off their connection to it, at least, I thought, working my energy around the atrament from afar, pulling at my auric core and from the connection between Elliot and I for fuel, needing all the energy I could use.

Despite his lack of training, his auric reserves were deep, and his auric core was strong. I used our combined energy to feel for the spinning door filter that surged the redirected energy pulled from the auric haze filling the canyon and into the predators' corrupted energy blast. The filter didn't feel like a switch that I could flip, but like the auric architecture of something similar to a dam or an aqueduct, changing the physical reality of the world around it. The predators' structure allowed the atrament to pull in energy, corrupted it with a pass through in the atrament, and shot it right back out to feed the predators auras.

Once I felt the structure in the pinhole pull of the atrament, I expanded my energy around it, pulling more energy from Elliot as I fought against the atrament's energy vacuum until I penetrated the filter's form, while the predators remained distracted by their focus on the blast and he fight Kana and Hypatia were putting up behind them. The auric filter responded to my will as I worked to constrict the flow feeding into the predators' blast, successfully slowing the flow the more I replaced the filter's energy with my own. It took every ounce of focus I had to keep my power too from being sucked into the atrament filter as I worked against the tug of war of the pull, but my energy felt almost immune from corruption in the way the predators were.

I think I can cut off their atrament energy supply, I thought. *I understand how they're using it. It's more sophisticated than Joshua's use of the caves.*

Cut... them... off, then, Kana thought, struggling between blows as she and Hypatia fought back to back. *We could use some backup.*

I worked my energy deeper into the atrament filter, clearing out the chaos charge of the structure's energy, and filled the space of the pinhole, finally closing off the push and pull of the atrament's energy motions.

They're cut off, I thought. *They just have the energy of their auras now. Their stream of power is gone. It's blocked, and they won't be able to find it again.*

Good work, Leibniz thought. *Everyone get ready for their attack to slow and to get in there.*

As the energy from the atrament stream wore off, the beam of energy blasting from Oshun, Caesar, and Hannibal started to wane, but grew more corrupt as their fury raged from burning such high amounts of their own auras at such a fast rate.

"Let's go," Moremi called to Cleoseléné and Frederick, and the three of them ran through the shield that Leibniz held up against the weakening blast of chaos energy.

"We might win," I said to Elliot, not taking my eyes off the battle as the gold and moonlight forms of the trio of immortals sprinted across the canyon. But Elliot didn't respond. Behind me, to my horror, he was fetaled on the ground in the sand looking gaunt and shaking.

"Leibniz!" I called out, desperate for help as I rushed to Elliot's side. He was panting, which meant he was at least breathing, but his energy levels felt so low that I could hardly feel a vibration coming from his auric core.

"I'm here, what happened?" Frederick said, taking Elliot's other side. Down the canyon, Cleoseléné and Moremi launched themselves into battle with the predators, now outnumbered aside from the yolky energy missiles Leibniz shot at the predators to even the assault.

"I don't know what happened," I thought. "It might have been me. I might have done this. I needed his energy to help me with the atrament."

"Don't worry," Frederick said. "Don't worry. This happens. This is overextension, burn out, self-consumption. I've seen it many times."

"Unfortunately it's time for us to go," Caesar shouted down the canyon, taking flight in a cloud of his corrupted aura as Moremi cornered Oshun, while Cleoseléné barraged the furious Hannibal against the canyon wall. I didn't want the predators to escape, but looking at Elliot's petrified face, I was happy that the battle was ending, and my heart lifted. We were all going to make it out of there alive, even if broken.

"Pleasure seeing you again, Moremi," Oshun said, soaring up to meet Caesar in the air after scooping up Hannibal by the hand. It was only Elagabalus and the giant in blackened bronze left on the ground, both wounded with broken bits of armor and bloodied jaws as they fought back the agile blows from Kana and Hypatia who moved almost as one.

Let them go, Leibniz thought to all of us, sending a web of protective energy around Kana and Hypatia before the predators unfurled auric tethers that the two grounded predators grabbed onto and were lifted up with as the others flew higher.

"We might be done now," Oshun said from above. "But you all still might not make it to the next fight." And as the predators escaped over the canyon wall, behind us roared the crashing waves of the ocean flooding the canyon behind us.

"We need to get Elliot up," I said, lifting his arm. "Grab him under his other arm." I directed Frederick, and together we lifted him into the air with us as the wave of sea water slammed against the canyon's bend at our backs.

The other immortals took flight ahead of us, and we all lifted ourselves out of the canyon as the wall of water rushed in. The weight of Elliot was nothing for us as Frederick and I worked together, and we cleared the canyon's cliff as the wave crashed past, turning our battleground into a sloshing lake.

When we touched down on solid ground at the top of the canyon, everyone crowded around us. The predators had taken off into the sky in the direction of the concert and ship docks, and we were all too concerned about each other to worry about chasing them. I was still too concerned about Elliot to think about anything other than holding his face in my hands after we laid him down.

"What happened to him," Hypatia asked, joining the rest of us around Elliot. She and Kana had dropped their armor. They too had some bloody cuts on their arms and legs, but nothing gushing or terrible looking. It looked like Elliot got the worst from the battle, and it was all thanks to me.

"He's overexerted," Frederick said, holding Elliot's limp hand and wrist for comfort and to follow his pulse. Elliot's head was in my lap, as I made sure to support his neck. All I wanted was for his silver eyes to open so I'd know he was okay.

"I've got this," Moremi said, making her way over to us.

"I'll charge you, sister," Cleoseléné said, coming around and placing her hand on Moremi's back as she started channeling healing moon energy through her hands over and into Elliot.

"Our back-up is here," Leibniz said, staring into the sky.

The concert crowds by the stages were all retreating to the cruise ship docks, where the predators' two ships stood like cities with their own tetris'd skylines, making it look like our fight was for nothing.

Ow, Elliot thought inside his head as his body shifted. *Help*.

I'm here, I thought back. A wave of relief washed over me like the wave in the canyon. I could have kissed him, I was so relieved.

"What's this?" I heard Antonio say from behind us. He was hovering in the air above me in his blazing sky blue auric armor, plastered with a mask of fury.

CHAPTER EIGHT

LEIBNIZIAN LESSONS ON THE IMMORTAL UNIVERSE

Antonio wouldn't talk to me while the rest of the immortals reunited with us on our way back to the beach. All but Aurelius was with us. Oshun had flooded the canyon with a surge of ocean water that left the beach eroded around the rock path as it spilled back into the ocean. The atrament was still blocked up from my seal, which was the one highlight I could feel good about while I helped Elliot as he struggled to walk. These predators were powerful, skillful, and more creative than Joshua ever was.

I hoped my seal would hold if they tried using the atrament again. I also hoped the atrament wasn't still capable of luring in unsuspecting mortals to turn them into predators. But I didn't know how well my seal would hold without me present. I couldn't turn it into an auric well with everything else going on, but I did feel that it might be something I'll be able to do if I came back with some time and some extra energy from Antonio to use without having to worry about exhausting his reserves while I still trained my aura to hold more power.

On our way back across the water to the White Seahorse, we watched the enormous concert crowd fill both of the docked cruise ships in organized lines of synchronized movements and eerie silence. Aurelius swept onto the deck of our ship shortly after we returned, looking panicked and breathless. His auric robes were shot through with bullet holes and slices where blades or light beams must have cut through.

"We're not leaving you alone again," Baldwin said to him, as the group of us gathered around Aurelius. Captain O'Malley was with us again, while Horus steered us out of the bay before the predators could pursue us. We went from chasing them, to feeling like they might now have the upper hand to chase us.

"Where's your next show, Elliot?" Aurelius asked, pointing to Elliot, who still hadn't fully recovered on the couch in the amber glow of the cabin off the deck. "What happened?"

I did it, I thought to Aurelius. *I pulled on his auric core too much by accident and depleted his energy.*

I see, Aurelius thought back. *He's lucky he's alive.*

"We've almost got him stabilized," Cleoseléné said, as she and Moremi worked their energies over and through Elliot to help his aura recover. Antonio hadn't offered to charge Elliot with his aura, even though we all knew his aura would probably help Elliot recover faster.

"It's been a while since we've had to pull someone back from this," Moremi said. "Auric recovery is not easy after you're drained. He's going to struggle tonight, especially with his aura being so undisciplined and weak. You'll need to start his training, Aurelius. Or he'll be a liability to us and himself for the rest of this mission."

"Oh, boy," Baldwin said, looking as battle haggard as Aurelius. "I think we could all use some extra training for what we're up against. These predators are the cream of their rancid crop."

"That's an understatement," Rumi replied, looking concerned for the first time since I'd met him, as he wiped his sooted brow.

"Antonio," Aurelius said, finding him behind the island counter in the back kitchen of the cabin. "Where's the next show?"

"Mallorca," Antonio said, and from the sound of his voice he didn't expect the question. At least not out loud. I'd never seen him try to be invisible in a room full of people. His magnetic, charming aura was turned inward and layering it into himself like folded metal.

"Mallorca?" I wondered, trying to place it in my head. I'd never been. Most of the Mediterranean was a mystery to me aside from the major countries around it. I wasn't sure I knew of all the countries inside of it, and Mallorca, though I'd heard of it in the past, was a mystery to me too. But what was really curious to me was how Antonio knew what Aurelius had asked Elliot for first. Something felt off.

"Horus, set sail for Mallorca," Aurelius said, circling a finger up high, as if to 'wrap it up,' but Antonio still looked troubled.

"The concert starts in Mallorca," Antonio said. "But it ends in Menorca later tomorrow night."

"What?" Aurelius asked, looking Elliot over as Moremi and Cleoseléné bathed him in moonlight on the amber couch. "Are you sure?"

"I've never heard of such an island hopping concert," James said. "And Rumi and I have been to so many shows, it's hard to count."

"Shows on the 'Orcas could inspire love songs and epic sagas, themselves," Rumi reminisced. "But even I haven't heard of a two port show."

"The two of you," Frederick said. "Are the reason why I stopped going to the 'Orcas in the 90s. You two still need to disguise yourselves every time you go? Or did the ones who ban you die already?"

"I don't like talking about the years so close to the end of my first life," Baldwin said with a haunted tone. "I dropped the disguises for everywhere go. I just keep up my more youthful appearance, and rarely do people ever say I look familiar anymore."

"But..." Aurelius said, getting caught in a thought.

"And I use a disguise every time I go out," Rumi said through a muted giggle. "The secret to attraction is to be everything your target admires. And I'm not above reflecting to the girls and guys what they desire exactly to their wishes. I rarely maintain an image through the night in the jungle of lust and love."

"And now this is out of hand," Hypatia said, putting her hands on her hips.

"Horus," Aurelius called out.

"Yes?" the voice of Horus begged through the air around us.

"Take us to Menorca," Aurelius instructed.

"But, then we're not going to be able to stop them in Mallorca," Antonio said. "All those people..."

"All those people will be there in Menorca when they arrive to meet us," Aurelius said. "And we've failed to stop them every time so far. I'd rather take them by surprise. Set a trap if we can. Take us to the port of Menorca, and we'll wait there, Horus."

"They're not going to the port of Menorca," Elliot sighed, finally slitting open his silver eyes. Everyone looked surprised except Moremi, who grinned with success.

"Take it easy, Elliot," Moremi said, sliding a hand against his cheek and checking on his eyes with gentle prying fingers. "You'll be feeling better, but don't overdo it."

"Thank you," Elliot groaned. He sounded as weak as he looked, and a little dehydrated with crusty lips that seemed alien compared to the ones he used to kiss me the two... or three or more times that he did. It was hard to remember what was becoming so frequent, but I did remember how he held me against him the night before, with my head resting on his chest. With his sweet smelling, silver aura filling the room with his sleeping breath before I faded into his rhythm and the sleep of the night.

He grimaced as he shifted his body against the couch in a painful way that made me feel worse for what I did to him. I didn't know what else to do but sit beside him while the two healers worked their magic. I just wanted what I did to him to be over.

"They're going to a beach," Antonio said. "Cala Macarelleta."

"What a place," Cleoseléné said, looking at Juba with a smile.

"Ah," Rumi said. "Quite a romantic spot. I've had a few immortal dates there. Dating immortals is always more work, but always more fun. To have power alone is a curse, but to have power together, that's a gift and a blessing."

How do you know these things? I thought to Antonio, but he wouldn't look at me and didn't answer. Elliot was waking up more and fixed his silver eyes on me and me only. I knew he'd be needing me more after this, and I knew Aurelius would charge me with tending to him. The thought of being needed by him made me feel warm but frightened by how Antonio might react. He'd keep hating me and keep distancing himself, but I was starting to believe there wasn't much that could be hidden from him. He seemed to know everything.

I know everything, Antonio thought back to me, turning my suspicion into a heavy coldness in my gut that sent my heart into overdrive pounding in my chest. His directness used to refresh me. I could depend on it, but now it stung and made me feel like a target.

"We'll trap them there, then," Aurelius said, watching Antonio's face as I tried to figure out how to respond.

"Setting course now," Horus said, and the ship careened slightly starboard.

"Excellent," Aurelius said, crouching at Elliot's side to get closer to Elliot's pale, drained face. "You're going to be okay, Elliot. This is a flesh wound in our world. Actually, it's the soreness after a marathon. It feels like it could kill you, but you inevitably come back stronger than ever. It's a sadistic strategy in some circles, to repeat auric depletion in order to grow the strength of aura faster, but it's never worth it in the end. Power isn't the same as the show of power."

"I'm good," Elliot said, sitting up. "We were going to start in Mallorca and end in Menorca at night. First island hopping concert ever. There's a beach in a cove on Menorca that Jordy and Gabirol wanted to fit all three ships in to use the beaches and cliffs as the stadium for the fans."

"Three ships?" Kana said, looking at everyone else, as everyone else looked around each other. "We couldn't save one ship of people. We couldn't save two ships of people. Now we need to save three ships of mortals? Why are they even doing this?"

"I'm guessing we'll find out there," Aurelius said, turning to Moremi next to him. "I saw Oshun, Moremi. Did you see your son?"

"I didn't, Aurelius," Moremi choked, clutching her throat

and turning to the sky. "I'm going to find him, though. She won't get away next time."

"Caesar was there, too," Cleoseléné said to Aurelius, as she comforted Moremi with an arm around her shoulders. "Hannibal, as well."

"I saw Elagabalus and Hano too," Aurelius said, charging Elliot with his tyrian purple aura through a hand on his chest. "They all fled to the larger ship. The one we saw leave the bay in Málaga. This is a bigger operation than I expected."

"What happened to you all? What did you discover?" Leibniz said, taking a seat on the other curved couch. "We had some progress with Dylan's atrament training. He saved us, really. I don't know how, but they were channeling the corrupt energy from the atrament. If Dylan hadn't cut them off, who knows what they could've used it to do to us?"

"That's good to hear," Aurelius said, smiling at me. "I'm proud of you, Dylan. You saved us again from terrible losses. At the concert, we found a normal scene of fans, but the crew of the ships and security were as suspicious as we suspected. They were unresponsive and unreactive to anything except moving silently into position where they just waited. Like mind controlled zombies, almost."

"Then, Jordy appeared on stage in the image of Elliot, with Gabirol behind him. Cast in Gabirol's manipulative golden aura, Jordy started to sing. He sounded unlike himself, but not quite like Elliot either. But what stood out was Gabirol's energy influencing the music."

"The two of them took control of everyone in the crowd except for us, and they all started filing to the boats shortly after the singing started. Then Calamity and a few other predators joined them on stage. I recognized Dragut, but

I'm not entirely sure about the others. The four I mentioned gave us a hell of a battle, but then I sent everyone to your aid and stayed behind and hid to see what they were doing to the crowd."

"Unfortunately, they discovered me and almost got at me, but I was able to escape. At least I can always count on that trick. I overheard them saying they only have a few more stops before they'll have what they need, so they need these people for something. It has to be for their energy, but I don't know what could be worth such a craven display of mass abduction. It's sounding like Menorca might be where they'll have everything they'll need."

"We were supposed to head to Malta after, though," Elliot said.

"If we're headed toward Malta with Dragut at our back," Aurelius said. "We better hope we stop them in Menorca."

"We should try for Mallorca, then." Kana said. "We know what we're up against now. They'll be stronger in Menorca." Hypatia and Captain O'Malley stood behind her, but everyone had an air of uncertainty about our next steps.

"We should try," Juba said, looking untouched by battle, still in his navy auric armor. "We'll have control of the sea."

"I'm not sure of that," Aurelius said. "They already used the tides and the sea against us, and now we know why. They have Oshun, Dragut, Hanno the Navigator of the oligarchical republic of Carthage. All known for their control of water. I might have recognized another pirate queen too, Captain. Sayyida al-Hurra. Did you know she was still in our world?" he asked Captain O'Malley.

"She, I had a hunch was out there," Captain O'Malley said. "I've heard rumors of a ghost ship with 'Sayyida al-Hurra' on the back of it. Were you shot at though? Like, with guns?"

"Yes," Aurelius said, laughing to himself as he pulled at his robes. "Men in black suits like the FBI. Some of them might have even had badges. It's bizarre to see outside of the US. I never would have guessed men's fashion would die in the 'birthplace of modern democracy.'"

"We can still put up a fight in Mallorca," Juba said. "You have all of us. There's no way they can take us all."

"You're right," Aurelius said. "But our best shot is at night under the moonlight, so the lovely queen of your life will be at full strength and able to control the sea better than any of them could dream of. We need the recovery time, and will be better off for it. They'll be on high alert, using their energy to surveil for us even without us being there. I want Dylan to have another lesson with Leibniz, and I want Elliot training his aurics with Antonio and I. We can't leave any of us defenseless. Antonio and I will take Elliot for training immediately. Cleoselené, Juba, Grace, help Horus stay on course. Moremi, if you could join us and keep healing Elliot through our session, it might help a lot."

"Of course, Aurelius," Moremi agreed, smiling down at Elliot as she worked her aura into his.

"I've got a pot of chili on the stove if anyone wants some," Captain O'Malley said, and all of us joined in a chorus of thanks.

I hadn't realized the emptiness of my stomach through the rush of adrenaline and auric power, but all that work made my stomach feel depleted. When Aurelius directed Elliot to separate from me for training, I felt his enthusiasm drop through our auric connection, but I figured it might be good for me to get away from him for a bit. He stood up fine as everyone went to grab food, but I felt bad for him. Mostly for what I did to him, but Aurelius was right about him needing to train. He needed a master, and I clearly wasn't good enough yet.

You'll be fine, I thought to Elliot.

Antonio hates me, he thought back, and I couldn't argue with that. And I hoped Antonio was listening then, since he seemed to be listening to everything else we said to each other.

He's upset with me, not you, I thought, in attempted support, but I knew Antonio wouldn't hold back how he felt in training.

Dramaaaaa, Horus thought in my head, and I actually felt relieved to have him to talk to for a change.

It's growing more and more difficult, I thought back to Horus.

And it will continue to do so, Horus thought.

Wish me luck, Elliot thought, as he left to gorge on some chili, looking a little more back to normal than he was a few minutes before. Everyone else was already en route to the food or Aurelius, so I chose Aurelius to find out more about his plan. He'd pulled over Juba and Captain O'Malley to discuss something privately.

Good luck, I thought to Elliot, as Cleoseléné guided him to the lounge kitchen.

"I'm going to be a second with Aurelius," Leibniz said, brushing past me and cutting me off. "I have to run something by him with Frederick and Baldwin."

"I'll be joining your lesson," Frederick said, following with a bowl of chili.

"As will I," Baldwin said, following after the other men, but offering me a smile, warm and wrinkled with mischief, which I appreciated. The bowls in their hands looked like exactly what I needed.

"And I'll be there to make sure they're not mystifying you too much," Rumi said with smooth humor, getting in my way as well.

"Thank you all," I said, giving up, and turning to find Elliot and a bowl of chili.

Antonio was over by the pot in the kitchen, spooning chili into bowls for Kana and Hypatia with Cleoseléné, Elliot, and Moremi in line behind them.

Why don't you bring me a bowl, I thought to Elliot, nodding at him in line. *I want to talk with Aurelius and Leibniz if I can get the chance to.*

Oh, Elliot thought, looking back at me with tired surprise. *I guess I can, yeah. I'll bring it over to you.*

Thank you, I thought, catching Antonio's eye. *I'll need a full bowl.*

I'll fill it, don't worry, Elliot thought back, and smiled the smile that made him millions. He was spoiled, that's for sure, but he wasn't beyond learning new ways of being. I felt a calmer shift coming over him as the influence of Jordy wore off. The energy the Immortal Philosophers emanated was like a brainwave meditation for those unaccustomed to it.

You know, I care about you, I thought to Antonio, watching him as he served the chili.

I know you do, he thought back without looking up.

We need to talk about this, I thought to him, hoping I could get some insight on how he felt. *Help me with him later. He could use your charge.*

I don't know, he thought, locking eyes with me across the lounge.

I think you should, I thought. *And you think you should too.*

"...it's imperative," Leibniz said with ringing passion, pulling my attention back to Aurelius and feeling I should leave my thoughts with Antonio where they were.

"We can't rush things," Aurelius said, running a hand through his thick black curled hair.

"Things happen in due time," Frederick said. "In inexplicable ways."

"I'd love to argue," Rumi said. "But Leibniz and Frederick are correct. If we're being moved fast toward opportunity, who are we to fight against it?"

"There's nothing more important than surrendering to the nature of change," Baldwin added. "Let us train the boy in this. He can clearly handle it."

"Fine," Aurelius said, scrunching his lips into his nostrils in thought. "I want you all to guarantee his safety, but train him as you see fit. You're all his masters as much as I am."

"And the universe gasped in shock," Baldwin said, bringing a hand over his mouth. "Change really is the nature of things," he continued, his fingers stepping through the air.

"To have even moved the rigidity of Marcus Aurelius," Leibniz said. "Your sentiment must be correct."

"Trying things a little differently than you did with Antonio, eh?" Rumi questioned Aurelius, thumbing to the back of the lounge

"Every student, as with every son, needs their own special treatment," Aurelius said. "I've always understood that."

"As have we all," Rumi said. "True too with lovers, dancers, poets, and philosophers."

"It's the story of humanity," Frederick said. "Our individual uniqueness."

"It's the story of the universe, but we'll get more into that later," Leibniz said, pulling me into their circle. "How are you feeling, Dylan?"

"Good," I said. "I'm surprised I was able to find the atrament, but I'm not sure I closed its aperture completely."

"We'll work on that," Leibniz said.

"I'm having Leibniz bring new focus to your training," Aurelius said. "You're a quick learner, and your aura is eager to adapt to being exercised, so it's time we see what you're really capable of."

"I'm ready for that," I said, feeling my aura flare as a response to the thought. It didn't feel like my aura had a mind of its own, but, like any muscle, it was responsive to my feelings. How well it responded was the trick that needed training, though.

"An eager student," Leibniz said, clapping my back with a palm. "This is exciting. I'll be ready after some chili."

"Yes, everybody, eat," Aurelius said, and Leibniz, Baldwin, and Rumi went off toward the kitchen. "The chili smells delicious. Grace really cooked up a good one for you all."

"Thank you, Aurelius," Captain O'Malley said. "Maybe we should head to the brig, though. We can't get off course again this time."

"I agree with that," Juba nodded. "We'll catch up with you all later. Dylan, good luck in your training with those guys. I'm always learning more than I ever want to know around them."

"Thanks," I said, laughing and feeling good about it. The more the battle stress wore off, the more normal I started to feel.

"Here's your chili," Elliot said behind me as the two navigators departed.

"Thank you," I said, turning to him for my lunch and to check on how he looked.

"You doing alright?" I asked, looking up at him. "You

really scared me."

"I feel better, actually," Elliot said, holding a spoonful of chili over his bowl. "I felt drained, worse than any hangover ever. Worse than being dried out by a dehumidifier and the sun in the desert. But now, I feel clean. Every part of me feels clean. Tired and empty, but clean."

"That's normal," Aurelius said. "But there might be something more to that feeling. Dylan might have actually purged you of the predators' influence without even realizing. If they're corrupting their own energy with the chaos energy of the atrament, it's possible they've used that energy to infect you, too. And with it now gone, that would explain the clean feeling."

"Could that be their whole plan?" I asked, taking the logic to the next conclusion. "Corrupting the energies of everyone on the ship?"

"Oh boy, and there's no telling the devastation that could cause," Leibniz said, back with a bowl of chili himself. "Each mortal corrupted would be at grave risk, and our chances of saving them would be even more risky."

"Handling these predators will not be easy," Aurelius added, and with that admission I knew we were going to be in deep trouble next time we saw the predators. Especially if they were all together.

"This isn't sounding good," Elliot said. "These guys sound worse than I thought they could be. That magic was intense."

"It was dangerous," I said, thinking back to the heat and corruption of the chaos energy.

"Dylan, meet up on the top deck after you eat," Leibniz said, turning to find a seat as his bob of kinky hair shifted back and forth behind him.

"I'll be happy when we're all safe from this," Aurelius said, pouting his bottom lip.

Keep our secret safe for now, Aurelius thought to me.

I will, I thought back. *It's not easy, you know? It's destroying Antonio's love for me.*

Ah, there's nothing that can do that, Aurelius thought back. *Antonio is a strong philosopher. His reason will save his love for you before falling.*

I wish his reason would overcome his anger with me now, then, I thought back.

You two will figure things out, Aurelius thought, walking away too. *We're almost to the finish line of this mission, and then we'll all have time to explain ourselves.*

"Now I must eat too, before we start," Aurelius said, leaving Elliot and I to eat our chili.

"Let's eat at the bow," Elliot said, slinging his nautical terms like a pro.

"The bow?" I asked. "Sure. You must be experienced on the sea, knowing these words."

"Yeah," Elliot said, leading us up the starboard side of the deck in the direction of the front of the ship. "I've been on many boats with Jordy and Calamity. They love to tour by boat, especially for island tours."

"That's interesting," I said, remembering that they were my enemy and not just social figures. Every shred of information was valuable, and if Antonio was in his head, I wondered if I could get in there, too. If Antonio was going to help me recharge him, I'd have him help me try my mind-reading, too.

"They usually like the big ships," Elliot said, his voice trailing off in the wind and the churning of the ocean around our boat. "Cruise ship size, or even cargo ship size. They don't like small ships for some reason. I never asked why. Never was something I really thought about. I get so focused on what I have to do that I haven't really had time to think. This is new to me. I think you cleaning my aura really helped, though. My mind isn't as cloudy anymore."

"Isn't as cloudy, anymore?" I repeated, stepping next to him as he reached the point of the bow. He took a seat on the rounded curvature of the boat's floor, and I followed him to the ground. The sun was still bright in the sky and warming on my skin even as the wind blew back our clothes and hair.

"Yeah," Elliot said. "Like, I felt so afraid all the time. I felt the weight of every decision I had to make, which made feeling good about any decision really hard. Sometimes I'd be so consumed for weeks with regret over a decision I made, and I wouldn't feel paralyzed or anything, I'd feel frantic. I would just act without thinking, because all of my focus was on the past or the future or the potential future that I might have to deal with. Some of that distraction is cleared now, though. It could just be because I met you, though."

"Wow," I said, chewing on the savory spiced beans, corn, and potatoes of the chili. "I didn't know that you suffered like that. You always seem so confident in yourself. I thought you were full of yourself, which I feel might still be true. But you have to stop with the flirting. I love flirting. I'm a flirt. But Antonio is my boyfriend, and I don't want to change that."

"Yeah, I hear you," Elliot said, looking hurt into the horizon. "I didn't want to complicate things, but it is a shame you're taken. I really do like Antonio, too. But what about the kiss? You didn't pull away. You kissed me back. I thought..."

"I'm sorry for that," I said. "This is my first relationship, and I just fully came out to living my truth. I just joined this group, and I'm just trying to make everyone happy. There's a lot more you don't know, and I'm just trying the best I can. You frustrate me in all the ways I like. I used to even fantasize about meeting you one day and you actually being gay, like the rumors suggested. I imagined you'd actually be interested in me. And then it happens, but I already found what I love having. Wanting, having, and not wanting are almost so biological that they often don't make sense."

"But life doesn't have to make sense," Elliot said. "That's the beauty of living. We can just trust our natural instincts. If you, me, and Antonio all want each other, we might as well try to see what that looks like."

"What?" I asked. "You mean like a..."

"Like a throuple," Elliot said, looking over at me with his silver saucer eyes.

"You're joking..." I said, looking at him with the stone mask of neutrality I used with Joshua and the guys. But Elliot's face grew red and hot around his cheeks and ears, telling me he didn't expect such a response. "You're not out yet. How can you be enthralled in a throuple at the same time?"

"I always knew I'd have to come out some day," Elliot said. "I just never had a guy to do it for. I never had anyone to love like that. Like how you and Antonio love each other."

"We're just figuring things out too," I said to Elliot, afraid of the troubling routes the conversation could go down.

"But you have stuff figured out," Elliot said. "You have love figured out. You won't be with me because you love him. Love has aligned with you both, and you both aligned with me. I think this could work. It feels like destiny."

"I'm not sure anything is truly destined," I said. "I mean, for a while I would've said the only thing that is destined is death, but look at us with immortality now. This world is what you make it, and your life is what you will it to be. I'll see if Antonio will spend the night in your room with us, though. He might agree to that. But, as you already see, he doesn't exactly scream 'throuple type.'"

"Okay," Elliot said, relaxing his shoulders as if he got exactly what he wanted, but I could still see the wheels of thought turning behind his eyes and smile. "I like the idea of that first step. He *is* pretty jealous, I guess. Or hurt. I kind of just threw myself at both of you. I see that now. I'll try to smooth things over with him during my training session."

"You are more and more full of surprises every time we talk, Elliot Cutcas," I said, watching him scrape the bottom of the chili bowl with his fork for the last bean.

"I even surprise myself," he said. "Way more than I want to. The throuple idea isn't silly, is it?"

"No, not at all," I said, lying. But what else could I do? This mission was making a big liar out of me, which I was starting to worry about for my auric integrity. I didn't want to be a magnet for all of the chaos energy we were bound to go up against, but I didn't want to hurt him or lose his allegiance. His heart was more pure than most. "We should get to training, though," I said, steadying myself against the tilt of the ship as I got up.

The top deck was the slick white roof of the second story, above the brig. The evening exhaled a brilliant pink, orange, and soft blue view of the retreating Ibizan beaches and of the Mediterranean horizon around us. The sea breeze was warm, even with the speed of the boat, and I welcomed the feeling of the air on my face as I focused on getting into the mindset for training. I wasn't sure if I'd get another session with Leibniz before or after Menorca, so I needed to make this one worth it.

"How was supper?" Leibniz asked when I met the group of him, Rumi, Baldwin, and Frederick in the middle of the deck. They all looked refreshed from their food, with a renewed sense of joy from the short rest. It amazed me how well the immortals balanced their emotions against the danger of the situations they're seemingly always placed in.

"It was good for a chili made outside the US," I said, my mouth still stinging with the hum of spiced heat. I wasn't *that* kind of American, but I knew chili was as all American as it gets. And the comment brought smiles to their faces that I felt good about. "When we got back to the boat and we were talking with Aurelius, you mentioned the dark things the predators could've done to us with the chaos energy. In the canyon, I felt it trying to infect your energy shield the way it had infected their auras. The chaos connection made them strong, but there was a madness to the energy that they seemed compatible with. I felt that it could drive an immortal crazy if it were to infect us."

"Hmmm. Well, crazy is a relative term," Leibniz said. "I was called crazy in my first life more times than anyone would like to admit, and I'm still called it. So, what exactly do you mean?"

"I mean, it could turn one of us into someone like them," I said, making everyone take a second to think.

"Then, let us get to work," Leibniz said, his hairy brow

scrunching. I knew he'd be thinking about what I said, if not communicating with the others mentally. The thought of one of us being turned into one of them would have been devastating. Not only for our fight, but for the sake of confidence in always being who we determine ourselves to be. If something so external could change us so internally, I wasn't sure anything, about anything, was certain anymore.

"I'm ready," I said, crossing my legs into a seat. Leibniz sat in front of me with the blue haze of the horizon behind him. While Rumi, Baldwin, and Frederick sat so that the five of us made a circle as the boat charged forward.

"To start, forget everything you know about everything," Leibniz said.

"I think I have that down at this point," I said, closing my eyes and thinking about my life before I left Manhattan.

"Immortals need a million minds to think from," Baldwin said. "Start a new one for everything Leibniz teaches you. You might have to use this mind a lot, considering your auric dispositions."

"Thank you," I said to Baldwin, and Leibniz smiled.

"Thank you for those kind words, my friend," Leibniz added, and then turned back to me. "I want you now to keep your eyes open. This world is a canvas for our magic as much as for the darkness of our imaginations. And it's from the world that we need you to be able to see and feel. You've done well in hiding your power, I can tell, but now you need to flex them and expand them. We're heading out into the sea under a blue sky of sunshine. The battle of our day is already fought. There's no fear of our enemy reaching us, and we have every advantage by showing off some of the power of the Immortal Philosophers. Let me see you light up the sky."

"Light up the sky?" I said, confused, and feeling less enthusiastic about my lesson than I wanted to be. I couldn't get the thought of Elliot and Antonio being together out of my head. Even if I knew Elliot didn't need me, I wanted to know what was going on. How Antonio was being. What Aurelius was saying and not saying. And what I needed to know to prepare for when we all came together.

"Like fireworks," Leibniz said, flicking his fingers around in the air about his head. "I want to see how far you can expand your power. You need to see how much you can feel. This is lesson one on how to handle the atrament, yes, but space, time, present, past. Even here and there, they're all parts of the same thing. Feeling for holes into other dimensions should be the same as searching for immortal souls across time, as Aurelius believes you're capable of doing."

"There's everything in everything, and I mean that sincerely. Each monad of existence, which I call existence's smallest particles, are all reflections of the totality of universal possibility. The ravers and sunbathers we saw on the beach are all evidence of the complexity of existence's variety. Look here," Leibniz said, and in his hands appeared a bone-china cup and saucer full of inky black coffee that stained the porcelain where it sloshed up the sides of the cup's walls.

"Inside this single cup of coffee is the totality of the universe," Leibniz said. "And, at the same time, is a cosmic universe all its own, if only we had the time to travel throughout it."

"You make it seem as though you have," I said, prodding with simplicity while I wondered about what his theory actually meant for me.

"I did, at a time," Leibniz said, but my mind was on to

what didn't add up.

"How can things be themselves and the variety of the universe at the same time?" I said, conjuring my own cup of tea while Leibniz sipped his coffee with a smirk. "Wouldn't that mean everything's the same?"

"Now, what is something without everything it isn't?" Leibniz said. "Logically speaking? If logically something needs everything, it's not a part, but a function of its whole. Then, how could not the same principles apply for the perceived physical expressions we experience as *matter*. Add thoughts as well, and auric energy. Auric energy is, by my experiences, to be the most basic nomadic structure that binds us other than time and spirit of life in general."

"Your affinity to all of it is what makes your power so important for you to master. And part of that is in seeing yourself as no different from the breeze or the air around you. Or the energy currents that we exist within. The energy that belongs to you is no different than the energy on the other side of the ocean or floating around in space. Distance is a fallacy that power can overcome when applied wisely and with practice. Some have even joined that omniscient presence, and you've met at least one who did within his first dozen years of life. Ikkyu. His early enlightenment is proof to us all of the existence of the unknowable forces of our experience. Now, you don't have to reach nirvana for us, but reach for what's out there. See if anything speaks to you in a language you aren't sure you can understand. That usually means you're onto something worthwhile."

"So, just reach out?" I asked, taken by the notion. "Just feel for things? Same as I did on the beach?"

"Deeper than on the beach," Leibniz said. "Feel for the

monadic cores of existence through the noise of what existence creates."

Be sensitive, I thought to myself. *Be sensitive. I'm sensitive. Sensitivity is power. Like the antennae of a radio, feeling for frequencies.* I tuned my internal auric sensitivity dial against the comforting blackness of my now quiet mind. Channeling my aura helped silence the anxieties that otherwise filled me, and I pulled as much energy as I could out from my core. I sprayed my power out into the sky above and around me, feeling the space with every particle I reached.

I felt the immortals sitting around me. The serious and distilled energy of Frederick, the spiced energy of Baldwin, the erotic tickling of Rumi, and the library-esque feel of the tome that was Leibniz. The energies of the other immortals below us all mixed in the auric current like the oils off bodies in a neighborhood pool. I caught strands of identifiable essences, but my mind was beyond our ship, soaring with the yellow legged seagulls over water and land.

What a view, came Horus in my head. Bringing me a feeling of deeper calm that relaxed the strain between my eyes.

It's breath taking, I thought back to him.

You're on the right path, he thought. *I'm here if you need me. I'll guide you a bit if you get stuck in this noncorporeal state.*

Thank you, I thought, not sure if I knew what I was doing, but confident I'd get to where I needed to.

I didn't think I'd find an atrament by just expanding my aura and feeling the energies around me, especially being so far from land, but I did want to see if I could feel for the chaotic energy of the predators still boarding their boats behind us. Julius Caesar, Hannibal, Oshun, and Elagabalus. The first two I had heard of, but the latter two were a mystery to me, but horrified I was to have met them all.

As I expanded my aura, my senses sharpened to the point that I wasn't feeling the breeze inside my auric space, my aura *was* the breeze. I did what Leibniz said and felt myself as one with everything around me. As the totality of the universe, and as a unique reflection of its entirety.

I fused myself with the monads until I became the birds coasting through my aura in the sky. Until I became the bird's eye view receiving lightrays and imaging the data into the cinematic experience of the biological optic to mental theatre. And as my mind focused on the predators, so too did focus the eye of the bird. But with every bird within my field, until the birds exited my auric air space.

For once, my mind was quiet and working with me in greater harmony than I'd ever experienced. My months of auric training got me far outside my mind, encompassing more than I had ever held at once. I didn't include the immortals around me the way Leibniz did with his shield in the canyon, but there was something else that was pulling at me.

Something far below us, pulling at my attention. It wasn't the tight pin prick of an atrament or the lifegiving spring of an auric well. It felt like the whisper of a lost friend, one too soft and too far away to hear. It felt like a message more than a location, but I couldn't be sure. I focused on listening and expanding the perimeter of my auric reach, wondering what to do about the itching presence.

I've found something, I thought to Leibniz and the others.

He's a fast learner, Frederick thought. *Reminds me of myself, young. You can't extinguish the flame of a bright mind no matter how hard you try.*

And brighter, through darkness, it shall glow, Baldwin added.

If only we could still publish under ourselves, Rumi thought back, but I was as focused as ever. The presence of them felt supportive of my aura like, if I were to slip, they'd be there to catch me.

Let's give him a charge, then, Leibniz thought. *Leave your fantasies for later, you three. We could be on the brink of something here. Dylan, in the way the atrament is a void for filling, open up space in yourself for the message of what you feel to be received. It might just need a little more of pull in a certain direction. We'll enhance your efforts. We're not picking up on anything except the predators behind us. Is it them?*

No, I thought, thinking about it. *Maybe, though. I'm not sure yet.*

I felt like a dolphin or shark using echo location through the depths of the crystal blue water, searching for a message in a bottle lost hundreds of years ago. But if it was the energy of a predator, I needed to know, and I needed to find out before it was too late to alert everyone else.

I took Leibniz's advice, and felt for space inside the places of my mind as they each fueled me with more power and focus. Visually, all I saw was the color of dense cobalt aura where the darkness of my closed eyes would be if my energy wasn't also pouring from my eyes, but I felt in a visual way everywhere my aura reached. So, as my energy sank into the Mediterranean deep, so too did I. Luckily, my aura could move faster than I could swim, so it was better that my body stayed behind atop the ship.

As I stretched my aura through the light beams and fractals of the upper ocean, I started feeling cold. The warmth of my aura wasn't enough anymore. I felt the chill of the oceanic tundra that was the rocky seafloor. Below us were the inky, oil-like depths where a submarine would explore in a sci-fi horror flick, but staring at the trench, I felt like I had learned all I needed to know.

I was in the womb of the Mediterranean. Between light and dark, above and below the sea, and all I wanted to do was to see. See beyond the limits of all I knew or could speculate. To see the trueness of everything and everyone in every way they could be seen. To love the many versions of every potentiality, equally. To let go of myself and embrace the totality, and to let the totality embrace me.

And that's when it hit me. The signal wasn't a beacon, it was a signal. One maybe even from the ocean or Earth, herself, but it wasn't the corrupt energy of the predators at play here. The energy was different. Timeless, mystic, and terrestrial all at once. But no matter how hard I pulled, pushed, or focused, I couldn't connect to it.

With no other direction to go in, I reached out a hand to pull back the curtain of time and flick through as much of the past as I could. And it worked. I watched the sun retreat back into dawn and the moon brighten into focus. I saw trails of ships swallow their own wakes, like a zipper pulling closed, and I waited and watched.

Storms pulled together, tossing the sea and the ships in it against the wind and mountain sized waves, before dispersing back into skies of starry nights and blue haze. The cosmos of the Mediterranean were like no other, with a chaotic beauty as if painted by the brushstrokes and pinpoints of humanity itself. But there was no reason for the cosmos to be any more responsive to humanity than the storms that take shiploads of lives to the bottom of the seafloor. Even the signals I received, whether sent consciously to me or not, were subject to my understanding. It seemed true for mortals and immortals, that objectivity wasn't something achievable for a subjective mind, even a mind relinquished from subjectivity. Even for a noncorporeal entity, like Horus. The whole experience of existence felt like a collection of attachments, even as I watched ships blast, crash, and sink each other.

I wondered what attachments time might have had, as sailors sank, too tired to keep kicking their legs or moving their arms. Too tired to feel their attachment to the fear that reminded them of their connection between body and mind. But watching them in reverse, their bodies lifting back up through the depths of the water, watching the shreds of life blink back into their stone-milky, to alert again eyes.

It seemed to me, moving further into the past, that the only thing outside of the experience of subjectivity, was time. I watched an island grow from reverse erosion, back into a small sand island between two surging currents, but time didn't care if the island was here, there, or nowhere at all. Time, simply, was. The island was, too, but the island struggled to stay together, while the currents blasted it apart, pushed to for some reason or another outside of its control.

While it took time for the forces to establish the balance of non-existence, time's existence wasn't dependent on anything else or attached to any of its states of being. Time was the constant, and only in the direction we experienced it in, was it determinative. Because in how it is, it is something as fluid as liquid in a test tube, flowing this way, then that, depending on the direction it's tilted.

But something did catch my eye as I flicked through days, months, and years. It was a structure that I couldn't quite make out through the haze that surrounded it every time it passed by. All it brought with it, other than the blur, was the feeling of familiarity. Like stumbling upon a letter from an old friend written long ago, when you were both very different people. It emanated the feeling of being lost, too. In the way we often look back at our younger selves as being lost, and in the way we often see ourselves as ships, lost at sea and guided only by the currents of our times and the quality of our company. Lost, and pulling at the strings of time, the way I had learned to navigate the complexities of my own life. When attachment was a luxury I felt I could never afford.

CHAPTER NINE

THE CHILDREN OF THE MOONLIT KINDOM

After hours of traveling through time, the White Seahorse was well on course for Menorca, and Leibniz was the only one still with me on the top deck. The night was dark off the side of the boat as it hummed its way through the water. While other ships had to crash into waves to keep pushing forward, our boat glided through flatness, as the water around the boat was in a constant state of ease. Even big waves crumbled into glassy, astronomical reflections when they got close, but there was no morsel of anything on the horizon to help me understand the mysterious traveling presence that I kept seeing as a blur moving through time and space.

"I think that's enough for one lesson," Leibniz eased into saying. His voice was as rough and scratchy as mine felt from the silent hours of meditation.

"Yeah, I agree," I said, turning from his moonlit face to show my whole face to the moon. Moonlight and sunlight were always so curious to me, and it wasn't often I took in the moon's rays, but it felt satisfying. Where the moon shined, my skin tingled with delight from the inherent activation of my aura.

"And just look at the two of you," came the voice of Cleoseléné behind us. "Basking in the ambiance and power of the moon's reflection."

"What an astute observation," Leibniz said, moving to see past me, but the pull of the moon was too strong for me to look away from it to greet her.

"If you want, I can take him back to his quarters and oversee him until I do," Cleoseléné said to my teacher.

"Still keeping up your moonlight meditations?" Leibniz asked her, getting to his feet.

"It's not a choice, if I want to feel alright," Celoselene said. "Espeically with all that's going on. Caesar's presence is a poison to this world and to my soul. The anger... the sadness. It all surfaces like the painful reminder of a tragic wound by the brush of a sensitive scar."

"I understand a-plenty," Leibniz said. "We just finished up. He could use a good moonsoak. I'll leave you three to it. I need to get some sleep, too, before Aurelius starts barking more orders. Our resident emperor never lost that quality. I don't envy the position he's in, though. It's doubtful that he gets much sleep these days, either."

"Ah, well, he's not one to let us know his worries," came the voice of Moremi, as the two queens stepped into the moonlight on their way to rails where I stared. "A true leader never sleeps or leaves worries to wonder. Especially when hard truths and answers are required to save the many."

"That's why I gave up trying to lead long ago," Cleoseléné said, leaning back against the ship's rail, with the moon full and bright behind her as Moremi joined her. Both wore white swaying gowns of heavy silk that rippled against the breeze.

"Well, I wish good night to the three of you," Leibniz

said, and he scurried off between us.

"Good night, Leibniz," the women said, in the near unison of two of Charlie's Angels.

"Matching nightgowns?" I asked. "This is looking more like a gay cruise full of upside down pineapples the more I'm here."

"You'd know, better than us," Cleoseléné joked, mirroring Moremi's smile back at her at my expense.

"That's a good one," I said. "Unfortunately, I don't have experience."

"Too bad for you," Moremi said. "But the gowns are in every bathroom on the ship. Complements of Grace and Hyp. For all guests, not just the horny lesbians or bisexual, free sex types."

"Thanks for telling me," I said. "I'll be sure to hide them before Elliot throws one on."

"Couldn't be the worst end to either of your nights, after almost killing him, that is," Moremi said, raising her brows at me as she walked over to sit on my right, with Cleoseléné taking a seat on my left. "Could be a good way to say sorry."

"I'm sure he wouldn't mind," I said, feeling my chest collapse with stress at the admission. "I'm trying to forget and ignore everything to do with that thought, though. Antonio is going to kill me one of these nights if things don't get better between us."

"Ahhh, leave the talk of the night for the decks below us," Cleoseléné said, breathing in a deep breath of Mediterranean air that looked so satisfying, I took one too. Drawing into my lungs the salinity and moisture that hovered above the warmed ocean water.

"I didn't mean to nearly kill Elliot," I said. "I'm kind of scared of myself for doing what I did."

"Such sacrifices are transcendental," Moremi said,

looking at me hard, but with the softness of a friend. "Every sacrifice is. Every sacrifice carries with it generational consequences to the point that we cannot imagine as we move forward in time. Do you think the traders who traded their neighbors foresaw hundreds of years of violence and oppression for their sacrificial subjects? Nothing's safe from the men who say you must sacrifice. But that's all in the past," Moremi said, her face glowing in the moonlight. "Stay minded in the future, and the more bountiful will be your future. You learned from your experience, and that will make you a better Immortal Philosopher."

"Wise advice," Cleoseléné said. "Moon-like, advice. Always foretelling the next day with the data of the past."

"And what do we foretell, tonight?" Moremi asked, activating the moonlight dazzle of her aura around herself.

"Let's see," Cleoseléné said, activating her aura in turn, leaving me blanketed within their merging energy fields.

"Hands," Cleoseléné said, grabbing my hand as Moremi grabbed my other, sparking my aura to life, and adding cobalt to the center of our field against the moon and black sky filled with pinholed stars that all mirrored off the inky sea.

Two bright cylindrical beams shot out from the moon and stretched to both of the foreheads of Cleoseléné and Moremi, and one more beamed right between my eyes.

A cold, arctic energy started piping into my skull. The nights Antonio and I laid on the beach staring at the moon came back to me. Me in his arms on the soft, cold wetness of the midnight dune sand. The crook of his arm was the perfect place to rest my head, and he didn't mind it no matter how long we laid. At night, the beach was more social than during the day. Night walkers paced like city

LOST BETWEEN THE LANDS OF HERE AND THERE street walkers, greeting each other as they passed through the swinging cones of their flashlights. Us, undetectable in the darkness of the rustling sea grass, listening to the rush of the waves crashing at the wave break and the fizz of the bubbles popping against the sand.

"I saw something in my lesson with Leibniz," I said, losing myself to the current of memory. "I don't know what it was."

"There are thousands of things in the Mediterranean to see," Moremi said, her hand warm and pulsing in mine. "And thousands more that only come out for the moon."

"What a truth," Cleoseléné said, breathing in even rhythmic cycles. "And thousands more on the Island of the Moonlit Kindom."

"The what?" I asked, unsure of what she meant.

"The Moonlit Kindom," Moremi said, her delight lifting her voice. "Has Antonio taught you nothing?"

"He's taught me some stuff, but there's not enough time to learn everything," I said, understanding that truth more now than ever before.

"The Moonlit Kindom is a Mediterranean island that Moremi and I oversaw as matriarchs for lifetimes at some points," Cleoseléné said. "A place guided by women, wisdom, and the collective. Where business and life is conducted under the moonlight and in the few hours surrounding the moon's ascent and the sun's rise. It's a place governed by the maternal nature of Earth, and it's survived hidden for centuries because of those pillars of civilization. Unfortunately, it moves with the tides and the astrological changes of the moon. And the Kin make sure to cover their moon dusty tracks so they can keep it hidden from the rest of the world."

"It's a much more peaceful place to live than out here," Moremi said. "Much more of nature is alive at night than it is during the day. Nothing beats being barefoot in a field of flowers and hills on a full moon without a cloud in the sky, or walking on a beach. The cities and gardens, though. Those were my favorite places in Moonlit Kindom."

"That place sounds dreamlike," I said, feeling punny.

"We still do like to laugh, Dylan Eaglegod," Moremi said, smiling at me. "But you have to actually be funny."

"I don't think it was that island that I saw, though," I said, feeling the truth in what I was saying and not wanting to lose my thoughts. "It was not like an island. It was much smaller. Not quite a boat, either."

"Like we said," Cleoseléné said. "It could be a thousand different things. Give it time, and it will become clear to you. The same way your path forward with Antonio will become more clear to you, too. Now, silence. Drink in the moon's gifts before you head back to your boys for the night."

The two queens hummed together in a rhythm that moved the aura and air around us, and tuned into the beams pulsing into our foreheads. They played the energy like an instrument that made me almost dizzy behind the blackness of my shut eyes, as I felt the world around me spin. For a while I felt weightless, as my aura charged with the energy of the moon, tingling my body from head to toes, and restoring my body with the healing energy that Moremi channeled into Elliot earlier. I drifted, submitting to the moon's rays and felt more and more in balance the longer I hummed along with them, allowing their vibrations to penetrate my vocal box and take the reins of my own vibration, until I mimicked them without a thought.

"You should head back and get some rest now, Dylan," Moremi said after a while. "We'll be up here a bit longer, but you need your rest."

"Farewell, student of the moon," Cleoseléné said, letting go of my hand without breaking her focus on the moon.

"Last I saw your boys, Antonio was escorting Elliot back to Elliot's quarters," Moremi said, letting go of my hand too. "And they both looked like they needed some help."

"Then, I guess this is where I leave you both," I said, getting up. "Back to the war between broken hearts, I go. Thank you for this experience. It was everything I needed tonight."

Then I took my leave, back down the stairs at the back of the roof deck. I would have much preferred to meditate the night away under the beauty of the night sky on the sea, but every second Elliot and Antonio were together made me scared that one or both of them would explode, leaving a hole in the side of the ship that would make us all stranded and shipless in the water.

"Yeah, Dylan buried the guy at the bottom of the ocean," I heard Antonio say as I opened the door to Elliot's quarters, making me sound more badass than I ever felt.

"He never said anything about that," Elliot said, sounding amazed. Antonio was laying on the couch, and Elliot was sprawled end-to-end on the bed in nothing but his white undies like the night before. "I knew it, though. I can see it in his eyes. He's got what it takes to kill."

"That's not how we think about things here," I said, stepping into the room and making for Antonio, hoping for some kind of reaction from him. And keeping my eyes averted from Elliot's smooth and muscular body.

"It's about time," Antonio said, picking himself up off the recline of the couch-back.

"Oh, so you missed me?" I said, hoping to keep him in the room or have him take me with him. The romance of our Mediterranean mission was already spoiled, but we still had time to turn things around if he let me. I felt bad for Elliot, but it sounded like training might have at least brought them closer.

"Yeah," Antonio said, eyeing me up. "Of course I did."

"Well you're both sleeping here tonight," Elliot added, pulling himself into the conversation with a flash of silver auric sparkles.

"You taught him a new trick?" I said to Antonio, sitting into the space beside him and kissing his cheek. I pulled his hand into mine, and leaned my head against his shoulder as he relaxed into a recline again, giving me more space to connect with.

"You two are the cutest gays I've ever met," Elliot said, leaning back into the pillows behind him with his arms crossed. "You know, I haven't really been introduced to any gays who were a couple. And I couldn't dare be outed, so I never met a guy in an honest way like that."

"You're missing out," I said to Elliot, looking into Antonio's eyes. I knew what it was like inside the closet, and I knew what I had now. They were worlds of difference. There was nothing that could make me go back into hiding. Antonio helped me see what I couldn't see on my own and filled the parts of me that needed someone else's hands of healing.

The tickle of the spiced scent of his cologne sent me back to the heat of the summer when we had nothing on but perfume and bedsheets. Drunk on the sunset-to-sunrise lifestyle of the drunk-in-love gay Jersey Shore immortals and the feeling that it could all end at any second. I truly appreciated every minute we spent together. I knew, in those moments, that life was something worth living. If not for my own self desire to be loved by Antonio, but to also love Antonio in the ways that he liked to feel love. Learning each others' languages came easy to us.

"Well, you know I want the both of you," Elliot said, turning our heads to him. I look to Antonio, concerned about the smile on Elliot's face, and wondering what Antonio will say.

"You can have me," I hear myself say. I feel my lips make the words and my tongue fling them forth. "Anytime you want."

Antonio looked at me, brows high, jaw tight. Disgust, washed across his face.

"Now we're talking," Elliot said, scooting to the edge of the bed. "Where's this energy been the whole time?"

"It hasn't been between us," Antonio said, staring hard at me, as he got up. "That's for sure."

"I don't even know how I said that," I said, truly dumbfounded by the statement. "I don't even feel that way."

"I'm sure you don't," Antonio said, crossing the room to leave. "I say things I don't want to say and don't feel all the time. And you do, too apparently. I'd know better than anyone. But maybe I'm still learning. I don't know. I need to sleep, and you need to... do whatever you need to do to keep *him* happy, I guess."

"Well, if we're on the topic of keeping me happy," Elliot said, as Antonio left out the door. "Come back and join the fun! I'm so ready for this! I've been biting my lip for you two since I saw you backstage!"

Antonio didn't come back, and the door shut between us. Leaving me feeling cold in the room I made heartless. Elliot's feet were silent across the floor as he lifted me to my feet and bent my arms around his neck. He hugged me as we stood, and I leaned into him, feeling the loss of all my happiness in life flood away from me. Feeling only arms and hands. His body on mine. His hands lifting me by my thighs, and carrying me across the room as I held back tight tears in the crook of his sweat-fragrant neck as I felt myself lose control. And we kissed in the darkness between the pillows, my body moving against his in a way that felt musical against the silence of the moonlit night.

CHAPTER TEN

WATER WALLS AND WATER FALLS

Everybody UP! came the voice of Horus in my head, jumping myself and Elliot awake and alert. Sirens blared around the ship, and I called my aura into armor around my... naked body? And seeing me, Elliot did the same. *We're under attack! Everyone to the deck!*

On deck, the immortals are scattered and running about, checking the boxes of unspoken orders given by Horus, Grace, Aurelius. I wasn't sure why, but the boat was rocking, with mountains of waves being deflected by the water wielding of Kana and wind power of Juba, who both stood firm against the side rail of the ship, commanding the elements against our unseeable enemy.

I found Antonio straddling the starboard railing, frantic as he worked his aura into the sea to steady the ship and keep us from rocking or capsizing against the torrent of waves building around us. Aurelius was in the water, soaring atop a water funnel, thrashing mountains of waves back at the ocean, as it seemed the whole sea was attacking us.

You going to start seeing the future, or what? Antonio thought, looking back at me in relief.

"Fuse your aura with the ship to ground yourself!" I shouted at Elliot over the spray and crash of waves coming overboard made every step feel treacherous. "I have to help!"

Elliot looked at me horrified, and then down at his glowing silver hands.

"You got this!" I said, pushing him back inside the deck lounge and slamming shut the retractable glass door.

When are you going to start believing me when I say I don't know how things happen sometimes, I thought to Antonio, gathering a hot tub's worth of ocean water from the deck and riding it like Aurelius did, over to Antonio. *It's just recent. I don't know what's going on.*

Well, help me keep us upright! Antonio thought back, and I crossed over into the sea, lifted by the water cyclone spiralling underneath me. Just how I did in Ocean City for our Oceanic Battle Class.

You're crazy! Antonio thought to me as I focused my energy on lifting up the ship with the water around the hull of the boat. I pulled in water from the base of the waves that the other immortals were battling and fed the accumulating area under the boat, causing the boat to rise out of the valley of mountainous crashing waves. Water sprayed me from all sides, to the point I couldn't see, but still I lifted.

Feed me, I thought to Antonio, needing more power. As the boat rose, so too did my need to focus. One slip, and the ship would fall slower than the water holding it up, which would leave us all tumbling into the sea with the boat capsized and sinking. It was a risky tactic, but I felt I could do it.

With pleasure, Antonio said, and a fluorescent beam of cyan auric energy shot out of his chest in my direction, hitting me smack center in my chest and filling me with what

LOST BETWEEN THE LANDS OF HERE AND THERE
felt like an endless stream of charged power. I funneled it
into the growing pillar of ocean water keeping our boat
afloat and lifted harder until the boat sat atop a pillar taller
than the everest-esque waves that munched at the horizon
like whale mouths.

Good work, Antonio thought, as I settled back onto the
deck of the raised ship, putting all my focus on keeping the
pillar stable beneath us.

*We have to keep it raised on the water pillar until the
waves calm*, I thought to everyone around. *What's going on?*
I thought to Antonio.

These wave surges came out of nowhere, Antonio thought
back, soaked and scared looking, but smiling at me despite
himself. *We're a few hours out from Menorca.*

Great work everyone, Aurelius thought from his water-
spout, right before a wave crashed over him, from which he
emerged unmoved. *Keep the boat raised, and beat back these
waves! We need to get the ship moving forward! If we can
keep moving, we'll get out of this mess.*

Everyone who can, Grace thought from the brig, I
assumed, because she wasn't on deck. *Move the pillar forward. Great thinking Dylan!*

Dylan and I will keep the pillar standing, Antonio
thought to everyone, nodding at me. With both of our energies, I knew we could do it.

Got it, I thought, feeling the water under us as if it were
a straight leg getting kicked from behind the knee with
each wave that hit us, and threatening to buckle. Against
the push forward from the other immortals, the feeling
grew more severe, but we kept it standing. I felt and saw
the dazzling rainbow of auric colors imbuing the air and

water around us and inching us through the waves crashing far below. There was a way out of this mess, even while the funnel was battered by the fury that only lighthouses during hurricanes were used to enduring.

Is this Oshun? I thought to Antonio, searching for the energies of the predators in the mix of the storm, but I couldn't find a trace of any predator influence.

Moremi said it's not, Antonio thought. *We don't know what it is.*

All these immortals, and no ideas? I thought back, feeling lost.

And it's taking all of us just to get out of here, Antonio thought back.

Does Aurelius have a death wish for all of us? I thought.

He's just as susceptible to corporeal folly as the smartest among you, came the thoughts of Horus.

Aren't you included in that? I thought.

My origin is not of your concern, Horus thought back.

He's sensitive about being non-corporeal, Antonio chimed in.

So, the White Seahorse isn't your body? I thought, hoping for a rise from the bodyless immortal.

If I could retract all the help I've given you, I would, Horus thought in defense as the ship moved forward. The plan was working.

You could at least get your ship moving a little faster if you graced us with your help this time, I thought back. *For your own benefit, if not ours.*

I'm doing everything a true god can do, Eaglegod, Horus thought, with a stronger lurch forward than before, that brought us closer to the calmer waters ahead of us.

"Good work," Moremi said, drifting onto the deck beside me as the water spout she rode splashed back into the sea.

"Your quick thinking got us out of the worst of that mess."

"We were getting out no matter what," I said, surprised by the recognition.

"I mean it," Moremi said, her striking eyes connecting with mine. "The sea is a dangerous foe. We hardly know its powers or its limits."

"Well, that feeling I can relate to," I said, keeping focused on the pillar's stability. We were about a hundred yards up, at least, and a few hundred from the sanctuary of the calm sea.

"Don't lose that sense," Moremi said. "Immortals and predators often lose their sense of vulnerability and die from their underestimation of nature and humanity."

"I always feel like I overestimate every obstacle I come upon," I said, feeling the weight of my fear like a pit in my gut.

"Don't lose that instinct to survive," Moremi said, adding her power to the energy moving us forward. "After the loss of my son to Oshun, I spent centuries trying to find them and bring him back to me. I lost myself around the world. Drinking, sailing, and a whole host of other ways people cope when the hurt inside of them is too much to hold in."

Moremi's eyes filled with the moonlit glow of her aura, and I felt an auric shift around the ship. From behind us, a wave grew, far below, but lifted the sea behind us, and crashed into our pillar, lifting us high on its surface, and lurching us forward, like a surfboard riding a wave crest.

The moonlit tinge of the water shone through its depths, so I pumped my energy into hers. She pulled on it, and Antonio did the same. The other waves around us couldn't even tug at Moremi's control of the sea. My aura was a laser of blue connecting us, and through that connection I felt the love and loss that filled her heart. I recognized that pain, and let it fill me as it charged her.

When we reached calm waters, and it looked like the storm would be behind us, the sky cleared, and any sign of the storm was gone. As if it had only existed in the past, long ago. The day ahead, behind, and all around us was blue skied, with land coming up on the horizon, making me wonder if we'd all just imagined the terrifying event.

You did good, Antonio thought, looking at me and grabbing my hand before pressing the tips of his fingers into me. His hands did more than touch, though. I'd gotten used to how they seemed to dig in and become a part of me that I never want to let go of and in a way my body yearned for even when he was out of sight.

Thank you, I thought back. *I learned from the best.* I pressed my fingers into his hand as I squeezed back and leaned in to kiss him, long and slow. He let me, and kissed me back. For the first time in days, which felt like it could have been a lifetime in itself. The plazas of Málaga felt so far behind us, that all I wanted to do was return to that night he made a point to make the most special birthday night of my life.

You're right about that, he thought, getting the last hard kiss in before pulling away.

"Very impressive, my boys," came the voice of Elliot behind us. On the other side of the deck, the other immortals were gathering as they returned from their sea spirals or positions on the upper deck. Elliot looked shaken. Both physically with his hair and clothes ruffled, but also mentally. His eyes were wide and red with panic as he clapped for us, trying to hide his shaky hands.

"You did well in training yesterday," Antonio said, sounding... genuine. "Soon you'll be out here showing storms what you got, too."

"I don't know about soon," Elliot said, unsure of his words. "Training is one thing. Watching you guys in action... It really is magical. Beyond any show any star has ever given. But the danger you get into... I don't know if this life's for me. The high life was always my thing, but this is death defying."

"They don't call us the Immortal Philosophers for nothing," Moremi said, walking up to Elliot and placing a hand on his cheek. "Calm yourself, by the power of the moon."

From where Moremi's hand touched Elliot's cheek pulsed with a lunar glow that shone on the surface before sinking into his skin. Causing Elliot's whole posture to loosen and relax. His face settled into the normal, world-famous, serious-aloof look that was his own. Before tears welled into the crooks of his silver eyes and his face crumbled into tears.

"Thank you," he said through a half-smiled frown. "Everything's been changing so fast. It's hard to keep myself from feeling scared. I just... Half the time I don't even know if I'm in control or myself or not. I never felt this way before."

"You will find your way with us," Moremi said, as Antonio squeezed my hand again. "We're all learning as we go along, and we all pretend to have ourselves put together the way we want to be. It's the bravest among us who transpare themselves to those around them. Be open to us, and we will show you how to be strong in yourself. Strong enough to feel okay in your power, but you must find the peace inside yourself to settle your rustled existence into a new state of life and being. This life is just as hard as being a world famous pop star. Trust me, I've walked both lives too, once. Come with me for a while."

Then Moremi wrapped her arm around Elliot's shoulder and walked him over to the group of immortals, as we sailed on toward land.

"I stand by what Moremi said," Antonio said, taking my other hand in his too. "We don't know what happened this morning, and if you truly don't know what's going on in your head sometimes, I get it. The Mediterranean is the home of uncertain waters, and there's more we don't know than what we do know. You're really showing how strong you can be as a part of the team, though. You're proving yourself a lot more than some immortals ever achieve."

"Thank you," I said, feeling like I could cry too. His acknowledgement was what I needed, and what I hoped would help me figure everything out for once and for all. "I'm still trying to figure things out, and I don't want to mess up for anybody. But there are so many things that have happened now that have felt beyond my and our control. It's starting to become more of a feature of this mission rather than just a pattern or coincidence."

"Tell us more," Aurelius said, walking the full group of immortals over to us. He was the only one still soaked with ocean water from his wave battling. Everyone was in a mixture of pajamas and night gowns, with Captain O'Malley the only one in full leather boots, vest, and hat. True to a captain's form.

Antonio looked at me with a curious flattened brow, along with everyone else waiting for more answers.

"A few things," I said, not wanting to bring my moments with Elliot in front of everyone else. "Every instance of it has felt like this morning and the morning we veered off course, though. There're so many unexplainable things happening."

"I've felt it, too, Aurelius," Cleoseléné said, looking between us in a worried way that I hadn't seen on her yet. Her strong, angled face rippled with the slight of fear.

"I've felt something around you, too," Juba said, walking up behind her and taking her under his arm.

"Let's not get ahead of ourselves," Aurelius said, tamping down the air around him with his hands as if he could tamp down our fears. "The run-ins we've been having with these predators are getting to all of us, but we can't let them turn us into speculative bags of panicked anxiety. We need to keep our heads. We often live without the answers we feel we must know, and this is very much like that. We must continue on."

"We must, of course, Aurelius," Moremi said. "But something's off, and we might end up dead without an answer to what's going on. This isn't like a typical mission. We're not fighting on our terms. We're surviving despite whoever's coming for us, and I don't think those predators could have done something like *this*. In all my time with the Moonlit Kindom I didn't even see such power, and our powers over the sea while there are unmatched."

"I hear you," Aurelius said, scratching his chin through the wet clump of his beard. "Where are we, Grace?"

"A couple of hours off the coast of Menorca," Captain O'Malley said, inspecting the guardrails of the ship for damage.

"Do either of you feel anything off right now?" Juba asked of Cleoseléné and Moremi. Then he looked at me.

"No, I don't," Cleoseléné said, up at Juba.

"It feels fine right now," Moremi said, sounding uncertain.

"The feeling is different though," I added. "It's like, you only notice it while it's happening or right after it happens. There's no sense or logic to it. Something happens, and you have no control, and then you have to fix it or survive it. I spoke last night without even thinking about what I actually said."

"And my body moved without me moving it," Elliot added, with a renewed sense of subdued worry under Moremi's arm.

"This is outside of my experience," Leibniz said, clearing his throat. A piece of dark green seaweed was stuck to his forehead like a fresh press on tattoo in the shape of what looked like a whale tail fin.

"Except maybe the atrament energy," Frederick considered, scanning everyone with a hard look. "The corrupted infection of our auras could potentially produce such an event without our doing."

"The chaos energy?" I wondered aloud, with Antonio's hand tightening around mine. "It could be, but the chaos energy had a very specific and different feel. Like a vacuum and a true corruptive infection. The waves felt... natural. Like some kind of other force. Could a natural storm do that to the sea?"

"We've seen our fair share of stormy nights upon this boat," Captain O'Malley said. "Never have I seen waves like that in the Mediterranean. If it weren't for aurics, we would be gone. At the bottom of the seafloor. Done for."

"Did you sense an atrament back there at all, Dylan?" Leibniz asked, seeming to land on a thought he was working at.

"I really can't say. I wasn't thinking about looking for one. I just wanted to get the ship out of that mess," I said, regretting not tuning in to find an atrament before jumping into action.

"I want you searching for an atrament everywhere from

now on," Aurelius said, not looking up from the wood of the deck. "It could be the secret to our ability to defeat these predators. Especially if they're using them to attack us face to face and possibly from afar. We have to learn more about this, and, maybe, it might even help you train on peeling back the pages of the future as well as turning them into auric wells for our benefit. Let's continue to Menorca and establish a plan once we get there. We'll have to use the land and the sea to *our* advantage this time. Especially now that we know we're dealing with something outside of our collective experiences. Dylan, as soon as we get there, I want you searching for an atrament hole."

CHAPTER ELEVEN

THE OCEANIC AMPHITHEATRE OF WORLD RECORDS

When we reached the cliffs of Menorca, we weren't the first group there. Thousands of Elliot Cutcas fans were already gathered. Crowded in tents and mobs along the beach, and in boats bobbing atop the two pronged bay that lead to two beaches separated by a shark toothed cliff right between the perpendicular inlets. The larger inlet was a cape to the North, with the smaller inlet, tightly nestled between cliffs to the West. The bay water, though, was the bluest I'd ever seen, surprising me with how well I could see down to the bottom without even using my auric powers. I could see how a few cruise ships could fit in the cape, and the boats gathered made sure to nestle as close to the shore as possible without hitting swimmers to make sure the ships could enter. Nobody wanted to get kicked out of the Elliot Cutcas concert. Nobody except, maybe, Antonio.

"I wish we were here for fun," I said to Antonio as he, I, and Elliot stood at the bow of the White Seahorse, scanning the boats, beach crowds, and people nestled into the rocks of the cliffs for strong auras and predators that might be hiding in sight.

"How do you think I feel?" Elliot said, wearing a broad brimmed hat with droopy sides to conceal most of his face that made him look like a wine mom touring a winery. "These people are here to see *me*!"

"Don't get too upset, now," Antonio said, toying with Elliot, but I couldn't bother to police them. I was doing what Aurelius told me to do, and that was looking for the atrament above anything else.

"You two keep searching for signs of predators. I'm going to tune in to feel for an atrament while we cross the bay," I told them, closing my eyes and leaning forward against the bow rail.

"I'll keep you steady," Antonio said, getting his body behind me and grabbing the rail in front of us to hold me tight.

"Let me know if you need a break," Elliot said to Antonio, making Antonio snort out a laugh.

"I got him," he said. "Keep searching for the fans that wanna kill you."

"It's not my fans that want to kill me. It's my friends," Elliot said, as I struggled to silence them both in my mind.

"Knowing you, I don't blame them that much," Antonio said. "But, hey, you're really not that bad. And you're learning a lot here. By the time I'm done with you, you're going to be a completely different person."

"Whatever," Elliot said. "I'll do whatever it takes. I'm ready to feel okay again. Let me see if I can find any of them out here. I'm sure at least one of Gabirol's stooges is somewhere. They always are."

"Yeah, do that," Antonio said. "Just don't get noticed, or we'll be in deeper trouble. I'll keep your energy cloaked since you can't do it yourself yet."

"Thanks," Elliot said. "Doesn't the ship cloak us, too?"

"Horus keeps us all cloaked," Antonio said. "But once you start moving your energy through the bay and around these other boats, there's a chance you could be detected. But I'll keep the outer reaches of your aura secured. It's been a constant task of mine with Dylan up until we got here, really. He's pretty good at it now, though."

"I'll need to take more lessons with you, then," Elliot said, the smoothness of his flirting always filtering back into his speech.

Tea ceremony on the top deck in a bit, boys, Aurelius thought to us, reminding me of Zenda and Ikkyu back in Ocean City.

I like the sound of that, I thought back, longing to be back under Zenda's protective roof.

"What's a tea ceremony?" Elliot said.

"It's tea, but from ancient, aura charged trees. It'll start to show you what real power's all about, if you can handle it," I said, toying with Elliot too, since I could.

After a while of fruitless atrament searching, we gathered on the top deck for the tea ceremony as we traversed around the crowded boat filled bay as if on coast guard patrol. Each boat we passed was like its own village with grills, coolers, drinks, and music. I didn't know all it took was keeping up a beach ball for everyone to get on the same page. The red and white striped ball travelled from boat to boat, never touching the ground. Drones flew overhead, no doubt recording and documenting the once in a lifetime feel of the monumental Elliot Cutcas occasion, even if he was replaced by the poor body double of Jordy Portendorfi.

"What if I just perform before they get here?" Elliot

asked as we knelt down in a circle with Kana, Aurelius, Moremi, Captain O'Malley, Hypatia, Juba, Cleoseléné, Baldwin, Rumi, and Frederick. It was an all hands on deck occasion. Kana had in front of her a collection of matcha tea instruments. A bowl, bamboo whisk, bamboo tea scoop, a clay and metal lidded jar, and a cast iron water pot. Antonio, Elliot, and I were the last to arrive.

"If you performed here now, how would you explain the Jordy clone of you performing on Mallorca?" Antonio asked, highlighting the definitive obstacle. "We'll let the experts figure out the plan for now," Antonio added before Elliot could figure out what to say.

"I'm glad everybody is here," Aurelius said, taking command for the circled gathering.

And every-unbodied is here with you too, if you were wondering, came the thoughts of Horus to me.

I'll check you in, I thought back. *Will you be sipping for one or for two?*

Very funny, Horus thought back, sounding hurt. *I won't bother anymore.*

"I wanted to share a matcha session with you all," Aurelius continued.

"We could share a lot more, if you'd like," Rumi offered, weighing the options with his hands.

"This will be fine for now," Aurelius answered back, sliding Rumi a side-eye.

"Kana, tell us about this tea and why we're drinking it today," Aurelius finished.

"Well, this tea comes from a very select lot of tea bushes," Kana started. "There's a lake, shrouded by auric magic that Ikkyu and I oversee with a couple of charmed farmers. The lake is the very spot that Ikkyu found enlightenment, and the energy around a place like that becomes imbued with power, much like the way Elliot created his auric well. The energy from the auric well fuses into everything that fills the area, even into the tea bushes we use to craft this matcha powder."

"It should be enough to charge our auras for the rest of the day without us tiring or wiping out. The energy might be a lot to handle for you, Elliot, so sip in moderation, but it can potentially save you from overexertion again. As for the rest of us, there's really no overdoing it, so drink as much as you see fit. I have a whole jar here that we can finish. The compounds in the matcha stimulate, but also offer focus and a greater sense of control that we'll need if we're going to keep these crowds safe and survive the battles we're headed into. It should help us in the bay, on the beach, and up the cliffs. "

"What if we evacuate everyone?" Antonio asked, which seemed like the most logical option to keep everyone safe. But Aurelius didn't seem taken by the option.

"They won't come if we evacuate the venue," Aurelius said, looking down at Kana's hands as she rinsed the bamboo whisk with the steaming water stream from the kettle over the matcha bowl, then set down the whisk on the folded red towel and moved the rinse water around the bowl, cleaning the sides, before sending the rinse water overboard with the flick of her hand.

"So my fans, the people who made me what I am," Elliot said. "Are our bait?"

"That's not exactly true," Aurelius started. "We didn't make them bait, but we are going to save them from being abducted while saving the rest of the already abducted fans of yours. Their fate is being rescued by us, not threatened by us."

"That's an incredible way around logical reasoning," Baldwin said, showing genuine concern as the wind picked up and kites took flight across the bay, turning the sky bright with different shapes and sizes of soaring geometry.

"Ah, the kites on the Mediterranean are a beautiful site," Rumi said, tracking different kites as they lifted with ease into the sky.

"Now, this is a site to see," Frederick said, taking in the view of the sky.

"Let's hope we don't need a quick get away with all those kites up there now," Captain O'Malley added.

"Every second waiting adds more complication," Baldwin slipped in.

"I care about my fans," Elliot said, looking to Rumi for help.

"I, being a performer myself," Rumi said with an out-stretched hand he brought to his heart. "Understand how he feels. His fans are a reflection of himself. They are what makes him. They are to him what our hands, arms, and legs are to us. No offense, Horus. But, he truly cares. I see that. That's rare in humanity these days."

"Well put," Baldwin said, clapping his hands.

"Thank you, Rumi," Elliot said. "I'm new to people actually listening to me."

"Are we having a tea ceremony, or not?" Kana asked, again holding the kettle over the brown-glazed stone bowl.

"Yes, of course," Aurelius said, regaining control of the group. "Pour away, and we'll pass the bowl."

"Pour away?" Kana said, cocking her head at Aurelius. "I'll *lead* a *ritual*, and we'll all take part in it. Is that agreed?" Kana looked each one of us in the eyes as she waited for responses.

"Definitely," Aurelius said, clearing his throat. "Everyone?"

"Yes," came from all of our mouths.

"Now, everyone, everywhere," Kana said, pouring fresh water into the glazed bowl. "Sit for the spectacle of enlightened tea powder."

Kana unscrewed the metal lid of the mint green ceramic container, which opened with a flash of pink auric energy that shot out as the seal of the lid broke.

"This tea powder," Kana said, holding the jar with one hand and scooping out the vibrant green, baby-powder fine, matcha with the bamboo scoop over the bowl. "Is grown from the most secret and revered bushes in all of Japan."

The energy off the tea itself puffed out into the air around it, glowing the purest green I'd ever seen as she hovered the scoop before dumping it into the bowl. The powder spiralled around in the small bit of water as she scooped from the jar again. Two, three, four, five, six scoops she scooped and dumped with precise and deliberate movements that mesmerized us all into silence.

"And from those bushes, were picked the finest and most tender leaves, that were then auricly processed into the fine powder that we mixed today," she said, laying down the scoop and picking up the bamboo whisk. She circled the whisk in the powder and small amount of water, once, twice, three times around. Soaking the powder into a thick and smooth emerald paste before a vigorous whisk that produced a dense foam in the shallow murky lake of the bowl.

Then, Kana dripped spouts of water against the inside bowl from the kettle in a sequence of a first, second, and third longer pour. The tea mixture rippled and spiralled below the surface as the water lifted the foam halfway up the bowl's walls.

Kana then dipped the bamboo whisk into the top of the mixture, pushing and pulling back the bristles to rub against the sides of the bowl after a quick cleaning swipe of the bottom. As she moved the whisk, the aura of the tea glowed bright green against the clay as the liquid creamed into a dense duvet of tight-bubbled tea foam that held over the brew as Kana laid down the whisk.

"Allow this powder to inject you with the auric power locked inside. Straight from the filaments of life itself. From meadows to sunshine, to the locking shade that greens the leaves further. We drink and pass. We drink..." Kana said, lifting the bowl to her lips, and as she pulled in the tea mixture, the sound of bursting foam bubbles was faint in the air.

"And pass," she said, passing the bowl after dabbing where she sipped with the red cloth. The green stains of the tea were trapped in the corners of her mouth, and as each one of us sipped, the energy from the tea lit up around each of us. Starting with Kana, a green light tinged the perimeter of her aura, then that of Aurelius, and the rest of us. When the bowl was returned to Kana, she took it, and with the cloth that was passed around, wiped the outer sides. Then she restarted the ceremony.

She whisked, we sipped, and we passed. Until all of the powder was drunk from the jar and our auras surged with the power of the powder. The green tinge permeated our auras all the way through with solid green radiance that aligned my mind, soul, aura, and body with a power that emanated from me with the control of a focused master.

In a cloud of green aura, the bowl returned to Kana empty for the last time, where she lifted it above her head and bowed to the gift of the ceremony. We all followed her lead and bowed too, feeling complete and connected to not just the Earth and the tea or the plant it came from, but to each other through the sharing of the ceremony of the power. Complete in ourselves and complete in our unity. And most of all, complete in the mission we all knew was coming. Fully aware, fully understanding of the risks and in reverence of reality. Fully present for each other over the selfishness of any one of our singular desires.

"We've pulled from your roots, the power of the ancestral prayers of times before remembrance. We call on the timeless bond between humanity and Earth herself to nurture us as we employ ourselves in the guardianship of those unguarded. As you brighten with us the light needed to combat this darkness, lead us. For in the realm of existence, we must remain. Charge us with the power of life herself, and meet us everywhere our auras touch."

As Kana spoke, the green tinge to our auras intensified to the fiery glow of hot charcoal, deepset and white-hot. The green energy oozed like magma around the circle, connecting us further in its thick, gooey glow that carried with it an almost radioactive vibration that jittered into our bones.

"Whoa," Elliot said, leaning forward onto his hands as his muscles and aura struggled to absorb the extra power.

"Take it all in," I said, patting his back to comfort him. "It's tough the first time. I thought the vibrations were tearing me apart during my first ceremony, but they're just shimmying up the atoms you're made of and enchanting each one of them with a little extra energy support."

"Monads," Leibniz said, wiping the green stains of the matcha from the creases of his mouth with a delicate finger.

"Either way, that's right," Kana said, lowering the bowl onto the towel. "And as we become one with the force of life, so too does life become one with us. And who we are becomes less and more dependent on that connection itself. To the point that we, ourselves, become a confusion to us. So, I leave us with this message: Self isn't what you do, it's who you are when you're not doing. It's that person inside, behind the addictions and obligations that we call personality and purpose. To connect with your true self is to reach past those smokes and mirrors to embody a true state of being. Like a pensive monk, rising in silence, to sit in silence, and to return to bed in silence. Then, to wake and do it all over again for the exact amount of days it takes to acknowledge the human debt owed to existence and how little we would be without her. May we go under this light."

"Nicely done," Aurelius said, bowing his head to Kana.

"Thank you, and I'll let you take the lead now," Kana said, sitting back on her kneeling legs. "What's the plan, man?"

Aurelius's smile faded as we all turned to him for guidance. Feeling ready and powerful didn't matter unless we had a plan to get the upper hand against the predators. Otherwise we'd be better off fleeing to the next island without even trying.

"I've put a lot of thought into this plan," Aurelius said. "And most of you aren't going to like it."

CHAPTER TWELVE

A CONCERT FOR THE AGES

As the afternoon stretched the sun across the sky, more and more boats filled the inlets, and more and more fans filled the beaches and the cliffs. We got word that the first concert finished as Elliot stalked his own, compromised, social media accounts. Jordy, wearing the likeness of Elliot's body, posted a selfie he took from the stage with the massive crowds behind him. 'History will be made tonight,' he captioned. 'Everyone in Menorca, we're coming for you.' The zoomed in eyes of the crowd were tinted gold.

"That's Gabirol's aura," Elliot confirmed, pointing at the screen. "It's all over them."

"Calm down," Antonio said, looking out at the crowded bay and beach from where we stood on the Northern cliff.

"You don't get it," Elliot said, looking worried as strands of his dark hair fell over his face. "For most people, words hit only sleeping minds, but my gift is words that raise armies out of thin air. I've known the power of my voice since I was a kid. I've known the power of how I leverage my… energy. I never called it that, but I felt something, always, even if I didn't know how to use aurics. I always gave off this energy that affected other people. I always knew how to control it and how to control them. To see my gift turned against the fans that got me to where I am… They're the only reason… for anything. Now…"

Elliot crumbled to his knees at the cliffside, and I knelt down to help lift him up. But he wouldn't budge. Antonio kept his face cloaked for everyone else, but I still saw him as Elliot Cutcas. The cliff path we found to take up from the beach was narrowed by the amount of people taking up every spare rock, bush, and cliff side space.

"You're not responsible for what they're doing," I told him. "I blamed myself a lot when I lived my lie. I let my friends drive me crazy. It took distance and the help of new friends to get me through it, and you're going to get through this. But you can't blame yourself. You're with us. You're on the right side of history. They're predators. This is what they do. They often look for the best, most kind hearted among us because they know our authentic nature. They know how much we care, and it's that energy that feeds them and gives them what they crave. They physically can't live with it."

"Why me though? These fans are all I have!" Elliot cried, tears streaming, fist clenching at his heart. "I don't have a boyfriend or even a true friend. My music, I have that. But with nobody to listen to it…"

"You'll be fine," Antonio added, kneeling at Elliot's other side. "You have us, and I mean that. We're going to help you. We might not be your boyfriends, but we are true friends. We are family. And in a few years, you'll be more a part of us than you will be of your past. It's never too late to start a better life. We'll show you how, but you need to help show us how to survive this fight. You need to rescue your fans. I see the cruise ships on the horizon over there. It's time. Your words will raise armies again. To save everyone."

Elliot looked up to where Antonio was pointing, and sure enough, four cruise ships were emerging into our visual horizon.

"We've got like an hour or two," Antonio continued. "Let's find that atrament and close it up before they get here. Dylan, you ready?"

"Yeah," I said, feeling through the ground the atrament I felt from the ship after the power of the tea ceremony charged me. Only, this atrament felt deep inside the rock at the bottom of the inlet, so I was still struggling with how to locate it exactly. I had two hours to close it up before the predators got here, no doubt knowing they'd be using it.

"Four ships?" Elliot asked himself, as I sunk into the auric energy of the cliff and reached through the rock to where I felt the quiet, absent space below the seafloor where energy seemed to disappear.

"Yeah, looks like it," Antonio said, sounding casual.

"Then they're going to try to take everyone from here," Elliot said. "They're not leaving anyone behind."

"You're probably right. That's if we can't pull this off," Antonio said. "But I'd still put my money on us, over them."

As the cruise ships moved across the Mediterranean, the murmurs and cheers over Elliot's impending arrival grew louder. The night was growing dark as sunset came to set the world ablaze with the oranges, purples, and reds of the lowering sun. When I could finally wrap my aura around the atrament vacuum, I felt the pull tighten. It wasn't a black hole to nowhere. It felt more like a vacuum into a reservoir, which I struggled to keep my aura from being sucked into.

"Antonio, I need some energy," I said, keeping my mind

focused on the pull. "I've got it, but it's pulling me in. The filter they used in Ibiza is different here. It's like an auric tank, collecting all the energy it pulls in before it reaches the void. I have to close send the power into the void before closing it up, or they'll have all the energy they'll need once they get here."

"Here," Antonio said, placing a hand on my shoulder and flooding me with the warming essence of his familiar and pure auric power. My aura drank it in, enhancing my control of the energy I held around the atrament and the reservoir mechanism of the predators.

"You better hurry," Elliot said. "They're almost here. They must be using their power to speed up the ships."

"Well, I have it contained within my aura for now," I said, feeling the fear of battle rising in my quickened heart and breath. "If I can hold it, they shouldn't be able to find it or use the energy they've harvested from it. If Joshua had power this easily available to him, we might not be here right now."

"These predators are frustratingly impressive," Antonio said, sounding more annoyed every time he spoke. "I'll hold the charge over you, but try to get rid of that chaos energy and close up that atrament for good. We can't take any risks with these assholes."

"I know," I said, struggling to figure out how to send the energy through the atrament without it infecting my aura too. The crowds were getting louder, the predators were getting close, and I was feeling less and less prepared and feeling more and more frustrated with the feeling of failing no matter how hard I willed for what I needed to happen.

I get it now, I thought to Horus.

And what's that now? Horus thought back from where

he was on board the ship.

The god thing you keep mentioning, I thought back, understanding him more than ever. *A god can will and can create. They can provide, they can define, they can threaten and destroy, but they cannot force will against its nature or reverse the laws of reality itself. Gabirol might think himself a god as he controls people's minds, but they're still themselves underneath and outside of his influence. In the same way I cannot will the chaos energy to my command without fear of it turning against or corrupting me. I must fear the nature of reality even more since I bend it, and if I bend it, I must deal with the conse-quences of not being able to put it back into its box.*

And now you know the curse of the gods, Horus thought back, sounding satisfied for the first time I'd ever heard. *I know your current struggle, and I'll help you as much as I can. I gift you some of my ancient energy, and hope you can save us all. Fear the chaos energy, but don't let it keep you from living up to your Eaglegod name. Reaching for great godliness, and I believe you will attain.*

As Horus finished, I felt a wave of deep power come over me like the warmth of the sun after getting used to the shade of a passing cloud.

Last time I manipulated the enchantment they were using, I thought to Horus. *Maybe this time I can make my own enchantment?*

It's worth a shot, Horus thought, considering the idea himself. *The high priests of Egypt enchanted items and crypts through my power, so I don't see why you can't do the same with your own power.*

Maybe you could send Leibniz to help? I considered, feeling like the more help I could get, the better.

How can a man help, when only a god has access to such

a thing? Horus riddled me, leaving me with the most honest answer he could offer.

You're right, I thought, feeling the weight of my fear in my gut as the raging fury of the chaos energy around the atrament boiled inside my cobalt cloak. Taking a deep breath, I settled my energy again around the atrament, feeling the pinhole in the center of the chaos energy reserves. There was no mechanism I could feel, so I penetrated my energy through to the center of the vacuum, manifesting with it the funnel I needed to pull through the chaos energy around it.

"They're almost here," Elliot said, as I finished half the fixture. A slow trickle of chaos energy started releasing into the void, making me hopeful that my plan might actually work.

Horus, I thought, feeling the energy of the predators approaching. *Reach Leibniz and Aurelius and tell them I have the atrament contained. I'm draining the chaos energy reserves around it, but it's going to take a lot longer to drain it and close it up. I'll try to keep it cloaked while I work as best I can, but I can't make any promises.*

Got it! Horus thought, and went quiet for a second. *They've got the message! You're doing fantastic, young Eaglegod. Keep it up.*

Thank you, I thought, opening my eyes for the first time in a while. With the atrament contained inside of my auric protection, I needed to know how much time I'd have before we started coming under attack. I continued feeding auric energy into the funnel structure that vacuumed up the chaos energy, feeling the trickle turn into a stream, but knowing there was so much more chaos energy to clean out.

"They really are close," I said, gritting my teeth at the sight of the four cruise ships a few hundred yards outside the inlet, as they slowed down their approach into the boat-spotted bay. The deck of the ships were already lined with the zombie-starring 'cruise worker' army.

"Yeah, no duh," Elliot said, kneeling down at my side.

"I feel the predators on the brig," Antonio said. "A few of them per ship."

"What about Oshun, Caesar, and Hannibal?" I asked, more worried about them than any of the others. Even without access to the chaos energy reserve, their auras were infected with the poisonous energy.

"Yeah, they're up there," Antonio said. "Channeling though, scanning for something. You better hold your cloaking down while you work. I hope Aurelius knows what he's doing this time, too. Ibiza was a shit show."

Everyone in position? thought Aurelius to all of us immortals.

Yes, I thought back, feeling the roving energies of the three infectious predators as I drained the reservoir little by little. I almost had it a quarter drained by the time I got the full funnel complete, making me more confident in draining it completely if we could hold them off a little bit longer. Now, it was Elliot's turn to save us.

Elliot ready? Aurelius thought out to us all.

I can support him over the cliff to get started, Antonio thought back.

I could use Leibniz's help with the atrament, if possible, I added.

No time for that, Aurelius thought. *Do the best you can to keep the predators from reaching the atrament. We need all the senior immortals keeping Elliot safe if we hope to win this fight. Everyone except Dylan, channel protections over Elliot as he takes to the air.*

I see Jordy! Elliot thought out. *Looking like me!*

Sure enough, an Elliot Cutcas duplicate emerged from the roof of the second cruise ship in the line as the boats of the bay bobbed around in the massive shadows as the ships approached and crawled to a halted line, leaving little space for any of the other boats to escape.

And that's Gabirol! Elliot added. *Are we too late?*

Nope, we're right on time, Aurelius thought. *Send him out, Antonio, Elliot, your voice is now... amplified. This is your show, now break a leg!*

I'd be lucky if that's all I do break, Elliot thought, as Antonio lifted him off the ground with his own aura and hovered him over the cliffdrop toward the center of the inlet.

Antonio bent down beside me, seeming to lift Elliot with his knees as he pushed out his arms, moving Elliot further and further away from us and the cliff, over a clean drop of a hundred feet over the water. Not enough to kill him if he landed in the water, but over the bay full of boats, there was no telling how he'd end up if he fell.

"How my people doing tonight? If you can hear me, make some noise!" Elliot spoke, his voice cascading over the crowd and erupting his fans in endless waves of screams and applause as Antonio moved him further and further to the center of the bay. An auric ball of protection was the only thing keeping him in the air and away from the alert predators on cruise ship roofs.

You got this! I thought to Elliot, in one last show of support before the fun or horror show actually started.

I think you're right, Elliot thought, smiling back at me from his now fifty meters away. *I'm finally back in my element.*

They're readying an attack, Antonio thought out, and sure enough the predators were collecting their auric energy around themselves.

Calamity and Gabirol are with Jordy, Elliot thought, checking out the threat behind him, before turning back to his fans below.

"I've got a new song for everyone tonight!" Elliot said, and his voice rang around what felt like the most perfect natural arena. It would have been epic for his plan to play out the way he originally wanted it to, but a feeling in my gut was telling it'd be a night to remember either way. The fans cheered again, oblivious to the threat of the predators preparing for their abduction.

"I wrote it after someone I thought was my friend turned out to be my enemy," Elliot said, and the crowd listened. Seeing him at the top of the world, and still so hurt, felt almost humbling. I didn't think people could maintain vulnerability behind money, fame, and fortune, but without the love we all so desperately crave, he wasn't a monster like the others. He might have been manipulated by monsters, but I couldn't blame him for that. It's often those who dream the biggest who are living to escape the darkest hells inside of themselves.

Gabirol, Calamity, and Jordy were flailing their arms at each other, no doubt blaming each other for Elliot beating them to the performance and figuring out what to do next.

On the furthest boat, I recognized Julius Caesar, Hannibal, and Oshun and felt the chaos energy they channeled from their own auras. So, I strengthened my cloaking with the energy charge from Antonio and Horus, but as Antonio moved Elliot further and further into the middle of the bay, I received less and less from him.

I've got Elliot, too, came the thoughts of Leibniz. *Supported in suspension and protection.*

Thank you, Antonio squeaked with relief. The two energies of Antonio and Leibniz swirled around Elliot, as the crowd settled back down from their cheer-ruption.

Everyone harden Elliot's defenses with as much energy as you can spare, Aurelius thought out, and in the next instance, Elliot was swirling in a rainbow of auric colors over the bay.

"That person taught me that sometimes," Elliot said to the crowd. "You have to sail away from the one who caused you hurt. Far away from their abuses and lies to find yourself whole again. Especially when you know that person can't be any better. It's called 'The Epic of My Life.' So... here we go."

With the magic of the immortals, the whining sounds of the strings symphony filled every ear, hushing everyone in the crowd.

"I wish I had a real life / I didn't have to run / Or a place to fit just so / I didn't have to hide," he sang.

And with the last word, I recovered from the trance his silver aura stole me into, his voice charming everyone into the smoothness of his tones. Everyone except for us philosophers, and for the predators preparing their attacks. Luckily, my auric work around the atrament held steady while my focus slipped.

On the nearest ship, the flaunty Elagabalus snapped his black and red auric armor and longsword into auric existence around himself, looking vengeful and depraved in his movements. He pointed across the bay at... Antonio and I... The predators around him I didn't know, but the masked giant in blackened bronze armor from Ibiza was with them, standing tall over the others like an impervious wall that I did not want to end up fighting against.

"I howl again to settle down / The beast I cage inside /

The sinking ship I patch around / The sea of all your lies," Elliot sang, impressing me knowing he must have written the song over the last few days of non-stop running, fighting, and learning.

"Dragut, Hanno, Sayyida al-Hurra," Antonio said. "And Elagablus. I didn't think we'd be targeted so quickly. You know the giant will be a problem."

"So fool me once / Or fool me twice / Once makes me / Not enough," Elliot sang, and as he did, his aura streaked down in tendrils into the crowds of boats and crawled through the sky in the direction of the beach.

We might need back up, Antonio thought out, as Hanno and Elagabalus stepped off the brig roof, floating over the water in our direction as the other predators all took aim at Elliot.

"The world I want / And where you'll end up / Will never / Be the same," Elliot sang.

Blasts of auric energy beamed across the bay in the direction of the singing star. The gold of Gabirol, scarlet of Calamity, radiation green of Jordy, and the chaos beam that Oshun charged through the circled energy of Julius and Hannibal.

"So pull the ropes / And set the sails / And let me / On my course," Elliot sang, his silver aura blanketing the crowds on the beach as the predators' beams smashed into the protective barrier around him. The white hot plasma clumped in the air and slopped down into the sea as the immortals fought back the attack. For now, the sphere of protection held strong, and the atrament had vacuumed fifty percent of the chaos energy out into the void.

"Your anchor's down / In sinking ground / And dragging / Me no more," Elliot sang, his silver aura glowing in protective waves over everyone it touched.

As Oshun, Caesar, and Hannibal continued their attack, from the cliff across from us, Kana, Hypatia, Moremi, and Cleoselené were armored up and preparing to get in the fight. But Hanno and Elagabalus were about to reach us, too.

Horus, don't leave me, I thought. *I'm going to need help if I'm to keep the atrament hidden and stay alive.*

Gods never abandon one another, Horus thought back, with appreciated comfort. *You have my word.*

"So fold again / Into the sins / That fill you / With sad thrill," Elliot sang, and the group led by Kana took to the sky, shooting through the air between the cliff and the ship with Oshun, Caesar, and Hannibal. Kana, decked out in powder pink armor with her two katanas raised, clashed with the sword of Hannibal. Moremi, unsurprisingly, struck a blow with her sword to the staff that Oshun conjured out of the chaos energy she wielded. While Cleoselené and Hypatia took on Caesar, who blocked their blows with his gladius and shield.

Jordy, Gabirol, and Calamity kept up their beamed attack on Elliot, watching the battle happening one ship over, while Aurelius, Frederick, Juba, and Baldwin shot up out of the bay waters on spiralling water spouts to start their attack on the three ringleaders of Elliot's manipulation.

That left Leibniz, Rumi, and Grace unaccounted for, until I noticed Rumi and Grace scaling the side of the cruise ship nearest us, where Dragut, Sayyida al-Hurra, and the mystery predator in blackened bronze stood, shooting their own beams of energy at Elliot and watching Elagabalus and Hanno reach the lower ledge of mine and Antonio's cliff. The audience was too entranced by Elliot's silver aura and voice to notice anything, but I braced for combat.

"They're here," Antonio said, armored up and double sworded with a haze of defensive sky blue light around us.

"The epic of / My life awaits / Only after / Your goodbye," Elliot sang, as Rumi in his parchment colored aura and Grace in her amber glow launched into battle against the sharply dressed pirates Dragut, in mustard yellow, Sayyida al-Hurra, in sage green, and the lumbering giant. Rumi's daggers redirected sword swings and won him a few slices into Dragut's side as the pirate struggled to adapt to Rumi's speed, while Grace danced her sword in blocking deflections, taking shots at anyone she could hit with the auric blunderbuss she held in her other hand, shooting bullets of auric energy that ate away at the auric armors of the predators.

"We're going to have to fight," Antonio said as our two pursuing predators made their way through the crowds to us.

"The battlefield of love is made / For two minds forged as one / And two souls bent on breaking down / The fears between our hearts," Elliot sang, as sectioned a portion of my attention on keeping up my auric work while I got to my feet, armored up, and pulled my auric blade from thin air.

"I taught you, but you never learned / The lessons of the heart / Now watch my greatest lesson yet / As I sail into my sunset," Elliot repeated, as Hanno and Elagabalus centered Antonio and I in their sights.

"Now watch my greatest lesson yet / As I sail into my sunset," Elliot sang, as the maniacal thinned lipped smiling Elagablus blinked into the air and popped up right in front of me with the length of his thin bladed spear swiping straight down at me. I swiped it away with my blade just in time to deflect his strike into the ground, as Hanno took an arcing leap, his purple-pink aura trailing the air behind him before landing with his shield and spear into blows with Antonio.

"Now watch my greatest lesson yet / As I sail into my sunset," Elliot sang, as I moved my sword to block each blow Elagabalus tried to nick me with.

"Your fight is futile," Elagabalus said, giggling as he spoke. The mirth of his energy was unnerving and chaotic, as was his style of fighting, making it hard to take a chance at attempting my own striking attack when I saw an opening.

"The battlefield of love is made / For two minds forged as one / Not one soul breaking down the other/ Keeping both afloat," Elliot sang, feeling my cloak of the atrament slipping more every time I deflected with my sword. But the song was good and powerful, even. The crowd was fully subdued into calm. Elliot's power was impressive, even if it could be so dangerous.

"*Your* fight is futile," I said back to Elagabalus, pushing him back with auric force after staggering him with a strong block against a side swipe. His right hand pulled from his spear as he struggled for footing, leaving his right side open, and I took my chance.

I brought my sword around, from my right side, to my left, and struck him in the soft side of his armor between his ribs and hips. I put everything into the strike, but the blow bounced back at me, sending me flying back.

"The epic of my life has taught / Me the power of good-bye / And showed me all the epic ways / I know I will survive," Elliot sang.

Elagabalus stumbled further back, falling into a crowd of people a little bit down the incline, while Antonio and Hanno circled each other like gladiators in a ring, striking when and if they could, blocking when they had to, and undoubtedly trying to pry into each others' minds with telekinetic attacks that I wasn't sure how to see.

"The battlefield of love is made / For two minds forged as one / Not one soul breaking down the other/ Keeping both afloat," Elliot sang, and watching Antonio, I realized I too had a secret weapon that could help me turn the tides of my own battle.

It's time for the gods to work together, I thought to Horus, hoping he was still around to hear me as Elagabalus reemerged from the crowd of mortals with a hot, red, anger burning off his elven-like face. *I can't hold the atrament and fight at the same time,* I thought. Elagabalus's attacks and the people around us were so distracting that I the longer I was in battle, the more my focus on the atrament cloak slipped. I didn't want people hurt, but it looked like Aurelius, Frederick, Baldwin, and Leibniz were keeping Jordy, Calamity, and Gabirol locked in a battle of wind and oceanic attacks from the water spouts hoisting them around the top of the ship.

Atop the furthest ship, Moremi and Cleoseléné were now double teaming Oshun in a fury of blows and blocks. At one point, Oshun dove off the back of the ship, just escaping the moonbeams blasting from the eyes of the two ancient-world queens. The two queens then dove in after the water goddess, leaving Kana and Hypatia back to back in battle with Caesar and Hannibal in circling blows.

Help me with Elagabalus, I thought, unsure of how he could. *While I hold the atrament.*

You want me to take the corporeal reins? Horus asked, surprised.

Sure, I thought back, unsure of what he actually meant, but hoping it would help.

In the next second, Elagabalus was back in the fight, sprinting at me with his bladed spear trailing after him. Through me, Horus pulled the strings of my limbs while my focus was liberated back to the atrament. With a swipe of my hand, Horus ripped up big chunks of earth in Elagabalus's path, smacking the mad emperor with what grew into a wall of rock that moved in the direction of the cliff even after it hit him, threatening to send him tumbling over the edge.

Elagabalus leaned into the attack as much as he could, pulled at the earth stone behind him, and lifted onto the wave of rock like a surfer slapping over the earthly wave curl he rode down the other side. Behind him, Antonio had Hanno on his knees with his arms pulled back and cemented to the ground behind him by his crystal blue aura.

As Elagabalus rode his rock board down the rock wave toward me, I felt my arms lift my sword at the direction of Horus, while I held tight concentration on keeping the atrament hidden from the predators and vacuuming out the last thirty percent of the chaos reserves. Since Oshun took to the water I felt a presence surveying the auric current, and I didn't want her to even feel my energy cloaking the atrament.

Through Horus, I deflected a cross body swipe from Elagabalus with the flat face of the blade, and redirected the power of the blow in a way I hadn't practiced before. Elagabalus slipped right past me at full force and sent himself flying off the edge of the cliff. In the air, he caught himself, and locked my gaze before lowering into a dive into the air and flying in the direction of the ship where Gabirol, Calamity, and Jordy were under assault.

"The epic of my life has taught / Me the power of

goodbye / And showed me all the epic ways / I know I will survive," Elliot sang, and Antonio landed next to me, deciding against pursuing Elagabalus.

"You held up well," Antonio said, grabbing my shoulder from behind and pulling me close to him while he surveyed the rest of the battle. Aurelius was locked into a battle of purple and gold splashes of auric power that exploded against the surface of the water and in the air when they missed each other with their blasts. Him and Gabirol were both airborne, with Elagabalus heading towards them fast.

On the brig roof, Jordy and Calamity exchanged gunfire with auric hand guns behind walls of protection, as Frederick, Juba, and Baldwin torrented them with a spouts of auric charged seawater they pressurized beyond power-washer strength streams from the glug of water they hoisted in the air. Shredding everything they hit.

Where's Leibniz? I thought to Horus and Antonio, feeling the pressure of Oshun's energy closing in around the atrament through the auric current.

He's aboard the White Seahorse, *right below Elliot,* Horus thought in response.

He's helping keep Elliot protected, Antonio thought, searching the battlefield for his next move.

"Aurelius might need help, though," Antonio said, watching Elagabalus clash with him after Aurelius deflected a distracting blow from Gabirol.

Is Hanno contained for good? I asked, looking back at the sailor as he struggled against Antonio's auric restraints.

He's not getting out of my hold, Antonio thought back. *But something's up with him. It's like he's only half as powerful as he should be.*

"The work is hard / The work is long / The work is / Never done," Elliot sang, his silver aura touching the hundreds of boats and thousands of fans.

"We're almost there," I said. "He's almost reaching the abducted fans on the ship."

"The journey's rough / The journey's tough / The journey never ends / In the immortal epic of my life," Elliot sang, descending as he did.

"The journey's rough / The journey's tough / The journey never ends / In the immortal epic of my life," Elliot sang, and as he finished the song, he touched down on the White Seahorse with the orb of protection still around him.

The fans erupted in goosebump chilling waves of screams, cheers, and chants that left the air feeling static. But before Elliot could make it inside the ship, Oshun broke through the surface of the bay, sending the boats around the White Seahorse teetering onto their topsides. Leibniz blanketed the ship with auric energy, creating a dome the way he shielded us on Ibiza, and gathering Elliot close to him on the top deck of the ship.

"Elliot...," I called out, feeling my hold on the atrament slip and the energy of Oshun slip into my orb of containment. "No..."

Oshun's energy flooded into the reserves, bursting it open as I tried to hold it shut. I pulled energy from Antonio. I pulled at every shred of energy I could gather from my core, and I held the seams of my enchantments together as Oshun ripped them apart. The mechanism of redirected energy was an instant installation after she took control. Atop her mountain of water, she laughed deeply up at the sky as the White Seahorse struggled away from the pull of her consuming currents.

Oshun now holds the keys to godliness, I thought to Horus.

It appears so, Horus thought back. *But we have more than two god-like among us.*

Then Moremi shot out from the water mountain like a missile, connecting with Oshun and dragging her across the water surface, sending chaos energy spraying out from Oshun like an oil spill. Moremi dragged Oshun all the way to the beach, where the crowds under Elliot's control moved away from the two battling women in frantic sprints. Moremi's moonlight energy enveloped them as she beat into Oshun, draining Oshun of her chaos energy the more she beamed her cleansing power into her. The beach and bay filled with the oily black energy, as it spread atop the surface of the water and away from Oshun's control.

We have a problem, came the thoughts of Leibniz from the White Seahorse. *There's some kind of anomaly beneath us. I'm driving Elliot and I out of here.*

You're not driving my ship, Grace thought. *Horus, get them out of there.*

You got it, Horus thought, and full control of my body came back to me. I'd gotten so used to him holding me up, that I staggered from the return of control as I looked to Antonio for what to do next.

"Is that a...," Anontio said, looking in awe down at the sea.

We're dealing with a maelstrom down here! Leibniz thought, and it was true. A small spiral in the water behind the White Seahorse spiralled, as the ship raced off through the maze of boats across the bay. A smaller boat closer to the small vortex was sucked right into the vortex as the sky grew dark and sunset winked out of existence in an instant, leaving the night to take over.

The wind started picking up, pushing at our backs, pushing us closer to the edge of the cliff. Everything around us was in chaos, the air, the water, and the people.

"It feels like this morning," Antonio said, as lightning cracked overhead and the cliffs, beach, and bay shook. Screams rang out in every direction as people, awoken from Elliot's temporary hold, started running for the cover of the trees and the safety of wherever the parking lot might be.

"Yeah it does feel like this morning," I said, fearing the worst was upon us, while trying to understand what was happening while figuring out what to do next at the same time.

Within a minute, all of the small boats nearest the maelstrom were pulled down, without plopping back up to the surface. As more boaters noticed, they all started heading for the shore or the open sea, but crashed into each other in panic more than making and progress in escaping. The vortex consumed, growing in size and speed like the initial start up spin of a washing machine.

"Baby you mesmerized me /" came the voice of Elliot, in the amplified way it did before, but this time not from the sky and not from the White Seahorse. It came from Jordy atop the second cruise ship, basked in gold and cosmic chaos energy. The gold beamed out from Gabirol's palms from where he stood behind him in a golden auric hooded robe that gleamed against the storming night.

The beam met Jordy's back, and glowed through his chest in warm looking rays that radiated into the bay. The chaos energy beamed in from both of the ships on his sides. Caesar on one and Hannibal on the other, charging chaos energy into Jordy's outstretched hands.

"What happened?" Antonio asked, staring in awe at the state of the battle. "Where is everyone?"

"Rumi!" I shouted, noticing him curled up on the roof on the cruise ship nearest us. Grace had Sayyida al-Hurra secured to the top fin on the ship, and was making her way to Rumi's side. On the roof of the ship next to them, where Hannibal stood charging Jordy, Dragut and the blackened bronze clad warrior sparred with Juba, Baldwin, and Frederick.

"Grace has got him," Antonio said. "We should go for Jordy and Gabirol. We need to stop them. Don't let them charm you. They're more practiced than Elliot. The battle might get messy."

"Might get?" I asked, looking between the continuing fights on the ships, to the whirlpool pulling in and swallowing boats, and finally to the battle on the beach between Oshun and Moremi that lit the sky with lightning cracks and sent up torrents of dusty beach sand. The storm rolling in, or more so manifesting centrally from where we were, started even blowing down sail masts, and capsizing boats onto each other, turning the entire bay into a nightmarish hellscape of painful screams, croaking wood, crunching metal, and the blank stares of enchanted silence. The captivated fans along the cliffs were golden eyed and zombie walking towards, and off, the cliff. Supported by golden aura around their feet, they even continued their march through the air.

"Let's go," I said, taking Antonio's hand, and lifting off the ground for him to join me in the air.

"So many are already lost," Antonio said, staring down at the boats crashing into each other as they cratered into the maelstrom. "Is that from the atrament?" he asked, bringing me a devastating realization I couldn't bear to process.

"We can't be certain," I said, knowing full well that I was certain it was because I failed. "There are still so many more to save." I pointed to Jordy's Elliot cloned form and nodded. Antonio understood. "We can't let him finish his song!"

"You're right," Antonio said, looking me hard with his dagger-like stare, his eyebrows giving him his iconic seriousness that I've grown to find comfort in. "I got your back, if you got mine."

"For forever, and till the end of time," I said, pulling him to me, and up he came. Up, with an arm around my back, for a kiss that we both held onto with our lips. Like the pause button for a battle that only raged on, and in the next second, we were soaring up into the sky until we reached just below the clouds that let loose a drenching downpour.

"There's Aurelius!" Antonio said over the roar of the wind, and sure enough Aurelius was behind the cruise ships, fighting a two-on-one battle with Elagablus and Calamity J. With Hypatia, Cleoseléné, and Kana even further out, and all building up a wall of water with their teal, white, and pink energies.

"That's going to be a *big* problem," I said, pointing toward the horizon of the sea, where the big waves of the morning were now heading directly for the bay.

"We need to help them," Antonio said, pulling at my hand to go. "We need to help Aurelius."

"No," I said. "We need to take out Jordy and Gabirol. That's the mission we have before us. We need to stop them and what they're doing."

Grace, Antonio thought. *Is Rumi safe?*

Aboard the White Seahorse now, tucked in an aura-bed, came the thoughts of the captain.

Help out Aurelius, while we handle the pop star clone, Antonio thought, giving me an affirming nod, before reassessing the Jordy, Gabirol situation.

Sure thing, Grace thought back.

Now, do we go for Jordy or Gabirol first? Antonio thought. *If we go for Jordy, Gabirol, Hannibal, and Caesar would all target us. If we go for Gabirol, the others might stay where they are, powering up Jordy. Two on one is better than four on two.*

We'll see how long Juba, Frederick, and Baldwin can last, I thought back, wondering if helping the three men would be a better use of time. But nobody would be safe once Jordy and Gabirol smuggle everyone onto the boats. *Let's go for Gabirol.*

And the two of us dove straight for the golden hooded predator, manifesting our gladiuses again as we closed it. We only had minutes before the waves would wash every one of us away, but Kana, Hypatia, and Cleoseléné had their water wall buffer prepared, higher than the cliffs, in a 'c' around the cove. Higher than the height of the cruise ships Antonio and I came down on fast, and almost as tall as the waves that were inbound.

We took a course around the back of the fin of the nearest ship, where Sayyida al-Hurra blazed sage green fire from her mouth as she screamed and fought against the amber rope energy holding her tied tight to the fin.

"You two!" she screamed, tracking us from one side of the ship to the other as we passed behind her and on past the ship where our three allies were beating down on the two predators. As we flew past their ship's tail, we leaned up and toward the beach, angling ourselves as the final seconds before impact slip-streamed past.

I swung for his neck, and Antonio swung for his knees, as we flew into our swings. Gabirol broke his connection with Jordy right before I connected my blade, not with his neck, but with the wrist armor that sparked with golden streams of light so bright that it blinded me. In the flashes of my returning vision, I watched Gabirol cry out from the blow that Antonio landed on the back of his right knee. Between blinks, Antonio's whistle sharp auric blade sliced through Gabirol's golden wrist armor, and clean through. Gabirol recoiled in roiling pain, as the hand half of his forearm fumbled up into the air and over the edge of the ship as the storm downpoured harder. With his other arm, he sent Antonio flying back from a crushing armored fist to the chest.

Antonio slid back against the metal roof, buckling the metal where he slid. I lifted my blade to slice through Gabirol's chest, and pulled the edge of my blade through the edge of his ribcage as he failed to completely dodge.

My blade struck bone, then a gritty softness that felt like wet sand, as he peered through the black shades of his hair at me. His aura moved like oozing clay over my blade and the wound of his severed limb, reforming his forearm inch by inch.

"You Americans always think you can figure everything out," Gabirol spat, spewing spittles of golden mud from his mouth as he spoke. "Some things are *beyond* you!"

And with the back of his other arm, he shoved me back, giving me the thrust I needed to pull my sword from his body chest as I stumbled backwards. While, behind him, Antonio unleashed a beam of sky blue energy that glistened like the dazzling daylit sky. The beam hit him square in the back, making him cry out in initial pain, before turning to Antonio and screaming through the blast that tore through his chest.

"You've caused enough pain!" I shouted, considering ways around killing an immortal who could regrow limbs with mud. The mud of life?

The more I thought about it, the more I considered how Jordy could take Elliot's form, and came under the assumption that the mud could, in theory, be what Jordy was using to mold himself into different forms. Like a set of second skin.

You keep up the attacks on Gabirol, I thought to Antonio. *I'm taking Jordy down. Gabirol will be more distracted that way.*

Got it, Antonio thought. *I like this plan.*

I don't, but it's all we got, I thought back. Jordy still had his back to us, leaving me with the opening I needed.

Past Jordy, the bay was a hellscape of nautical collisions around the growing maelstrom, spiraling with the wreckage of the already destroyed ships. Every boat mid-bay to the beach would probably end up swallowed before the waves even reached us. The chaos energy of Oshun and the moonlight energy of Moremi flashed like flares as the two exchanged fire on the beach, lighting up the sky. But even the cruise ships were being pulled forward into the vortex.

As I readied my auric attack against Jordy, a growl grizzled into the night, turning into a booming yell as the predator in blackened bronze cratered into the metal roof, blocking me from Jordy. Without wasting time, I pulled down at the jet stream above me, and channeled the force of it over my head and into the mountain of a man. The jet stream force made him stagger as I charged it faster with my energy, but he stood as sturdy as the mountain he was, raising his long sword and readying a powerful strike at me.

I jumped to the side to escape his range, and nudged the

blade outward with a blast of auric power in a way Ikkyu taught me in our training sessions. My maneuver stretched his reach and redirected his weight away from where he needed it to be to deflect my next flurry of stabbing blows. But even with the auric enchantment of my blade I couldn't pierce the armor of the predator, reminding me there was so much about auric combat that I still didn't understand.

The jet stream current kept the predator slow in his movements and attacks as he fought against the wind, making him just fast enough to block my useless sword strike, but it gave me time to figure out what I needed to do next as Jordy sang into his song.

I'm with you, came the thoughts of Baldwin, and in the next second he crashed into the battle behind the giant predator in a cloud of violet energy, keeping low to stay out of the jet stream.

Keep him busy while I get Jordy, I thought back to him, as he landed a slice into the predator's side that cut through the giant's armor.

Got it! Baldwin thought.

"You've met your last foe," Baldwin said, as I stepped back.

The predator charged at Baldwin, but Baldwin was fast on his feet. I lifted myself back into the air and lined myself up with Jordy. The ship was moving faster towards the maelstrom as the smaller boats in the bay struggled to reach the beach. Our ship's fate seemed doomed as the bow tilted forward into the vortex.

Gabirol won't die, Antonio thought to all of us.

We're having trouble down here, too, Aurelius thought from outside the bay.

We're all about to be washed away by these waves!

Cleoseléné warned, as I readied my blade, and bulleted toward Jordy.

You two go, came the thoughts of Hypatia to Cleoseléné and Kana.

"Hey Jordy," I shouted at him, and as he turned, the image of Elliot, mutated in a mix of their two faces. The chaos energy around him was now only coming from Caesar on my right, with Hannibal embattled with Frederick and Juba on the leftside ship. Despite Jordy's plan working until then as fans stepped across the sky onto the ship, he looked to be in more pain than it seemed worth.

"You!" Jordy shouted, spotting me with squinted eyes as he readied an energy orb between his hands.

You can't hold this wall for long, Kana thought, her sternness sounding drained.

I lifted my auric shield in front of my face, hoping to knock Jordy into the air, where I could attack him out of the energy beam of Caesar. On impact, though, he didn't budge. My whole body crashed against the shield, popped my lip with a painful slice, leaving me with gritted teeth against the slickness of gushing blood.

I can hold it long enough, Hypatia thought. *Escape before you all die! Go! These waves... I'm afraid nobody can survive.*

It might be too late for that, anyway, Antonio thought, as the cruise ship tilted further into the hydro vortex, and I knew he was right. In the next minutes all four cruise ships would be consumed, and all the thousands of fans would be swallowed up, along with us. Unless… unless I didn't know what.

I pushed back against the shield, struggling to win the fight more than to win the battle. Then, the rush of the vortex turned to gurgles, and the pull of its current reversed, gushing out with a wave that knocked the cruise ships back, knocking them into each other with the crushing force of destruction. Out of the maelstrom, spiraled into the sky a climbing stone tower of what felt like the only sanctuary in the area.

Everyone get to the lighthouse! rang out the thoughts of Horus. *It just erupted out of the maelstrom! It'll be the only thing that survives whatever that tsunami is.*

He's right, I thought back, feeling the pull of the white stone tower in all of its cylindrical beauty as it radiated a ghostly white light that whisked off the pillar as thick as fog.

Can everyone get there? Aurelius thought out, as Jordy beat his fists against my shield, but I too was unmoving.

No, came the panicked thought of Baldwin.

Behind me, the giant predator had him on his back at the edge of the roof. Baldwin's violet aura was spent out and clung to him like threads under the driving swipe of the predator's blackened bronze long sword coming down. There was no time for Baldwin to fly out, to scramble away, or to fall. His shallow breath was proof he gave everything he had.

Ahhhhh, came the cries of Moremi, and over my shield blasted a bright cascading sprinkle of starlike sparkles that filled the air, as if lighter than a sky full of snow. *I'm on my way,* she thought again. *With victory behind me.*

I feared the worst, turning back to Baldwin, but I found the sword of predator dug into the metal roof all the way to the hilt, over which he knelt in confusion. His body was wracked with sobbing tears as he dissolved his auric armor to reveal the sad face of a terrified man looking down at Baldwin.

Oluorogbo, I've freed you! Moremi thought to all of us, and every muscle on the man's body twitched. In the next second, the giant man was on his feet, then in the sky, and searching the beach.

Everyone get to the lighthouse now! Hypatia thought. *I can't hold the wall forever, and the waves have hit and keep coming!*

That was close, Baldwin thought, rolling onto his stomach and turning to me. *You wouldn't mind helping an old gay to the lighthouse, would you?*

Not at all, I thought with relief. I shoved my shield into Jordy with a two footed push that sent me flying for Baldwin. I picked him up in my arms, as Antonio stood over Gabirol's soaking, golden hooded form. The man's robes flickered in the wind as the hum of Antonio's energy forced him down.

"You're done with this... sick show!" Antonio shouted in his full, solid and undamaged set of auric armor.

Help me with Baldwin, I thought to him, hoping to save him from himself, as Aurelius, Cleoseléné, and Kana flew up from the now dry beach that was the sea outlet behind us. The escaping ships from before teetered in the sand, as people ran for the coastline in desperate fear. Hyp held herself in bright teal auric form, holding up the wall of water that was then taller than the icebergs of Antarctica, and gleaming with her teal auric energy like the northern lights. I couldn't imagine the amount of power needed to keep it up. But still, the waves coming in to shore were larger, and growing larger behind her wall.

As I rounded the tail of the ship in my wide turn holding Baldwin under his arms, Antonio caught him by the legs, and helped me carry him through the air back in the direction of the lighthouse.

I'm with you, Antonio thought to us.

CHAPTER THIRTEEN

THE LEGEND OF THE LOST SUN GOD

"What is this place?" Elliot said, sounding in awe as my vision blinked away the bright stain from the blinding light of the threshold into the lighthouse.

Outside I was flying, but inside I ended up face down in a gritty puddle on the cold tiled floor. My body hurt with the strain of energy use, but I was happy to have made it inside the lighthouse. I made it not knowing who else would make it too. I didn't know how it got here, and I doubted it could have come out of the atrament. But I couldn't rule out the prospect of me having caused the destructive maelstrom or the idea that I didn't somehow conjure the lighthouse from the atrament. Nothing was certain except that I was still alive and that Antonio was behind me before I flew inside and still was with me now, with Baldwin's shallow breathing between us. And from the sound of it, Elliot made it too.

"Everyone make it?" came the haggard voice of Aurelius behind me, as I finally found the strength to lift myself up into a seat against the wall beside the threshold.

"No," Cleoseléné said, kneeling at Kana's side, as Kana bowed into the smooth, sandcolored floor. She held her head down in her hands as she tucked into herself, her sides and back expanding and clamping down as she cried hard in muted grief. "Hypatia sacrificed herself for us. She told us to flee while she held the wall. The waves, the people. What happened back there Aurelius?"

"What?" came the voice of Antonio, as he lifted himself off the floor beside me, as he regained consciousness, too.

"I don't know, and I don't know how this lighthouse plays into this, either. The waves took us by surprise, and we had to stop them. Or at least try to. Why would they bring a wave such a size, when they needed to protect their cruise ships? Elliot, do you have any insights?"

Elliot was already half way down the hall, arms folded in astonishment as he ogled at the high arched ceiling with Leibniz.

"It's limestone," he said, surprising even Leibniz beside him.

"I'm sorry, everyone," Leibniz started, shaking as he spoke. "I don't want to be insensitive, but we must keep moving. That doorway is still an open portal to inside here, and as well as it worked for us, it will work the same for the predators we just fled. I tried to leave once we came in, to make sure everyone followed, but it wouldn't let me pass back through. We need to find another exit."

Around me, Frederick, Baldwin, Rumi, and Juba, nodded in agreement. Frederick and Rumi helped Baldwin to his feet. Aurelius took Grace under his arm as she stood petrified and too broke by the news of Hypatia to speak or move. Antonio rushed over to Kana with panicked tears, and I followed, my heart broken for her, him, Hypatia, and all of my new family.

"You're right," Aurelius said. "But we're still missing..."

Before he could finish, two more figures materialized through the threshold, sending us all scrambling back and readying our auric armor. When the light dimmed behind the two figures, it was the warrior in blackened bronze, helmetless, and... smiling. Holding the hand of the battle-rugged, but firm standing queen Moremi.

"My son," Moremi said, raising the hand of the solid jawed man. "Oluorogbo, our newest Immortal Philosopher. Saved at last. My boy."

"I'm sorry for fighting you all," Oluorogbo said, his face as muscular as his arms, and his voice a deep drum.

"How, Moremi?" Aurelius asked, holding Grace tight as the Captain sobbed into his shoulder.

"Oshun," Moremi said, smiling a bright and wide smile. The sweat on her forehead was caked with the fine powder of sand while the rest of her face glistened with gleeful tears and rain. "She's gone. Done for. Deleted, and never to return. Oluorogbo's curse has been lifted. Oshun's prisoners are free. And my boy," Oshun said, looking up at her son with a hand on his cheek. "He's back with me."

"What fantastic news," Aurelius said, getting caught up in the moment as we all sank for a second in the silver lining of our failed and tragic mission.

"We must hurry! We're not safe yet," Leibniz called from further down the hall, his voice echoing everywhere it bounced off of. The hall was about a hundred yards, which seemed to defy the size of its outside form, but I was too worried about surviving to be surprised by that magic. This felt like being trapped in a maze with predators in pursuit, and only one way out. "There's a room down here if we have to fight, let's go!"

"Let's go, everyone," Aurelius commanded, and everyone, even Kana got up to her feet to start running to safety. Leibniz and Elliot made it to the room at the other end first, and both looked back at us, watching with readied auras and obvious worry.

"Run," came the voice of someone I hadn't heard before. The word seemed to ring out from the walls of the hall in a way that Horus's voice might, but when I searched for him in my head and around us, I didn't feel him. But we all ran faster without needing to know who spoke with warning, because in the next second, the bright white light that came from the doorway we passed through, flickered again. This time, I didn't want to know who it was until I reached Leibniz and Elliot. We were two-thirds there when the hall lit up with the cosmic light of the chaos energy and the shouting of Caesar, Hannibal, Jordy, and Calamity rang out.

"Run! Before the portal closes," the voice called out again, and we were blanketed in a protective, rejuvenating light that was as warm as the daylight of the sun.

I crossed into the room, grabbing at Elliot's outstretched arm and swinging to a stop, pressed up against his body, as everyone else throttled into the room. Down the hall, the sunlight fizzled the chaos energy into a fog that blurred the other half of the hall where the predators still blasted their beams of hatred our way.

"Hold onto your bodies," the voice said from above, and the room went bright, blinding me in the same way of the threshold we took into the light house, but this time I didn't fall flat on my face at the force of the energy. This time, I felt lifted off the floor and pulled through a searing band of ultra violet energy that sizzled against my skin and deep down, though to my auric core.

"Aghhhhh," my body screamed as I lost control of my physical form. The pain, the shock, and loss of sight had me stumbling to grasp a thought inside of my own mind as the world fell away from me. As my body fell away from me, and as my heart stopped beating in the chest I no longer felt. I felt of myself only the wispy collection of particles of my aura. All, being squeezed in by the force of the unseeable vacuum around me. My aura, or I, moved like the air inside of a squeezed balloon, shifting as the pressure around me. Molded me into whatever shape I needed to be in order to key onward.

After a few panicked minutes of feeling pressurized, the overall sensation of the force started to ease, and I started to feel relaxed and... almost at peace. If not that, I at least felt like I was existing in the moment and not thinking of even a second before or after. Almost feeling like the ideas and experiences people explain when going to heaven.

Then my visual field started coming back, but from the center of my auric core. From the solid molten crystal like mass of concentrated auric energy particles. I was in a sea of fuzzy bright energy that shined out from the human figured molten sun being that all of the energy around us belonged to. Who, I assumed, the voice we heard in the lighthouse also belonged to. But I couldn't yet think beyond my feeling of awe as the concentrated energy of the being flared like the orange eruptions of sunflares, dispersing around us in warming rays.

The longer I watched, the stronger I started to feel. In this form, my visual field grew to encompass my front, back, and all around. And I noticed, thankfully, that I wasn't the only one who was transported. The tyrian purple, red-wine colored core of Aurelius's aura was above me, the sky blue of Antonio was next to me, the silver of Elliot's on the other side of me, Kana's cherry blossom pink, the two moon light glows of Cleoseléné and Moremi, the blackened bronze of Moremi's son, Oluorogbo, was beside her. The amber of Grace's aura, beside the eggy yellow of Leibniz, the deep royal navy of Juba, and the violet of Baldwin beside the gold of Frederick and browned parchment of Rumi.

"Welcome to the lighthouse of illusion," the voice spoke again, this time from the figure before us. The voice was warm, friendly, and excited. "It's been quite an effort to get you all here. I've waited quite a bit longer than I'd ever hoped to be here, but sometimes you don't always know what you're getting into before stepping your foot into it. In a second, we'll be somewhere else, so don't worry. We're all simply in a one way transit."

"It's been a pleasure connecting with the especially impressive immortal you're all traveling with. Dylan Eaglegod, it's been a treat working with you, even if you never knew I was there. Your abilities are a strength, I assure you. It's not weakness that allowed me to connect with you and the physical world we all come from. You were my antennae through time and space, and so conductive you've been in helping me carry out this self-directed rescue mission."

"I brought you all here through the only way I knew how. Through the way I took long ago. But the lighthouse of Alexandria, as epic as she is, is but a mystic portal to the prison we'll end up in. Now, don't be upset by that news, please don't fret. Because now that you're here, we can free us all from this tragic war between the forces of here and there. I'll explain this all until it's clear. But I must ask for one more fight to share the answers that you need. And I'll assume you're all on board since helping others is your whole deal. My master plan's final stage was set with all the utmost care. So don't you worry or disdain the means of how with ends like these. I am the pawn, I'm not the queen or godly king, who sits enthroned for all that's wrong for everything that you've endured. I'm but a cog in all the wheels, another victim with my appeals, a lowly actor pushing buttons with preset features I can't control."

"I've already spent so long just waiting for the day I'd slip into your minds to bring you here for not just me, but there are three that we can save, and many more who you will see. For those of past and future days, this place is hell and heaven all the same. I know your stories and your minds, I've learned the history of all your times."

"The sickness of depravity still plagues the world of your reality, but here it too exists and through to your world, but that we can stop. So, lift up with me humanity just like the rising sun, warm us with salvational love into the future we can reset."

The figure's molten form moved in plasmatic swirls of orangy lava lamps as he looked down at his hand.

"Cruelty over love is a choice that bankrupts the morality of people for reasons that are beyond the realm of explanation, but which we together can help humanity overcome. But that fight starts here, in the heart of the start of civilization. The lighthouse, through its secret travels, rescued you for a reason. It appears only for the weary and lost philosophers and heroes, but brings us to this prison of history."

"After I set us down, we'll stand before the true gates of the Babylonian Ishtar, and beyond those gates we'll be in the realm of Marduk and Mushhushshu," the sun being continued as we lowered to the ground in the white and golden auric haze. My body came back under my control once my feet touched the solid light beneath us, and the sun being's auric form melted around himself and disappeared into the floor, revealing a handsome man of about my age with striking similarities to Cleoseléné, but with golden amber eyes instead of the queen's silver.

"Helios!" Cleoseléné gasped as she broke from her paralytic

hold and rushed to him. Her face broke into tears as she threw her arms around him in a violent hug.

"Where? How?" Cleoseléné cried, and Helios held her with a smile, delighted by his sister, but also unable to hide the worried brow he harbored as he looked over his shoulder and back through the Ishtar gate.

"I love you sister," Helios said, patting her back. "But we are in danger here."

"Why didn't the moon lead me to you?" Cleoseléné asked, touching her brother's smooth cheek. "So many girls I saved for her."

"You're not the only one the moon's misguided for centuries," Moremi said, looking over at Olulorogbo with muted joy. Her heart seemed to be so full as to have a presence in the gathering with us, but nothing could fill the sniffling brokenness of Kana and Grace being comforted by Antonio and Aurelius.

My heart hurt for both of them around the periphery of the overwhelming rush of adrenaline from the sheer panic burning throughout my body after what Helios had told us. Being imprisoned between here and there? It didn't make sense. How can salvation be another prison we'd have to escape from? How did he use me? Everything was already too much to process. My mind was still cycling through my fight with Jordy and Oluorogbo, losing my grip on the atrament, and the deaths of all of those people we were supposed to save.

"What did you mean when you said you worked through me?" I asked, wondering how, out of everyone he could have connected with throughout history, he connected with me. A novice immortal with more issues to sort out than things settled. The last thing I needed was another immortal in my head, 'connecting with me,' whatever that really meant.

My question surprised Helios and Cleoseléné both. But

made Cleoseléné push him away to arms length. Truth, even when reflective of good intention, always has the power to break even the strongest hearts and bonds.

"Somehow, your connection with the atrament and skill at moving between energy realms called out to me in my search for Cleoseléné and any other immortal I could reach," Helios said, looking nervous. "After connecting with you, I tried everything I could for you to notice me, but everything failed. I felt like a god, truly. Able to move the world around you, to get you closer to finding me, but unable to talk with you or communicate my calls for help."

"You were in my head," I said, running down the chains of possibilities of his involvement in my moments with Elliot and in the friction between Antonio and I. "I know what you did."

"I apologize for everything done to get you all here," Helios said, his brow creased with deeper concern. "Drifting you off track, the storm, the tsunami waves, and even the intimate moments I intruded upon, Dylan. I truly am sorry. It was easier to connect with you the more alone and confused I made you feel. Antonio, Elliot, I'm sorry. Kana, Captain O'Malley, I'm broken for your loss. I never meant for anything tragic to happen because of my actions."

"Aurelius, how do we feel about this? Manipulation, endangerment, isolation? Murder?" I asked, turning back to Aurelius as Antonio pulled me by the shoulder to him and Kana, whose aura flared with pink hot anger. The fear of myself that I lived with and the things I did against my direction. The rage I felt standing before Joshua rose in me again. It clenched its cold hands around my gut and wind pipe, making me dizzy. Antonio noticed as my body slacked, and he held me up closer to him as I leaned harder against his body.

I love you, and I trust you, Antonio thought, looking over at me.

I didn't know he was in my head, and still I justified everything instead of just talking to you, I thought back. *How can I be sure it won't happen again? If people can change because of cosmology and over biological time periods, and other dimensional interference, how can we trust in us? How can we trust our hearts and minds?*

Look at us, Antonio thought, hugging me tighter. *Our auras are two shades of the same color for a reason. When we met, we fell in love because our souls were always searching for each other, and our hearts filled in ways they never had before. Being together is a promise that no matter the struggles that make us wander in life, we'll always find our way back to each other. That's all there is to trust.*

I love you, and I trust you, I thought, tears of anger, love, and confusion spilling from my eyes. *I know that's true. More true than anything else.*

Then let's make it out of here, and we'll make the most of what immortal life has to offer. One day at a time, Antonio thought. *I love you.*

I love you too, I thought back, feeling the stress of fear start to wash away and be replaced by the warm, charging energy from Antonio's pulsing aura.

Aurelius stared dead into the eyes of Helios, the gates of the Babylonian Ishtar started materializing brighter in royal blue behind Helios and Cleoseléné, shimmering with a glitter that danced and sparkled in the thick, cosmic haze of the auric realm.

"We answer the call of every mortal and immortal in need, willingly," Aurelius said, stressing *willingly*. "You robbed us of that opportunity, Helios."

"I did," Helios said. "It was necessary. Feel free to willingly not help, but the right to ask is inherent in your modus operandi, as you laid out."

"He's not wrong about that," Leibniz chimed in, sounding hurt to agree, as he brought a shaky finger to his chin. His face was creased with worry where it wasn't smeared with the grime of battle.

"So we're just going to go along with this?" I asked, feeling my fear turn to rage as I searched the haze behind us for a way back to the lighthouse. But I wasn't exactly interested in returning there, either.

"I can't send you back, and even if I could, I rescued you all from a battle that you were sure to lose," Helios said, breaking the distracted sorrows of Kana and Grace.

"You made the waves?" Grace asked in disbelief, with a red faced and squinted glare that seared into Helios.

"I had to," he said. "It was one of the only manifestations I could achieve through Dylan."

"No!" Grace cried, beating a fist into Aurelius's chest. "You killed her! I'll kill you!" she screamed, charging at the sun god with her blazing amber aura alive around her.

"That won't happen here," Helios said, lifting from the ground, a wall of golden light around himself and Cleoseléné, who still held onto her brother's arms in stunned revelation, numb to everything external. "Here is a place beyond the confines of life and death and time and space and imperfect representations. Here is a place of authenticity and forms. A realm prophesied by Socrates and searched for by Alexander and Aristotle, and later myself. To kill me, we would first have to make it out of here for good. Even to kill me, you must help, otherwise the realities of this place will be the conditions of our immortality. This is the graveyard and crown of civilization in only its most sterile and perfect way. Without me, you will lose yourself to these conditions. The battle each of us faces in the realm of our former reality is unique, but here the warden of our prison has created conditions that mistakenly neutralizes all into the same endless cycle of struggle less existence. We have only as long as I can hold off his senseless magic and only one shot at returning us back to the there of where we came."

"Rahhhhh!" Grace shouted, banging on the light barrier Helios hid behind. "Aurelius!? Cleo!?"

"I'm sorry," Helios said. "But we have to get going. I ushered you through the lighthouse connection faster than the transit would have been without me, but your pursuers are still after you. They'll be here soon. Once inside the lighthouse, it's only a matter of time before they're materialized here."

"What is *that*?" Rumi asked, pointing at something in the sky over the Ishtar Gate. It snaked in and out of the pinkish-tan clouds with a long and skinny body, a long neck and tail and front limbs like lion legs, and eagle talons tucked behind its hind legs. Its heavy, slowbeating wings dazzled with the reflection of the sky's light against its shiny scales. Its head, snake-like and scanning the ground, swept back and forth as it flew over the vastness of the city.

"That's Mushhushshu, the pet creation of Marduk," Helios said, his calm tone unnerving. "It's his guardian. Immortalized in the bricks of this very gate behind me in order to protect the city. But now, the city is a prison of no escape, where Marduk and Mushhushshu feed off of the suffering of lost souls seeking the secrets of the universe. We must travel through the hanging gardens and reach the temple of Marduk without detection from Mushhushshu. There, we'll find our captor and the captives we must rescue. There, we'll set them free and make our escape from this prison. Stay on guard and ready to fight. Don't get separated."

"Let's go then!" Grace shouted, banging again on the barrier Helios still held up. "But when we get out of here, know that you're dead. I don't care how long you've been stuck here."

"Grace, my dear, come here," Rumi said, placing a hand on her shoulder and seeping a little of his aura into hers. She turned, looking at him with desperation until he took her hand, which she squeezed around his. The tension in her face eased, but there was no washing away the sadness from her eyes. "We are with you."

"And so are they, now," Helios said, pointing up at the sky behind us, where energy was starting to collect in the colors of the auras of the predators that were chasing us. "Everyone, through the gate!"

We all hurried after Helios as he dropped his barrier and led us into the ancient stone city. As we crossed under the gate, the weight of the world started to feel heavy, pushing down my shoulders and forcing me to straighten myself against the pressure.

Through the haze of auric power, the sandy colored baked-brick buildings emerged, placing us on the brick road of civilization, where even gutters were set into the structure of a seemingly rainless space. Behind us, the gate stood as open as it had before we passed through, and the predators were materializing more and more as they lowered from where their forms first emerged from.

"Keep your heads down," Helios said, turning his head in a crooked way to make sure we all complied. "I brought you here, and have cloaked us from Mushhushshu, but the guardian will come to collect the other intruders. He'll present them to Marduk for their initial processing into the kingdom, and they'll either become his soldiers or his subjects. If they survive Mushhushshu that is. The beast and Marduk are the only arbiters of life and death here."

"Well, it's Caesar and Hannibal," Cleoseléné said, looking gaunt at Helios. "With a few others, so let's get out of here, now, please."

"That's not good," Helios said, pulling his bottom lip between his teeth and chewing with nervous energy. "Heads down, and follow me. Do *not* look at the sky."

Helios led us with Cleoseléné's hand in his. Antonio took my hand as we started moving, while Elliot grabbed onto my other hand. There was no resistance or pulling away by Antonio, and there was no spell over me enchanting Elliot's touch. I wasn't a victim anymore in a world of unknown dangers and mismatching motives and obligations. I was the conduit that brought us here, of my own accord or not, and somehow I knew we wouldn't get out unless I could make it so. The comfort Elliot needed, I was happy to provide, in the way Antonio was the comfort I needed to survive.

I'm scared, Elliot thought to me, as we hurried deeper into the winding streets of the city.

I know, I thought back. *I am too, but we'll get out of this. I promise.*

"How far is the garden?" Cleoseléné asked, as panicked as the rest of us.

"Not too far," Helios said, leading us past mudbrick build-ings with clean plain facades that shadowed us from the sky. "We have to reach the center of the city."

"Who are we rescuing, as you mentioned?" Aurelius asked from behind Antonio, Elliot, and I.

Helios turned down a side street that led to a grand avenue

where cloth topped market stalls stood empty in fine crisp colors off the sides of the buildings. The tables held no wares. And the stalls held no merchants. Throughout the entire city, there wasn't a soul anywhere.

"Are you sure you're not just imagining things?" Baldwin asked. "It doesn't look like anyone's here"

"He could be a conjure of Caesar," Frederick said, meeting my eyes as I considered what a perfect trap it would be. "If he's as willing as a predator to sacrifice thousands in the ocean, he'd be willing to sacrifice us once he's done with us."

"I'm not a predator," Helios said, crossing us into a side-street on the other side of the avenue. "I'm taking us to the hanging gardens, where all the greatest souls of humanity end up after being swallowed up by the lighthouse."

"You didn't make the cut?" Rumi questioned, with a scared edge to his voice where his humor usually was. Being trapped in a prison wasn't making anyone happy, and I could feel Elliot's heart beating faster and his energy pulsing harder the more upset everyone else got and the more the truth of our situation became impossible to ignore.

"I'm a sun god," Helios said. "I am a form in myself. That's why Caesar wanted me prisoner. His self sacrifice was an act of necessity for his predatory immortality. Octavian was his puppet replacement he planned to feast off of for as long as he could, until he needed a replacement. But once he tasted my energy, it became his most potent addiction. He planned on using Ptolemy as a battery system to mummify and pre-serve my energy inside of him to be dismembered and saved for Caesar's travels away from me. Ptolemy had the ability to hold vast amounts of my energy naturally. I cared for him before arriving in Rome, and I had to get us out of there. I just couldn't tell anyone."

"Not even me?" Cleoseléné said, her voice shaking with weakness. "And what of Ptolemy? Tell me he's here with us, too. Tell me he's the one we're set to save."

"He's here, but he's not the only one we're meant to save or the reason I brought us here," Helios said. "I knew Caesar would find us anywhere we hid, so I had to find the two most lost souls to ensure we'd never be found. Aristotle and Alexander of Macedon, or the Great, are the ones we'll have to pull from Marduk's gardens."

CHAPTER FOURTEEN

A PRISON OF PLATONIC PROPORTION

"Is Marduk really a god?" I asked, deciding to stay close to Helios as we reached the threshold into the arched gardens at the center of the city. Vines of plump grapes and round white cantaloupe melons canopied the verdant stone walkways of the mud brick path between the never ending series of courtyards, all bursting with fruit trees ripe with apples and cherries and grapefruits and figs. Hanging flowers around the courtyards were bright halos of the purples and reds of the blue, ruby, black brightness of the berry bushes that ringed the lawns, where finally we found people lounging in the grasses under the sunlight.

"Only as godly as you and I," Helios said, scanning each face in the courtyards we passed. I tried to recognize faces, but quickly gave up. They were all silent or muttering to themselves. Some wore threadbare sacks of linen, while others stood adorned in shined armor with swords at their belts. All ages were present, but nobody seemed to notice anybody else around them. Even the children were still and staring up at the sunlight above.

"So, he's an immortal? Like everyone else here?" I said,

feeling uncomfortable the more muttering souls we passed.

"Everyone here," Helios said. "Is here because they're here, but not all were immortal before getting here. Marduk collects the greatest minds he fancies from humanity and keeps them here. Without purpose, or society, or politics, his utopia of abundance breaks them. After reaching the land of forms, there's no theorizing left after accepting the lie that Marduk forces everyone to believe. It might be a utopia, but even if this place was *attempting* to be his ideal of utopia, it fails. He's an immortal, dubbed the God of Civilization, who's spent nearly all of his existence in this prison of his own making. Rescuing Alexander, Ptolemey, and Aristotle are the only way we make it out of here," Helios said, marching us deeper into the endless courtyards.

"It looks like anyone could walk in or out," Baldwin said, bringing up the rear of our group with Rumi.

"You'd think that in the gardens of abundance," Rumi added. "They'd be getting a lot more dirty between the fruit trees. They truly do lack all passion. Reminds me of a few people I know, however. See what a dead heart means, Aurelius? A dead brain and no life passion."

"That's the core message of my music," Elliot said, moving a hand to his heart. "Vulnerability is a magic all its own."

I didn't think I'd see a change in Elliot for decades, but all he had to do was speak from his core and his heart and drop the performative garbage for his soul to shine through.

"Music is the hidden arithmetical exercise of a mind unconscious," Leibniz said, looking between Frederick and Elliot.

"I can attest to that, Leibniz," Frederick said. "Music is a spring of internal salvation that reaches deep into the roots of the ethereal and auric histories of humanity."

"So our plan is to free them?" Aurelius said. "What's beyond that? What's the next step? And genuinely, why is it so important?"

"Well, once we break them from their Marduk's control, Mushhushshu will come for us…," Helios said. As he finished his thought, the shriek of a falcon cracked over head like lightning, and clapped between the walls of the courtyards, jumpscaring us all as we all scanned the sky.

"We must not be alone anymore," Helios said, as Mushhushshu dove against the blue and pink of the sky in the direction of the outskirts of the city from where we came.

"Why didn't that thing come for us?" Moremi asked, Oluorogbo still at her side.

Oluorogbo had the aura of a man who could do anything to protect someone he loved. The confidence and strength of his scarred and tortured face were all the evidence of his resolve.

"Dylan and I are protecting us," Helios said, winking back at me. "But Mushhushshu *will* come for us once we break Marduk's other guardians out of their trances, or possibly before we even get the chance."

"I'm not doing anything that's protecting us," I said, searching my aura for leaks or his presence, but I was secure.

"It's not like that," Helios said, laughing like a prince, even though he was seeming more and more like a mad emperor. "Through our connection I was able to seep the scent of everyone's aura into this realm. I channeled it between where you were, directly into the air Mushhushshu breathes and analyzes daily. Just like new souls, he got used to the gradual strength of your presence here. Julius and the others aren't enjoying their welcome, however. He hunted Ptolomey and I all the way to the lighthouse the first time I escaped him, which I'm sure is why he couldn't let go of the opportunity to follow you through the threshold this time. I despise the monster."

"He's even more dangerous now," Cleoseléné said to Helios.

"So are we," Helios said back. "I haven't been wasting my time here or letting myself become complacent. The other reason we're protected is because my energy is so closely identical to the Sun's energy and to Marduk's energy. It makes me able to skirt Mushhushshu's surveillance for as long as I decide to, while also allowing me to not succumb to Marduk's contagious insanity. But one day, I did go crazy. I decided to go on the attack. I lost, died, and rematerialized back before the gate. The first time I lost, I wasn't sure what would happen, honestly. But I figured I needed to fight to win my way out of here or I'd go as mad as all the others eventually. It took me a thousand losses of so many ways to die by the snake, lion, eagle, scorpion hybrid to finally win, until I won thousands more times."

"So, if we die here, we come back exactly as we are? Right away?" Elliot asked, sounding as confused as I felt.

If he had defeated the thing a thousand times, why would we have to be afraid?

"If *I* die, *I* come back," Helios said. "It could be because the same energy holding the place together is the same energy I'm identical with, making me come back as easily as Mushhushshu and Marduk. But I never could tell how much time passed between rematerialization. Sometimes it felt immediate. Sometimes it felt like hours or weeks. It's as predictable as how you come back in the real world. If you can heal your body with your will, if you come back into a body a soul has left, or into a new body at birth or before. Will, the universe, and the auric alignments decide. All at the same time, I assume. No single body is a permanent story or asset unchangeable by will, in the way the impermanence of who we are is proven with every thought we explore that takes us into a new state of being. Our cells shed complete bodies, rebuilding everything from the matter that we feed it. Giving us hundreds of new bodies over the centuries for as long as it lasts. If you die here, and I'm not with you when you reenter, you'll be as lost as the philosophers around you."

"Helios," Aurelius said, slowing the sun god down. "Are Ptolemey, Aristotle, and Alexander in any of these courtyards?"

"What?" Helios said, pulling his head back in surprise at the question.

"Are they in these courtyards?" Aurelius repeated, catching Helios's eyes and not letting go. "Where are you taking us?"

"They're with Marduk in the center of the courtyard," Helios said. "We're heading there now."

"Have you fought Marduk before?" Aurelius asked, keeping his warm even tone that pulled truth out from anyone.

"Yes," Helios said, looking down at the floor.

"You haven't bested him," Cleoseléné said, sounding worried and turning to Aurelius.

"Mushhushshu comes back too quickly," Helios said. "Before I can defeat him, the beast is alive again and refreshed with fight."

"And?" Aurelius said, pulling for more. "You mentioned three guardians?"

"And, Marduk uses Aristotle, Alexander, and Ptolemy," Helios said. "He has them mind controlled or something. Way more than he controls the rest of the others here. They fight for him and with him, and all of them together have always been too much for me alone."

With that revelation hanging in the thick auric air, the bricks of the long hall started shaking, and the hanging plants above our heads dropped fruits and flowers all around. Then came the boom, and an explosion of chaos energy plumed into the sky over the mudbrick buildings and gardens.

"What kind of aurics is that?" Helios asked, captivated by the cosmic swirl of the energy's mixing colors.

"It's the chaotic energy Caesar and Hannibal have harnessed," Cleoseléné said, watching the sky.

"It's pure chaotic force," Leibniz added. "We have our own wielder of chaos energy in Dylan, but he's not well practiced, to say the least."

"I don't know if I'm quite a wielder of chaos energy," I said back, afraid of adding more responsibility under my belt. "Chaos energy feels too dangerous and contaminating to touch. All I've done is fumble with their auric mechanisms of conveying the chaos energy for use."

"That's an important distinction," Helios said, his gaze unbreaking from the plume of the dark energy as it hung above the buildings as more crashes and explosions of battle clapped across the city. The beast groaned, and the city groaned from the walls and floors like buildings do from earthquakes. Shaking and breaking, before the beast cried, and the sky split with purple lightning.

Out of the chaos energy plume, the beast shot into the air, covered from head to tail in the chaos energy that it had escaped, lurching its neck in all directions as it struggled to beat its wings to maintain flight. On its back, four figures clung to its body, holding on as the first rider blasted chaos energy into the beast's head.

"This is really bad," I said, knowing instantly what I was seeing. The chaos energy hold on the beast was exactly that, a hold that the beast was failing to fight off. A hold that would manipulate the beast in following the rider's every order.

"Mushhushshu's a direct link to Marduk," Helios said, pulling Cleoseléné forward, with the rest of us clambering to follow after. "He'll be readying for a fight. Any surprise element we might've had is lost. Hurry, we won't beat them to him, but hopefully we can save his prisoners."

As I followed, I watched the beast struggle in the air, flailing itself from side to side and rolling over in spirals, almost shaking a couple of the riders loose, but failing. In a last effort, the beast shot straight up into the sky at the speed a bullet shoots from a gun, pulled back as it nearly went out of sight from the distance, flipped itself over bringing its momentum into a downward dive that ripped the chaos energy from its face and neck like the flames off a falling meteor, and screeched like a falcon in pure unfiltered pain through purple lightning strikes.

This time, the lightning struck the beast with five snaking strikes at once. The beast froze in the air where it was struck, glowing with electrical currents that left the beast's neck and tail, wings, and legs limp as it fell through the air.

The predators held tight to the beast's back, insulated within their auric armor and linked hands as the first rider blasted a fresh flow of chaos energy into the beast, stirring the beast into a lift that pulled them up into the air over the buildings they nearly crashed into.

"The center garden," Helios said. "Just up ahead."

CHAPTER FIFTEEN

THE GOD AT THE START OF CIVILIZATION

Marduk stood in the middle of the larger center garden, blazing with golden sunlight energy around his dark bronze skin and charcoal black, long coiled beard and hair of layered spiralled columns of architectural curls that spilled over his shoulders. His strong aquiline curved nose, wide, large pupiled eyes, and powerful squared jawline gave the immortal the look of an eagle whose gaze seemed inescapable. He snarled at the sky as his three prized prisoners gathered behind him. Ptolemy, Aristotle, and Alexander the Great.

Ptolemy stood in a lavender cloud of auric power, with the sharp angled featured face of Helios and Cleoseléné, with a curved scythe and Egyptian armor and weaponry. His eyes glowed lavender across their surface, hiding his natural eyeballs behind the glow and telling me that something was definitely wrong with him. Aristotle was wrapped in the white wrapped himation of ancient Greece, that furled over his right shoulder like a greek column, leaving his right arm exposed but concealed in the pure white light of his aura. His brown beard and hair were dark contrasts against the blinding light of his aura that also shined off his eyes in the way Ptolemy's did with his aura. Alexander, the most menacing of the three prisoners, stood with tawny, lion-colored hair and aura, forming solid plate armor across his body that showed he was the king of conquest. He balanced a long pike-spear in one hand and a lion shield in the other, his eyes as overcast with his aura as the others.

"Ptolemy's lavender aura," Cleoseléné said. "It's as beautiful as I remember."

"You better hope he doesn't kill us with it," Helios said back. "They're always prepared to win every fight."

"Everyone get under the arches," Aurelius said, pulling myself and Antonio under the arch of the nearest side courtyard. Everyone tucked under the closest arch to them and looked to Aurelius for answers. Then we heard the beating wings and groans of Mushhushshu's overhead, the vibration of his energy shook the ground and stone of the arched walls loose of dust and crumbling pieces of ancient mudbrick that fell around us, clouding up the air. A wall of chaos energy moved down the hall under the beast, as it directed its flightpath for a descent into Marduk's garden. With the four predators still clinging to its back.

The chaos beam swept through the hall past us, and into the garden, where Marduk and his triad of immortals were waiting for them. Alexander charged the beast and riders with Ptolemy. Alexander's pike and Ptolemy's scythe-shaped khopesh-topped spear slashed before them in preparation, their faces as serious as stone. Marduk, confident despite his beast being turned against him, lifted himself into the air, swirling his sunshine auric energy into a bright cloud in front of him. In what looked like a move of defiance, Aristotle lowered himself into a seat onto the grass and into a cross-legged meditation. His bright white aura burned like the sting of the lit magnesium, threatening to blind all who stared, but I couldn't look away. Tendrils of his power snaked across the grass and into the air to meet his three comrades, connecting with them and charging them with its protective purity in the way Antonio and Leibniz did for Elliot and I.

"I'm here for my throne," declared the voice of Caesar from atop the beast, as it reared back its landing to avoid the pike and blade of the two dynastic warrior kings' spears from below. Then, Jordy, Hannibal, and Calamity J all dismounted into the garden for their ground fight. Hannibal and Jordy were both armed with swords. Hannibal's was solid and curved, while Jordy's was roman in nature, looking a lot like Antonio's gladius, only neon green in color to match his nuclearly toxic aura. While Calamity J snapped a scarlet auric whip in her left hand as she fired scarlet energy blasts from her auric, short barrelled shotgun at Ptolemy, who deflected the blasts with the swipe of his weapon with flashing speed, before angling his weapon for attack.

"Four fine additions to my gardens," Marduk's voice rolled like thunder over the walls, floors, and across the sky. "Thank you Julius. Your service goes unmatched in history."

"You're not imprisoning us," Caesar said, launching a flowing blast of chaos energy at Marduk. "We've already turned your little pet against you."

And with that, Mushhushshu reared back against the hovering push of his wings, blasting Marduk with an even stronger current of chaos energy than any I had seen.

"There's nowhere to run, nowhere to hide, and nothing you can do to stop us," Caesar shouted over the hum of the energy as Marduk countered the blast with his own torrent of gathered sunlight energy.

"I'm the god that brought you the civilization you destroyed, Julius," Marduk growled past his rigid lips.

"This is a catastrophe," Helios whispered to himself, but all of us around him heard what we all felt was true. We didn't just have Marduk and his guardians to worry about, we had the predators to worry about too.

"Your time of hiding is over," Caesar shouted down from the beast's forward bent scorpion tale, as the creature prepared a strike against its godly master. "It's over for all of you."

"How are they not controlled?" Aurelius said, grabbing Helios by the arm, pulling him for face to face answers.

"I don't know..." Helios said, looking disturbed more by the realization than by Aurelius.

"It's the chaos energy," I said, patting Aurelius on the forearm. "It's infected in each one of the predators. It does something to their energy, like shields them from vulnerability. I noticed it when we were in Leibniz's protection bubble. The chaos energy overrides them and keeps their auras locked inside their chaos bubbles."

"That seems to align with my observation," Leibniz said. "It acts like a shell, rather than a part of their whole. Like a tool and armor at the same time."

"Like the negative of auric energy," I realized.

"Well, aura is life, even if predators use it to kill," Aurelius considered. "The chaos energy must be death to the aura's life."

"So does it kill them to use it?" Frederick wondered aloud.

"It weakens their core auric power, look," Leibniz said, throwing his arms down the corridor, where a lens of his aura appeared like the glass of a magnifying glass. "Like a parasite. Peer through here. I'll show you what I see."

On the other side of the lens, the predators were fighting the gods. Marduk was fending off strikes of the scorpion tail and arrows Caesar shot at him from Mushhushshu's back. The other three predators were sparring with the other immortals. Ptolemy was fending himself off against Calamity, as he closed the space between them with a pole vault into a roundhouse kick that sent Calamity's chin hard into the ground. Her gun tumbled away from her in a cartwheel, making her whip her only defense other than the chaos energy she channeled into a fire around her, charring the grass. As she inflamed herself, though, the lens showed fire burning off her auric core like a flame off of a wick, evaporating her lifeforce the more chaos energy she spent.

Hannibal and Jordy wielded their chaos energy in the same way. Jordy blazed an inferno of chaos flames from his hands, while Hannibal sparred with Alexander. But Alexander's blade moved as if commanded by foresight, anticipating Hannibal's strikes three or four in advance, needing only the slightest of movements to deflect them while Hannibal grew more haggard and enraged with each chaos-charged blow. Each wasted attack ate away at Hannibal's auric reserves, showing just how dangerously low he was on power from the continuous use for battle from the bay to the garden. Even as Alexander deflected with his sword, his shield did just as much work fending off Jordy's flames, but the protective aura of Aristotle moved like a cloud, preparing to defend wherever the warriors failed to protect themselves, giving them and ease of battle that not many could enjoy.

"With no atrament tap source," I said. "The predators' auras will eventually be consumed by the chaos. If they don't win this fight, they're done for. Without the constant replenishment, they'll either die or eventually end up as brainwashed as the other philosophers in the garden, I believe."

"We need to win this fight before that happens," Helios said, breaking away from Aurelius's hold.

"Do we join now, or let them battle it out?" Moremi said, shaking two moonlight auric axes into her hands. "We can take them all. We have the numbers, and the beast seems near useless under Caesar's control."

"The beast *is* useless now," Helios said, looking between the beast and Marduk's attacks. "Caesar has no idea what that creature is capable of, and it looks like Marduk is just toying with them. He'll crush them all like bugs once he's had enough of his game. We need to take him down first. It's the only way."

"If the chaos energy is shielding the predators," I said, wondering aloud. "I might be able to use it against Marduk. To contain him enough for the rest of you to free Aristotle, Alexander, and Ptolemy. If it smothers auric energy into containment and uses it as fuel, it should work to cut him off from them at least. With them on our side, we might have a better chance of winning this."

"If you lift the chaos energy from the predators," Leibniz said, with the doubt of concern. "He might turn the predators against us before you can contain him."

"This might just be the only way," Helios said. "Marduk may not be a god, but he is the god of this realm. Tell us what to do, Dylan."

"Me?" I asked, considering the plan further. I knew what I needed to do, but I'd need time to lift the chaos energy from each of the predators. "I need more than a distraction. I need you to get the predators as close to Marduk as you can, and the connection from Aristotle needs to be severed. He's feeding them all with protective energy that's countering the chaos and balancing it out before it hits them. Get him in the fight defending himself. If you all go for him first, Ptolemy and Alexander will help him. Then try to push the predators to encircle Marduk. If they're in proximity to him, I'll have a better shot at this working."

"I'll stay with you here," Leibniz said. "For shielding and auric charge."

"I'll stay, too," Antonio said, with a hand on my shoulder, which I wished I could fall into and have him catch me. I was weak already from the battle on the cliff, but I was ready to give everything I had to this fight. Even if it burnt me out of existence, it'd save everyone who risked their everythings for me. "I'll keep your energy levels full as much as I can."

"Elliot will stay here with you three, too," Aurelius added, nodding Elliot over toward Antonio and I. "The rest of us know our jobs?"

Each of the Immortal Philosophers nodded their heads in agreement and armored up, materializing their weapons at their sides if they weren't already there. Each one of them looked as serious for battle as ever, and as ready to give every-thing they had as much as I was.

"I killed one god today, already," Moremi said, bouncing on her heels with an excitement I wished I could replicate. "One more, with all of you and my son? We've got this."

"Nothing like a truly deathly battle to get the heart pump-ing," Rumi offered, looking as nervous as I felt, but I couldn't tell if he was nervous for himself or for the rest of us.

"Let's go," Cleoseléné said, nodding everyone forward. "I have another brother to save."

"Yes, my queen," Juba said, following her and Helios who

took the lead.

"I'll shield us in my auric mirage until we reach the threshold into the garden," Helios said, conjuring the light of his aura as a blinding sunshine around them. "But when we break into the garden it will fall, and we'll all be on our own from there."

"He can collect philosophers," Captain O'Malley said through gritted teeth. "This time, I'm collecting heads."

"I'm with you," Kana added, catching up to Grace and taking her by the hand. "For Hyp."

"For Hyp," Grace said, her jaw sounding tighter than before.

Once you're all in, I thought to everyone. *I'll start working my magic.*

CHAPTER SIXTEEN

THE RISE AND FALL OF ELLIOT CUTCAS

As the philosophers entered into the garden, Leibniz's eggy yellow shield went up around Antonio, Elliot, and I as Leibniz stood in front of us, channeling his auric energy into me. Antonio did the same from my side, while I made sure to keep my thoughts far away from using Elliot's energy as a battery again. But both of them had grabbed my hands as I closed my eyes and opened myself up to the auric current.

I was warmed with the energy charges and sank fully into the focus I needed to see and feel the auras of the predators beneath the blankets of chaos energy around them.

I'm starting with Calamity, Jordy, and Hannibal, I thought to everyone, leaving Caesar and Mushhushshu alone for now out of fear of freeing Mushhushshu from Caesar's control.

Calamity was fending off more attacks from Ptolemy, now with a conjured auric rapier that made her look like a French harlequin, cracking her whip wherever she could aim it. But no matter where she struck, Aristotle's protective aura absorbed her attacks before hitting Ptolemy. As the chaos energy was absorbed, though, it fizzled and spat like a drop of water on a hot pan, vaporizing the chaos particles in fumes that rose into the air like a fine smoke that I wasn't sure if only I could see.

But seeing the chaos vapor gave me an idea. I materialized my aura around the particles and pulled them to me and through Leibniz's barrier of protection. To my aura, the particles of concentrated chaos energy felt almost dormant, like the auric energy of the auric current. It felt uncontrolled and neutral, waiting to be reactivated and controlled. Even if I wasn't able to... or wanting to take the risk of tapping into the energy, I was still making progress as the other immortals broke into the courtyard and launched themselves into battle. But anything I tried would be useless if Aristotle's protections were still up.

As I focused harder, I collected more fumes into a gaseous bubble inside my cobalt sphere of control as Calamity sped up her attacks against Ptolemy, who Helios charged for first. Sunlight energy bleared the air around him in hot looking waves of illusion, as he harnessed swords of fire in each hand.

"Hello again, brother," Helios said as he broke into the fight, singeing Calamity's hair with his first strike, and sending Ptolemy staggering back to the ground with a low sweeping ground kick that spat fire that seemed solid. "I've come to save you again."

"You're not making it out of here alive over us," Calamity shouted at the sun god, burning through an explosion of chaos energy as she channeled more of her auric core into her fight. I collected the spent fuel as Ptolemy, still lavender auric eyed, lept into the air and cratered between the two immortals, bringing the protective energy of Aristotle down with him.

I might be onto something, I thought, speeding up the conveyor belt of my collections. *Keep up the fight.*

You're doing great, Antonio thought, surging a stronger

wave of his energy into me.

You're on the right track, Leibniz chimed in. *I felt the particles enter our protection. You have control. You know what you're doing. Trust your gut.*

I'll try, I thought back, broadening my reach over the battlefield.

Aurelius, Rumi, Frederick, and Baldwin were all locked in battle against Alexander and Hannibal, separating them, but fighting them as a team as they spun to strike both with sword strikes and auric attacks that beat up Hannibal but were collected by Aristotle's protection where Alexander would have been hit.

"You'll die for this!" Hannibal's voice grated into the garden with auric waves of force that staggered Aurelius backwards and to the ground, where he landed, firm on his feet between Marduk, Caesar, and the scorpion tailed Mushhushshu.

"Marcus Aurelius, I've been waiting for you for a long time," Marduk said, with the stunned amazement of a wide-eyed collector as Aurelius landed before him.

Past them, Cleoseléné and Moremi channeled their energy into Juba, who they launched at Aristotle while Kana and Grace battled Jordy into a corner of the courtyard. Before Juba was atop the ancient philosopher, Aristotle flew back with white-eyed clarity, breaking his protective blanket into a wave of auric energy that tumbled Juba backwards in the air. But as the wave washed past him, he channeled his navy energy into a moonlight rimmed beam that broke through Aristotle's auric defense, causing the philosopher to focus his energy into a counter blast that struggled against the strength of Juba and the moon queens' combined powers.

And as my window of opportunity opened, Hannibal

and Calamity were pushed nearer and nearer to Marduk, as I moved the sphere of the collected chaos energy into the garden courtyard. Using the sphere, I worked into the sphere the will to pull in all of the chaos energy from around it as it moved closer to Marduk and Aurelius. Turning it into a mechanism like the auric structure I used to funnel the chaos energy into the atrament under the bay. The structure pulled from the predators the way I had separated my auric power from Joshua, peeling away from them as I struggled to keep it from infecting me with its dark, soulless power.

Below the orb, Aurelius steeled himself in his aura, as Marduk stood over him, glowing brighter with sunlight energy as he prepared some attack against our leader that I couldn't predict. But Marduk, with his focus on Aurelius, forgot the beast and Caesar above him. As the scorpion tail stinger of the beast came down over Aurelius, I saw the moment we needed as Aurelius raised his arms over his head, with a wave of his purple hued aura grabbing hold of the fast snapping scorpion tail. I pulled from the predators their chaos energy, throwing every ounce of power I could channel from my auric core, Leibniz, and Antonio, leaving the chaos aura around Mushhushshu, and watched as the power magnetized around Marduk. While Aurelius drove the scorpion stinger deep into Marduk's chest. Sunlight poured from the wound like the ichor of the gods, as the king of the realm staggered on weakened knees. His shock dripped from his widened eyes as golden tears streaked down his face, mixing with the sunlight ichor of blood dribbling down his chin.

His energy dissolved from the air around us, as the chaos energy vaporized into a grey mist around him to replace it, searing the chaos energy through the beastly Mushhushshu, and freeing the mental holds over his guardians and the predators at the same time. After Mushhushshu shook fraying last of the chaos energy off of itself, Aurelius let go of his hold over the stinger, and the beast pulled it from its master.

As the other immortal philosophers and predators watched on as Marduk and his guardians grabbed with heads in defeated confusion, Jordy scrambled past Kana and Grace, heading across the courtyard for either Caesar or us, but as the eyes of the guardians cleared of auric light, it was clear that the fight was over. The chaos energy slowly lifted from the predators while even Mushhushshu grew subdued, shaking Caesar off its back and into the slump of a defeated man looking up at his destruction. Oluorogbo, the only immortal to attempt an assault on the beast, cast blackened bronze chains over the length of its body as it curled into a yawning heap on the lawn. Cleoseléné met Helios where he held a palm to Ptolemy's forehead, surging a healing light of energy into the confused face of the still young looking ancient man. Cleoseléné charged the back of Ptolemy's head with her moonlight energy as the twin siblings stared into their younger brother's face for signs of recognition that were starting to process in his mind as he caught up to his present.

"Cleo?" he said, looking up at the moon queen with disbelief uncertain across his face.

"Yes," Cleoseléné said, as she pulled him into a full hug. "It's me."

"Jordy!" Elliot shouted down the hall from where I watched the battle, as the youngest of the predators scurried in our direction. The terrified panic of a defeated warrior awaiting capture by his enemy staggering his breath and fraying his nerves. The exhausted burnout of the other predators from the loss of the chaos power hadn't yet hit him.

Through his hand, I felt Elliot's heart break as he stepped forward before letting my hand go. He ran for Jordy, through Leibniz's bubble of protection, and thrust a shining silver sword in his hand like an auric master. My lungs squeezed with fear as Jordy's eyes got wide with the hungry relief that I saw in Joshua after getting a predatory fix at my expense.

Antonio, I thought to Antonio, unsure of what else to do or who to ask for help, but he was already on his way after Elliot.

"You're alive?" Jordy said, sighing with disbelief as his toxic green aura returned around him in wispy mist. "We can get out of here togeth..."

Elliot's blade cut him off with a deep skewer in the gut. Elliot pulled him into a hug as blood dripped down the hilt and around his hand. Jordy's last movement was to look Elliot in the face, confused and flickering with his auric light as it flickered out for the last time.

Elliot... I thought to the popstar, who looked back at me as he laid Jordy to the floor, and I felt the weight of my focus crash down on me from the distractions on the battlefield. I held Marduk still in the last reserves of chaos energy in the courtyard, keeping him closed off from everything else. My head split with a screaming headache, but I could hardly feel it against the rush of... my own recharging aura?

The chaos energy connection connected my aura to Marduk's, fueling me with all of the energy he'd put into his realm of history over the millenia. And for as long as I held him, I felt the entire lengths of the city. Every street, garden, and every story of every building he'd built, but what I found most interesting was the landscapes of all the minds of the philosophers trapped here. Trapped, or collected, as I felt in Marduk's truth.

Preserved for the betterment of existence, was the purpose that he lived by. It was his truth and gift to humanity.

You've lost your way, I thought to the god as I took hold of his mind and body through the shared portions of our connected auras. *You used to know your purpose, and lived by it.*

I used to be worshipped by millions, for generations, the god thought with weary lag.

You used to serve those millions, I thought back, as his mind fought against my hold. *You used to bless millions with your knowledge and your will, and now you bless yourself as the idol of records.*

I'm the idol of civilization, humanity, and protection, Marduk thought, as the other immortal philosophers took care of restraining the other predators who then started to wake up from their auric infection.

Philosophy lives in practice, I thought to the god. *Keep your knowledge and your collection of teachers, but put them to work out in the world. If not through their own hands, then through yours. Back in the real world, where doing good will matter, and where you will regain the purpose you've lost for all this time.*

How do you see me better than I see myself? Marduk thought. *How do you know such a future could be true to what I need?*

I see it in your past and in the truth of human need, I thought, feeling some inspiration from him and the innumerous philosophers I was tapping into, but mostly from deep within. *But we must leave this place, and you must leave, too.*

I believe you, Marduk said. *You're right about what I should do. But I can't leave this place on my own. I haven't left in thousands of years without the prayers I need to travel back and forth. But two of the group you travel with have exactly the tool we need to escape.*

Cleoseléné and Juba, Marduk thought to everyone. *It's time to take us to the end.*

To the end? Cleoseléné thought as if it were something she'd forgotten about but suddenly remembered.

The end, Juba thought, smiling through his mind's voice.

Dylan can power you with my energy, and you can take us all, Marduk thought. *Everyone, into the courtyard. Even the dead.*

CHAPTER SEVENTEEN

THE MAUSOLEUM OF THE IMMORTAL END

"After we ended our first lives," Cleoseléné said, taking Juba's hands in the center of the circle we all made around them. "We crafted an enchantment within our tomb, preserving it for our entire existences, and marking it as a return point for us if we ever needed a quick escape from some life we lost control of."

"And we've never used it until now," Juba said, pulling Cleoseléné into a strong kiss as I held my control over Marduk, the beast, and held back the energy of the place from infecting the three rescued prisoners, as the garden's energy was growing stronger in its attempts to regain hold of them.

"And now it will save more people than I ever thought I'd grow to care about again," Cleoseléné thought. "I'm grateful to help you all, but..." Cleoseléné's voice broke as she lost her ability to speak from the tear-jerked catch in her throat.

"But there's always been the chance that this enchantment could burn one of us up," Juba said. "Transporting this many people, it could burn both of us up."

Charge them with every bit of energy you can from this place and myself, Marduk thought to me. *All the energy you can move that's mine. Feed them, and they will live. It's all on you.*

I did as he said, and pulled all the energy from above, below, and around us as it came pouring in from the sky and our surroundings to the point that they started glowing like twin suns from the surge of it. They nodded at each other with the weight of centuries of closeness and understanding, closed their eyes, and then their hands glowed bright with auric light. Then the blue and pink cotton candy sky and lush garden courtyard of the realm dissolved into whiteness around them.

When I woke up, the air above me was dark and dusty in the dim light that filtered in from a cracked spot in the building's roof far spot above me. Every breath felt gritty with stone dust and stirred dirt. I wasn't alone, but I was one of only two of us to be awake. Antonio and Elliot were next to me, still laying with their backs against the hard stone floor, as the rest of everyone from the courtyard laid around the vast tomb with unconscious breathing whistling into the air. Even Juba and Cleoseléné made it. I was most surprised to see Mushhushshu with us, too. Hulking with labored breaths along the wall.

Did we all make it? I asked Marduk to make sure. He stood in the center of the mausoleum between the two stone beds where history imagined the bodies of Cleoseléné and Juba to have been all this time.

"For now," Marduk said into the room, his presence in the real world just as powerful as he was in his own world. "You were right about me, and I am indebted to you and your cause. The lot of you Immortal Philosophers live the purpose I pretended to serve. Your leader, Aurelius as you call him, has been a master I've been waiting to learn from for a long time, and I see in you how well of a teacher he is. There's not a single one of you who does not have a piece of him guiding you, and that is the magic of his work. That is the magic of the human story and the human influence from one generation to the next. The way he learns and is shaped by you all, too, is another strength I wish to learn from. You are lucky to have such company, and humanity is lucky to have you, Dylan Eaglegod. You might just be a god more true than even I ever was by the end of your story. I think that together, we will do great things for the entirety of humanity. May that be our most true and final focus."

$$\text{The End}$$

THE IMMORTAL PHILOSOPHERS

CHRONICLES OF DYLAN EAGLEGOD
BOOK THREE

MIDNIGHT IN THE CITY THAT LOST ITS SOUL

by

ALEXANDER ANTHONY CASILLAS

RELEASING
2027

TURN FOR A SNEAK PEEK

SUBSCRIBE FOR UPDATES:

FourElementsPress.com
TheImmortalPhilosophers.com

CHRONICLES OF DYLAN EAGLEGOD
BOOK THREE

MIDNIGHT IN THE CITY
THAT LOST ITS SOUL

PROLOG

The city groaned under the squeeze of Hoover's gripped hand over the arched palace window as he looked down on the dark-clouded Málaga city from his ancient palace vantage point atop the central city hilltop. So many rulers of different civilizations had looked down upon the same view of the sprawling, near immortal, city in the valley surrounding the natural fortification, that the view itself, under his iron grip guiding the direction of its people's future, brought him all of the satisfaction he sought from the world. But still, the architecture of his master plans were just getting started.

The Spanish avenues, old stone buildings, and eccentric churches were mere half way trophies that marked the potential he knew he could achieve. The brick and mosaic tiled halls built by the Moores, now called the Alcazaba and Castillo de Gibralfaro were the jeweled sleeves of the one armed cathedral

La Manquita, whose other tower funding had been transferred into the accounts of the conquest of the Americas. Which kept the port of the city shedding its blood to the New World. The single towered cathedral, still standing tall above the city itself, still evidenced that history by hailing up to the heaven Hoover knew he was too forsaken by the darkness of his deeds to ever reach.

He revelled in the transformation of the city already. From the endless days of sunshine, to the dark grey skies of industry, as he returned the city to its shipbuilding past. Knowing his steel fleet would bring him as much conquest as it provided for the crown of the nation so long ago. He longed for his return to power over the same lands that brought Spain to their pinnacle of glory, knowing now just how valuable the riches were that he missed out on the first time his dominion spanned to over the enchanted lands. He couldn't grip the rail of the window hard enough to bring him to where he knew he would find the exact salvation he was looking for. A heaven on earth, as it's been explained. A heaven only he, in his eyes, could subdue and attain. Where he could rule by his name, as the god he always felt he was inside the broken mind he fought.

A god to silence the plazas of pointless existence he turned into work camps and barracks across the city below as the cruise ships he awaited for sailed into the harbor by the burning fire of the lighthouse stretched out into the bay. His cheeks lifted with rare delight as he settled into the command center of the Old World peering past the hills to the west towards the playground of the New World he promised to himself. Knowing no promise was as powerful as the one given by a god to himself. Knowing the presence of his gunmetal aura touching everything he could see was all the truth he needed to believe in his power.

Loyalists sentried every corner, forging the obedience he needed to get there into everyone who entered the city, leaving no one to leave without putting in the work he needed from them.

"We've secured total control of the city and areas north and south of here," Gabirol said, entering the tower from the high ceilinged hall of the palace corridor, followed by the stout Gertrude Stein. "Dragut and Sayyida al-Hurra are bringing the ships into port. All passengers are aboard and prepared to get to work on construction of the warships."

"And we've funneled the new tourist arrivals to the work camps from the airport and the docks," Stein said, as if checking to-dos off a list.

"Oh Stein, it's so good to have you with me again," Hoover said, keeping his gaze on the city and harbor. The docks where the tourists were starting work on his warship fleet rang out with hammered steel that made him want to cry from the pleasure it touched him with. "The time of recreation is over, for us and for the world."

"The streets are quieter down there than I ever imagined they could be," Gabirol said, taking the space beside Hoover to look upon the city himself.

"Well, my propaganda helps, of course," Stein said, taking the other side of Hoover over the city. "The picture-banners of you, Hoov, and the banners with the slogans. It's all a part of the larger effect. The greatness of you."

"And are you liking what you're seeing, Gabirol?" Hoover asked, oozing with a wave of gunmetal auric energy that pulsed through the sea of sentries and workers across the city, showing the three of them just how powerful he had become.

Gabirol stared out at the bay, where he'd looked upon more times than he could remember. "The strongest of the tourists, we sent to the arena," Gabirol said, keeping his gaze on the city and the rolling sharp hills in the distance. "They'll be ready to fight for your weekend games. I'll be happy with all of this when I can stay home and walk the cities alone. Without you and your sentries stalking me with orders to do. You know my hand in this has always been for my own purpose."

"Ha!" Hoover cracked, slapping Gabirol's back with a thick palm. "We all want a vacation, especially after your triumphs of the sea, but that time you seek will come in due time. We only have *forever*."

"Our forever isn't as certain as it feels," Gabirol said, sneering at Hoover in discomfort of his logic.

"You need not worry about that with what we're building here," Hoover said, flourishing a cigar between his fingers from a puff of his grey auric smoke. "And this will all be yours once we reach the end of our journey together."

"If you remember, we made that same promise to the already fallen," Gabirol said, lifting the hood of his golden robe and taking off back into the shadows of the corridor of which he came.

AUTHOR'S NOTE

Lost Between the Lands of Here and There is a tapestry through time and history to highlight the human struggles of the heart and will against the forces of toxic forces and toxic history itself. Dylan's journey across the Mediterranean, all the way to the gates of one of the first ancient civilizations, is marred with rollercoaster love trials that often make little sense. Even when seeking advice from caring new friends, he struggles to understand his own emotions, even if the emotions of the ones he hurts feel more clear to him than his own. Whether driven by heart, soul, lust, or the moon and stars, for the first time in his life his distrust of himself grows. While for the first time in his life, the trust he has in those around him grows even more so. But even when juggling shoulders to lean on while managing obligations to others, being a shoulder for others becomes his greatest tool and greatest liability.

These struggles mirror the very real roles we play in our lives across the myriad of relationships we juggle throughout our lives when the ones around us are the ones we are desperate to keep close by our sides. Whether for wisdom, love, purpose, or pride, Dylan's journey to find himself in his new family pulls him in so many directions he loses himself to the waves of change, endangering everyone in his orbit even if unbeknownst to him.

It's my hope that this story helps you conquer the storylines that are cross generational and inherited, even if they are not our own.

The past is littered with trials and tribulations for those of us walking the present, like curses waiting for their moments to strike on us when the time is right. But just as curses come to doom, so too they come to be doomed. To be ended and silenced and made right once and for all. Opportunity is always a two way street of overcoming or perpetuating the trauma of the past. When these moments meet you, I hope Dylan's journey inspires the striving to overcome and put right the wrongs that do and don't belong to you yourself. The present is the only time for these moments to become those of transformation.

Look to your heart to guide you. Look to your closest allies, who understand you better than you understand yourself, to aid you, and look to the past to inform you as you take on the future you don't let define you, but which you will into the mold you know will fit you.

This epic across the Mediterranean is a testament to the power over the chaos that thrives in the uncertainty of life and the lies we allow ourselves to live, when the truth is the only path worth living and the only path that sets us free. So live your truth and craft your future, until the feet that carry you feel more comfortable in your present than they ever have. For, there lies the happily ever after you deserve.

May we not allow ourselves to fall into the trap of the collector of idols and allow for words and practices read to not move us to action. May we take into the world the philosophies of the better world. May we be led, and lead by their teachings and examples and wisdom to not only inform ourselves, but to inform our decisions and the networks of people around us. A better world hides behind the fear to be different. A better you, hides behind the fear of leading. And a motive of connection, positivity, and honesty with oneself and others in the way to get there. For remember, everything in the immortal universe is a reflection of the whole from a different point of the totality of it all. The thousands and millions and trillions of particles that make up your you are already in sync in their decision to support you. That power of alignment to all be working together and in sync to be you is not something anyone else could give you. It is beyond.

Enjoy, and until next time,
    Alexander Anthony Casillas

THE
IMMORTAL PHILOSOPHERS

Aurelius: Stoic philosopher and former Roman Emperor. Founder of the Immortal Philosophers and leader of its members worldwide. Hunter of thieving and murderous predators lurking among us who are desperate to manipulate the innocent to steal the auric life force innate in all of us.

 Unique Abilities: Vast Auric Reserves, Teleportation Expert.
Aura: Tyrian Purple

Antonio Antoninus: Adopted son of Aurelius was born and raised on his home island of Puerto Rico. Antonio grew up around extended family and the protective eye of the immortals. His Puerto Rican cafe in Ocean City, New Jersey is his heaven on Earth, until his world is upturned after meeting Dylan Eaglegod.

 Unique Abilities: Auric Energy Battery, Fast Regeneration.
Aura: Sky Blue

Dylan Eaglegod: New York born and raised, and one of the newest recruits, Dylan escaped the nightmare of living a closeted life around homophobic friends, who, unbeknownst to him, were predators extracting his energy and who sought to kill him. Until the Immortal Philosophers found him and taught him how to free himself. Now the boyfriend of Antonio Antoninus, and a powerful force within the circle of immortals.

 Unique Abilities: Strong Past Viewing, Locating Atraments, Creating Auric Wells.
Aura: Cobalt

Zenda: Oldest of the Immortal Philosophers, and the most in tune with ancient energy. Zenda was a leader of a group of Spirit Warriors in South China, North Vietnam before time was recorded in any organized way. Her tribe was known far and wide as the people to turn to when nothing else worked, or when the danger was too mysterious. They kept centuries safe from demonic predators as far as the Indus Peninsula to the plateau of Tibet. Wife of Ikkyu, Zenda organizes the American based Immortal Philosophers and spent time raising and training Antonio.

Unique Abilities: Conjuring Ancient Bestial Forms, Exceptional Auric Reserves, Healing Expert.

Aura: Emerald

Ikkyu Sojun: Bastard son of an emperor, Ikkyu was sent to become a Zen Buddhist monk as a child. At a young age, he achieved enlightenment and unlocked abilities he was told were legend. After fooling and chastising everyone he met in his life for their hypocrisy and extravagance, Ikkyu took to training his body as well as his mind. Becoming a master of all historic fighting styles over his long lifetime. Husband of Zenda.

Unique Abilities: Hand to Hand & Musical Combat Expert.

Aura: Light Mint Green

Kana: Powerful sibling of Ikkyu and a miracle in her own right. Kana was raised with love and care in an imperial enclave, before her history took a dark turn. She is one of the most battle ready Immortal Philosophers, and always has something to prove.

Unique Abilities: Hand to Hand & Musical Combat Expert.

Aura: Cherry Blossom Pink

Queen Cleoseléné: Daughter of Queen Cleopatra and Mark Antony, she is the Moon Queen of Mauretania. Ruling beside her husband King Juba II, she was a protector of her people and worshipped as a semi-divine leader. Now, a devout protector of the Immortal Philosophers and all of its members.

Unique Abilities: Moon & Tidal Energy. Water & Healing.

Aura: Moonlight

King Juba: Son of King Juba I, Juba II ruled with his wife over a Golden Age for his people. Channeling his power over the tides and sea, he was a master of aquatic trade and commerce. A protector and lover of all people, he is a fierce friend and warrior.

Unique Abilities: Tidal & Water Energy Affinity.

Aura: Navy

Leibniz: The philosophical Father of the Immortal Universe and master of auric forces, Leibniz continues the work of guiding humanity through physics, battle, and ethics. A teacher of aurics for all new members, his auric imprint touches all of the universe.

Unique Abilities: Protective Barriers & Remote Auric Use

Aura: Egg-yolk Yellow

Queen Moremi Ajasoro: Eternal Moon Queen of the Yoruba people, Moremi is a lover of the people. Having made the ultimate sacrifice, her own son, for the protection of her people, she is a Queen like none other. Her commitment to the many over her own heart, is the power of the Moon incarnate. She is now protector and warrior Queen of the Immortal Philosophers, as she still hunts, through the pain, the river spirit who took her son.

Unique Abilities: Water & Healing Moon Energy Affinity.

Aura: Moonlight

Baldwin: Harlem born James Baldwin is a hero of the Civil Rights movement as an author and thought leader for the struggles of Black and Queer lives, and is a voice for all the oppressed people of the world. Having secured his entry into the Immortal Philosophers, he works behind the scenes as a driving voice of change in the world and within the group. Often as counsel to all who need the nudge of his keen and logical perception.

Unique Abilities: Storytelling & Emotional Manipulation.

Aura: Violet

Frederick Douglass: Born into the horrors of American slavery, Frederick fought for the salvation of his soul and the soul of his brothers and sister in shared trauma. But no amount of violence or fear could break his will. Through sheer willpower and hardwon intelligence, he outsmarted his captors and catchers, and fled North to freedom. He shared his story with the world, and draws strength from the memory of how badly people can treat each other. With a mission to help in never letting such horrors happen again. And a grounding grandfather to the Immortal Philosophers both young and old.

Unique Abilities: Pure, Dense Energy & Undetection.

Aura: Gold

Rumi: Born into the heart and freedoms of Persian culture, Rumi found strength in the raw emotion of love, love making, and poetry. As a master heartthrob for all, he revels in the beauty of intimacy of all levels, shapes, and sizes. Truly seeking the beauty of life, and preaching such as his philosophy to touch the power of god. Now a friend and guide to all immortals, he is a beacon of life giving energy and an advocate for not forgetting how to feel alive in neverending life.

Unique Abilities: Channeling Intimate, Communal, & Almighty Energies.

Aura: Tanned Parchment

Hypatia: Having lived as a philosopher and been torn apart by the city she served, Hypatia is a fiercely loyal and devoted practitioner, teacher, and lover for the Immortal Philosophers. Often taking identities of others, she is a shapeshifter who changes with the seasons of life and desires. A solid sailor and warrior, her aurics is a match for those daring to stand against her, when not keeping ship and bed with Captain O'Malley.

Unique Abilities: Instantaneous Form Morphing & Mending.

Aura: Teal

Grace O'Malley: Captain of the White Seahorse and fierce Pirate Queen, O'Malley works with her partner Hypatia to keep the coasts of the Mediterranean and seven seas clear of dangers for travelers. Fervent defender of immortals around the world.

Unique Abilities: Sailing & Navigating.

Aura: Amber

Horus: The eye and ear of The White Seahorse, and non-corporeal immortal. Guiding and protecting his crew, when not acting as the resident God of the group, popping up in their heads and offering energy charge and Godly advices.

Unique Abilities: Non-Corporeal Spirit & Mind Migration.

Aura: Lapis Lazuli

Gertrude Stein: Pennsylvania born, American Literary Icon and resident hardliner of the Immortal Philosopher and defender of the Immortal Philosopher library and Headquarters. Vowed to the group's cause after outliving her wife.

Unique Abilities: Seeing Hidden Truths & Mental Snaring.

Aura: Murky Brown

Fernando Guerrero 'Strachan': Architect of many world-famous structures around Magala, Spain, Strachan is the keeper of the Immortal Philosophers headquarters, the Palacio Asturias, and devout protector of the organization's secrets.

Unique Abilities: Manifesting Eternal Auric Structures.

Aura: Milky Grey / Marble White

Elliot Cutcas: World famous popstar and heartthrob to all ages, Elliot is the newest member of the Immortal Philosophers, just months after Dylan Eaglegod's joining. Self-centered and superficial seeming, Elliot reveals himself to be a far more complex personality, struggling to find a place in the hearts of those around him and to serve the fans that adore him.

Unique Abilities: Mind Enchanting Vocals & Aurics.

Aura: Silver

Selena Sol-Valencia is an in-denial teenage werewolf battling for her life against family tradition, human traffickers, and teen crushes. But her biggest antagonist might just be her own mind. Could womanhood really be the most dangerous part of a girl's life?

Selena must learn family history, her Tío's rules of survival, and figure out how to make the most of the nightmare situations brought on by teen-wolf puberty and the intrusive world. Secrets lay behind everyone she meets, but once the claws come out, nobody's safe. Especially on the night of the Blue Moon.

Selena Sol-Valencia Episodio 1

AUGUST
2026

Selena Sol-Valencia is off on an institutionalized adventure where breaking free from the psych ward before her full moon transformation is a high stakes journey of self discovery, self control, and the 'pro-social' behaviors she must master as she adapts to her new neurodivergent diagnoses and medications. But the haunting figure of Cualli, La Llorona, is making it more difficult than Selena ever imagined.

Selena must dive deep into her family history and Mexican-Indigenous lore to figure out how and why the haunting spirit is so drawn to her. Friends and family are near and far, and help as they can. But Selena's on her own against the ghosts of her and her family's present and past. With freedom on the horizon is she can win a release before the full moon. While her future, if she fails, promises a life time of werewolf incarceration.

Selena Sol-Valencia Episodio 2